DOODLE BUG DOODLE BUG YOUR HOUSE IS ON FIRE

AN APPALACHIAN NOVEL

BY MACK SAMPLES

Quarrier Press
Charleston, WV

Copyright 1993, 2015 by Mack Samples

All rights reserved. No part of this book may be reproduced in any form or in any means, electronic or mechanical, including photocopying, recording, or by any information storage and retrieval system, without permission in writing from the publisher.

10 9 8 7 6 5 4 3 2 1

Library of Congress Control Number: 94-92149

ISBN 13: 978-1-942294-04-7
ISBN 10: 1-942294-04-2

Distributed by:

West Virginia Book Company

1125 Central Avenue
Charleston, WV 25302

www.wvbookco.com

I

Corley Malone slid the big john boat into the river, stepped into it, and felt the smooth motion. It felt good. There was nothing quite like a good boat ride. It had been a Sunday morning custom with him for several years during the warm months. There was a quietness on the water, a stillness that a person couldn't find taking a walk in the woods. The only sound was made by an occasional drop of water as he lifted the paddle. Just as he pulled out into the current his attention was diverted by a flash of white up on the railroad track that ran along the other side of the river. He first thought that it was a fluttering bird, but a closer look told him that it was Julie Meadow's white dress, showing through gaps in the underbrush. He knew about Julie Meadows. Her father had built a new house across the river and up the next hollow from the Malone place. He had noticed her getting on the school bus down at the swinging bridge. And, he had also found that he was having trouble keeping his eyes off her. He had noticed girls before, plenty of times. He had lately been fascinated by the rustle of their petticoats and by the flash of their eyes. But, none of them had really caught his attention like Julie. She had caught him staring at her on the bus a time or two, causing him to jerk his head away in embarrassment. He guessed her to be about his age and she was enjoying the full bloom of maidenhood. Her legs were well developed and there were pleasant swells beneath her dress where they were supposed to be.

She saw Corley too, but pretended not to. Her gaze remained straight ahead and her head bobbed a little as she tried to step on each crosstie. Walking the railroad was an art which she had not yet mastered. Corley had heard that she had been playing the piano for the Sunday morning services down at the Big Run Methodist Church.

The church was about a mile from her house if she walked down the track and crossed the swinging bridge. But, if she drove, it was probably six or seven miles because she would have to go down stream about three miles, cross the automobile bridge, then drive back up to the church. The beautiful spring morning had inspired her to walk, Corley figured. The walk was becoming familiar to her anyway because she had been taking this route to the school bus stop.

Corley was chilled as he watched her make her way along the track and pass from his sight. Her hair was long and dark and fell down her breast with a fluffy, curly look. Her complexion was fair and perfect and her lips were red and full. But of all the things about her that bothered him, it was her eyes that really got to him. They were a deep blue, bluer than most blue eyes that he had ever seen; and she could melt him with a flash of them. He had not exchanged a word with her yet but there was definitely something about her that upset his metabolism.

It occurred to him that he might start going to church again. He always admired a good piano player and one as pretty as Julie certainly rekindled his interest in religion. Church wasn't so bad. He had given it up only a couple of years ago. He always enjoyed the singing and the handshaking. When he and his older brothers used to go, they practically carried the singing. The sermons got a little long sometimes, but were never boring, not at the Big Run Methodist. The preacher always yelled and stomped around, and sometimes even broke into song. The congregation usually got pretty worked up also and there was never any danger of anyone going to sleep. Corley didn't mind going that much. He had just sort of gotten out of the habit when his brothers left home. His mother was always wanting him to go.

He cruised the river awhile and contemplated his place in the universe. He had just turned seventeen on April eighth and it was just beginning to dawn on him that the carefree summers which he had been enjoying since he could remember might be coming to an end. He had spent his young life enjoying the Vandalia River, the thousands of acres of woodlands that covered the hills through which it made its way, and the beautiful little hillside farm where his father, Ike Malone, had raised his family. But he was about to go through that transition that carries a person from the bliss of innocence to the realization that life is slightly less than perfect. And, like everyone else, he knew that changes were coming, he just did not quite realize how painful they were going to be.

He heard his name called from the house and made his way in that direction because he certainly did not want to miss Sunday dinner. The Malones always had an early breakfast, so dinner was usually around noon. As he pulled the boat up and secured it to a tree he wondered about food. His dad was always making remarks about how lucky they were to have so much to eat while much of the world went hungry. He was beginning to wonder why the world went hungry when it seemed so easy for them to have all the food that they wanted. The smokehouse was always filled with meat and the cellar was filled with canned fruit and vegetables. Corn, green beans, carrots, pickles, applesauce, peaches, and blackberries lined the shelves. The cows provided all of the milk and dairy products that anyone would ever want.

Sunday always brought a special feast. Canned pork, beef, or deer, sometimes a fresh chicken, provided the main course along with three or four vegetables. There was always home made bread and a choice of a couple of desserts. Almost everything on the table was produced on the fifty-six acres owned by the Malone family. It seemed so easy to Corley and he just wondered why anyone had trouble getting enough to eat.

But on this Sunday, Corley hurried through the meal and headed back toward the river. He thought he just might get back down there in time to watch Julie go back up the railroad track. He was afraid that his mother would be suspicious because it was his custom to fool around with his guitar after Sunday dinner. But, she did not say anything. He positioned himself on a big flat rock in the edge of the river and he immediately saw her coming with that haughty look that fit her so well. He got up and decided that he would wave at her if he could catch her eye. His dinner was not settling well at all.

She would not look his way for nothing; so he just heaved a rock in her general direction and it crashed through the limbs below the track. She stopped suddenly, turned and was looking right at him. He waved and smiled. But Julie turned and walked away briskly, leaving him shattered. He had now had his first encounter with the female mystique.

He went back to the house and mulled it over all day, wondering what her reaction would be the next time he saw her. Nothing in the world had ever bothered him as much as that tiny incident and he kept turning it over and over in his mind all day. What was it about her that bothered him so? He went to bed that night and lay awake a long time planning his strategy for the bus ride to Bolton the next morning.

Bolton, West Virginia was a small town of about two thousand people and it was the county seat of Vandalia County. It was located about ten miles down river from the Malone place. Since the high school was located there, Corley had to ride the school bus. He hated the school bus. It was crowded and noisy, and during cold weather when all of the windows had to remain closed, the body odor was terrible. The Saturday night bath was still considered the respected standard for personal hygiene in most circles in Vandalia County. Boys sat on one side of the bus, girls on the other so as to prevent any hanky panky while the bus was underway. There was always an inseparable couple who held hands across the aisle. All told, the bus ride was a generally nauseating scene.

Yet, on the Monday morning following the Sunday encounter, Corley was sort of looking forward to riding the bus for he knew that Julie would be getting on down at the swinging bridge. She always looked so fresh and Corley had a deep feeling that she violated the Saturday night bath code. She looked especially pretty that morning and he thought that he would smile and speak to her. But when she came up the bus steps and their eyes met, he froze, then looked out the window as she walked by. The rustle of her dress sounded especially loud and sensuous.

He decided that he would talk with her when the bus arrived at Bolton. The bus arrived at the school about eight thirty but late April kept most of the students outside until classes convened at nine. The students stood around in little groups, usually in accordance with their established social standing. The kids who lived in town considered themselves a cut above the rural children, and this fact accounted for one layer of the social stratification. The boys who participated in sports maintained their own esoteric group, and they strutted around like Greek gods going to war. The boys who smoked usually sat together along a little concrete curb just off school property.

Corley watched Julie move into a group of girls from town. While she lived out near him, she had been a big city girl prior to moving into the area and she definitely belonged among the well scrubbed and articulate. He put her out of his mind for a moment and decided that there would be a better time to approach her. He walked over to talk with some boys who were admiring a '55 Chevy. It was all black with whitewalls, standard shift, with a 283 engine under the hood. Awesome twin tail pipes protruded from the back. It was the first V-8 ever produced by Chevrolet and it was the talk of the country. In 1955, the short distance drag race was the true test of an automobile, and from zero to sixty, the '55 Chevy could dust off about anything in town.

Cars did not interest Corley much at this point in his life so he did not share the excitement of the Chevy. But he was comfortable with this particular group of boys. They were mostly rural and, like him, went to school because they thought they should, or because the law required it until the sixteenth birthday. To most of them the Chevrolet was something to be admired from afar. It belonged to Denny Lewis whose father owned and operated a building supply outfit in Bolton. Denny was the leading spender at Bolton High. Everyone accepted that and Denny carried his station in life pretty well. He was a big, good looking kid with a frock of blonde hair that was just slightly longer than the established length.

Corley had pretty much decided, or his mother had decided, that he would finish high school. Life at school was not that bad but learning was not the motivating force that kept him going every day. He had not identified a particular goal in life. And, except for English and history, the subject matter left him cold. The single most motivating factor that kept him in school was music. He participated in all of the music groups that the school offered. The band was his favorite. The band master, Frank Kerns, was a good man. He successfully conveyed the notion that being a musician was a manly art and managed to attract boys from every social strata. He fashioned them into a sound unit and his band was the talk of the town each year. He was a hard man, but Corley always found him to be a fair man.

History fascinated Corley but he was something less than fascinated by those who taught it at Bolton High. All of the history teachers were coaches. They usually made an appearance at the beginning of class, assigned the questions at the end of the chapter, then left for activities and conversation more in line with their interests. But, Corley enjoyed reading the material and usually managed an A on the standardized tests which were taken from the teacher's manual.

English was his favorite academic subject. The English teachers were all ladies and were very dedicated to their profession. Corley did not particularly like any of them, but he did like to read the assignments in literature, and, sometimes, the ladies pointed out some really interesting insights that he had overlooked.

It was after English class that Monday morning that he was standing at his locker exchanging books and getting ready for the next class when he heard a voice behind him.

"Do you throw rocks at everyone, Corley Malone, or just at people whom you do not like?"

There was no doubt who it was and he dreaded to turn around. He had never really talked to girls much and was sadly lacking in experience. He tried to think of all of the lines that he had heard in movies. He went to the movies a lot.

"Normally, I just throw rocks at pretty girls who won't speak to me," he managed to say.

"I didn't see you," she said.

"Oh, I think you did."

"Well, I'm just not used to boys who go around throwing rocks at people," she said as she walked away.

Corley was definitely shaken by the entire encounter and very disgusted with his poor performance. He did not hear anything that was said the rest of the day and dreaded to go to band practice that afternoon for he knew that Julie would be there, blowing her flute, and looking right at him with those eyes of hers.

Oddly enough, she did not even look his way all through practice. He stared at her the whole time but she just pretended that he was not in the world. He thought he would make an attempt to talk to her again after practice. But, she did not give him a chance. She flew out of there in a flash leaving a shattered country boy to lick his wounds.

II

Samuel Shenandoah Somerville was about the coolest name that Corley had ever heard and it belonged to a boy about his age who lived just up the hill and around the ridge from the Malone place. Sam's father was a mine tipple builder and he had moved his family into the area recently in response to the opening of some new coal mines. Coal production was not a major industry in Vandalia County, but there were a few small-time, independent operators around. Sam's family had traveled up and down the Appalachians in pursuit of his father's trade.

The Somervilles had moved into an old house that had been vacant for a long time. It was kind of a small house but the Somerville's had fixed it up until it was pretty nice. Sam had a younger sister who looked to be about thirteen. Old man Somerville had a weekend drinking problem which had caught the eye of the community, but Corley and Sam had hit it off right from the start. They shared an affection for the out of doors and for adventure.

On the last Saturday morning in April Corley had gone up to the Somerville place and hollered Sam out. It was a warm, beautiful morning, the first really summer-like day of the spring.

"I think I'm going to make a trip back into the hills today, see what flowers are blooming, and just fool around," Corley said. "Want to go?"

Sam was already coming off the porch. "Might as well," he replied, "I got nothing better to do."

Corley was looking forward to flaunting his knowledge of the flora and fauna of the area. He knew the common name of every tree and shrub that grew in the hills of Vandalia County. His father had taught him on a daily basis. Working with him on the farm was a continuous learning experience because he was always explaining which kind of wood was good for what and pointing out how to identify each tree or shrub. His father had very little formal education but he had plenty of savvy about how to live the good life in the Appalachian hills.

Sam had spent most of his time in coal towns and was not as familiar with what grew wild in the hills and what uses folks made of what was available, but he was an interested and willing learner. Corley introduced him to mountain tea as they topped the first ridge. The new leaves were just coming up and they were especially tender and sweet. The boys picked a good jaw full and sat back to enjoy the flavor and the view. It beat chewing tobacco all to hell, they decided.

The timber leaves were still not out very much and the view was practically unobstructed. They could see the river winding its way down through the hills. The meadows along the river were becoming lush and green. The houses were mostly white frame structures and were all well kept. Generally, there was a quarter of a mile or so separating the farms and each house was surrounded by several outbuildings. Livestock had been turned into the pasture land along the lower parts of the hills. By this time of the year, the stock could usually find enough grass to get by.

Corley could see their place and was proud of it. The house was situated in a grove of sugar maples and would be obscure once the leaves had grown to their full size. The yard itself was small and fenced. Mowing the lawn would be a chore with which he would have to contend, but there would also be many more demanding tasks. The lawn was kept small for that reason. The mower had become easier to push last year and Corley figured he would be even stronger this year. He had grown some during the winter and was now about five feet ten inches and weighed about 155 pounds. He was mature for his age and looked older than his seventeen years.

The boys chewed the mountain tea in silence for awhile, but Corley decided it was time to confide in someone.

"You know anything about girls to amount to anything?" he asked.

After a long chewing pause, Sam replied. "No, I guess not. I really haven't given them much thought until just recently."

"Neither have I," said Corley, "but one of them is really beginning to bother the hell out of me."

"Which one?"

"Julie, over across the river."

"Well, she is a looker, no doubt about that, but she is probably out of our class," Sam concluded.

"Probably so," Corley said, "but damned if she ain't something."

"I couldn't argue with that," Sam said as they got up to move.

As they started back the ridge Corley thought of old Blackie Osborne. He lived back on the ridge in the head of one of the hollows not far away. Blackie knew all about women. Perhaps they should go by and talk with him.

"We ought to go back and talk with old Blackie," Corley said.

"Hell, he's an authority of women, or so he says. "Want to go by that way?"

"Well, I have never met the man, but let's have a go at him," Sam replied.

Blackie Osborne spent most of his life sitting on the front porch of his house. It wasn't a bad house and the location was outstanding. You could sit on his porch and enjoy a view that folks in big cities would pay a big price for, just for a summer home. But Blackie lived there year around and it did not cost him anything. The place belonged to his father and had originally been built for one of his sisters. She had moved away so Blackie had moved his family in from an old shanty that they had occupied. The new place was luxury to them. It had running water and free gas for heat, not to mention an inside bathroom.

While Blackie had never worked for a living, he was not without virtues. His place was one of the focal points of the community. Everyone who happened to be in the vicinity would always stop by and talk with him and get the benefit of his wisdom. He knew everything, at least in his own mind. American foreign policy, baseball, the United Mine Workers, farm subsidy, automobiles, and the weather were among the areas that he lectured on. He could tell you about how dry it got back in '31. "You talk about dry," he would say. "Dry I reckon." Or, if he got on the winter of '36, "cold, you don't know nothing about cold. Now in '36 they drove horses across the river on the ice down there all winter. Now that was cold."

He played a little guitar but not enough to entertain anyone other than himself. He always kept it with him though. If he was on his front porch in the summer, he usually held it all the time. He would pick a little while he was talking. And, sometimes, he would hum along with his picking. The guitar was an old Gibson and a real jewel. No one knew where he got it. He would sometimes give little unsolicited lessons, making statements such as, "now this here is the G chord, but if you slide up the neck and note it this way, it's G again. There are a lot of ways to get a G chord and a lot of people don't know that," he would say.

He was also an authority on the stars and the heavens. He spent endless hours sitting on a bench on his front porch watching the stars. He didn't know the names of many of the stars, but he could point them out to you and show you exactly where they were a month before, or a year before. There was nothing scientific about his observations, but he knew what was going on in the heavens. He would give you an explanation based on local objects.

"Now you see that bright star to the north there, just to the right of the barn. Well, last month at this time of the evening it was right straight down the river, just about over that big white oak in the meadow there," he would explain.

But what the young boys in the area liked to hear him talk about was women. He loved telling the teenaged boys about his sexual escapades when he was young. He had a way of describing a woman that would captivate the young boys and they would all listen attentively.

"Now she had beautiful hair," he would say, "long and dark with a kind of silky glow to it. And, buddy she knew how to use her eyes. She could make you understand what she was thinking without saying a word."

Corley had heard all of the stories several times but he had never really asked him for advice. As they approached his house Blackie was setting on his porch with the guitar. He was picking a little of "Just Because" and humming along with it.

"Morning Blackie," Corley ventured.

"Well, Corley, what are you boys doing up this way so early?"

Corley decided to get right to the point so he plunged in.

"This here is my friend, Sam Somerville, and we wanted to ask you a couple of questions about women."

"Now that's something that I know about," Blackie said.

"What would you do if you liked the looks of one but couldn't get up the nerve to talk with her?" Corley asked.

"You just lock your eye on her, don't break your stare, and start talking. Tell her that she is about the best looking thing around and that you would like to spend some time with her. If you tell a woman that she looks good, she will talk to you. I know that to be a fact."

"Well, it sounds easy enough," Corley said.

"You just do what I told you and you will do fine," Blackie said.

Corley and Sam thanked him for his time and started back. Coming back along one of the lower ridges, the boys came upon a huge boulder that had been perched there for untold centuries. Corley had stood on it a hundred times and had always thought what a kick it would be to somehow get the thing rolling down the hill. It was a steep one hundred yards or so to the creek at the bottom of the hill.

"Sam," Corley said, "do you think we could get this damned rock rolling and give it a ride down the hill?"

"It looks awfully heavy," Sam replied, "but what the hell, let's give it a try."

They got behind the big rock and pushed with all they had. They managed to break it loose from the soil and tipped it just slightly, but they could not turn it over. They changed positions several times, but she wouldn't go.

Corley took his hatchet and cut them both a pole about ten feet long. He had read once where some Greek said that if you had a lever long enough and something to brace it under, you could move the world. The boys placed the poles under the rock, got their shoulders under the poles and begin to push. Veins popped out in their necks and arms and they pushed even harder. It was moving the way they wanted it to go and it finally toppled and started to lumber down the hill.

Brush began to crack in its path and it picked up speed with every roll. By the time it was halfway down the hill, it had become a formidable flying object, crashing everything in its path. They watched with delight as it hit the creek below, sending water and rocks high into the air. It had left a wide path of broken saplings and had skinned a tree or two, but really hadn't caused any serious damage. They rested a minute, talked about how strong they were and started home. They were extremely pleased with their morning.

III

Things were winding down at Bolton High. The late May days were warm and balmy and the entire area was a thing of beauty. The leaves were all out full and the school lawn was soft and green. Students loafed under the big maples in the yard during the lunch hour, and they groaned in agony when the bell rang at one o'clock for the reconvening of classes. It was a difficult time to concentrate on things academic, and for Corley's part, it was just a matter of going through the motions. He had exchanged glances with Julie Meadows on several occasions since the encounter at the locker, but he still had not said anything to her.

On the next to the last day of school Corley decided that this would be the day that he would put old Blackie's advice to use and make his move. He came out of the school building at noon to look for her. As he surveyed the scene he spotted old Charlie Calvert standing across the street, legs spread apart, hands behind his back, and a big chew of Beech Nut in his mouth. Corley decided that he would talk to old Charlie for a minute. They had gone to grade school together. Most folks would not talk to him, or did not want to be seen talking to him, but Corley always enjoyed old Charlie and he did not much care what people thought about it. Besides it would give him more time to think about what to say to Julie.

There were lots of poor people in Vandalia County but the Calvert clan was probably the most poverty stricken of the lot. They lived way back away from the paved roads. Folks called the place the Head of Blue Creek because there was nothing else to call it. There were four children in the family, two boys and two girls. There was no road available to where they lived, only a walking path, and it was a good two hour walk to anywhere from their house.

The Calvert children had attended the one room elementary school at Broad Run with Corley. They did not attend often and when they did it was usually ten o'clock or so when they arrived. Charlie was the oldest and he was the shining star of the clan, and almost a tragic figure. While the other children were incapable of learning to read and write, Charlie showed a definite spark of intelligence. He read pretty well and had a nice halting delivery when he read aloud in class. The room always became quiet when it was his turn to read because all of the children enjoyed hearing him. Many times, after he had completed a difficult line, he would smile, very pleased with himself that he had gotten through it. His smile revealed a horrible array of rotten teeth, but it was genuine just the same.

The Calvert boys dressed mostly in World War II Army surplus and the girls wore pathetic little dresses that had been given to them by some generous soul. None of them had the slightest idea of how to be social or to carry on a conversation with others. During recess, the two girls would generally hold hands and stand off alone in the corner of the playground. Charlie would hold his arms stiff and run a little circle, sometimes during the entire duration of the recess. If the other children tried to include him in basketball he would tuck the ball under his arm and run away. Football brought out the worst in him because if tackled, he would fly mad and want to fight.

None of the Calverts, including Charlie, was ever promoted on a regular basis. They usually spent two or three years in the same grade. In Charlie's case it was not because he was not bright enough, but because of excessive absences. The county truant officer was always after them but it never came to anything. So, when Charlie turned sixteen and was legally eligible to quit school he was in the sixth grade at the little one room school. He had become something of a curiosity for the children at the school, and he never returned after his sixteenth birthday.

Once out of school Charlie became a familiar sight around the town of Bolton. He would walk to town every day, a two hour walk from his house, and would stand around the streets all day. Often at noon, he would stand up in front of the high school where he should have been enrolled and watch the students come and go. He would just stand there until the noon hour was over, then walk back downtown. The tragic part was that he was intellectually capable of attending school, he just never had any guidance nor encouragement.

"What you up to, Charlie?" Corley asked.

"Not much," Charlie answered. "Want a chew?"

"Don't have time to get a chew going," Corley replied.

"How are things over in the Head of Blue Creek?"

"Things are drying out some," said Charlie, "not quite so muddy."

Charlie turned around slowly, leaned over and spit. He was very deliberate in his movements. Corley had noticed that he never got in a hurry about anything.

After a long pause in the conversation Charlie ventured another sentence.

"Might get me a job on the pipeline," he said. "They are hiring some people."

"Have you talked to them yet?" Corley asked.

"Not yet," said Charlie, "but I'm thinking about it pretty strong."

"I'll tell you what," said Corley. "I'll pass the word to them that you are interested and you go down there on the job in a few days and ask if they are hiring."

"Maybe I'll do that," replied Charlie.

"Well, I have got to get back to school. You take it easy now."

Charlie just nodded and shifted his chew.

As Corley went back into the school yard he spotted Julie sitting alone under one of the maple trees pretending to read something. With a sudden burst of courage he walked over and sat down in the grass beside her.

"You are not throwing rocks today?" she asked.

"Well no, I don't throw rocks all the time," he answered.

"What else do you do?"

"Well, I do all sorts of things, I suppose, but I doubt that you would be interested."

"Oh, I might be," she said.

"Actually, I was just wondering about your summer," Corley said. "Just wondering what you were going to do with yourself. We are practically neighbors you know."

"Yes, I'm just a stone's throw away," she said with a smile.

They both laughed. Corley decided that it was time to make his move.

"To tell you the truth I think that you are just about the best looking girl that I have ever seen and I was wondering if you would like to go swimming sometime. Do you swim?"

"Yes," she said. "I don't suppose that I am a professional, but I can stay afloat."

Corley was very glad to hear that because while he was not a great athlete of any sort, he could swim with the best of them. Swimming was the national pastime in his end of Vandalia County. The Vandalia River originated in the mountains and there were no towns of any size along its banks before it reached the area where the Malones lived. And, just below their home was one of the best sandy beaches that could be found anywhere. Folks drove from some distances to spend a Sunday afternoon on the little beach. It was a beautiful spot and Corley felt very fortunate to have it just a few steps from his house.

"Listen," Corley said, "after school is out and things settle down, I'll introduce you to the sand bar. All of the kids up the river come there about every afternoon."

"Yes, I've heard," she answered.

The ring of the one o'clock bell was a welcome sound because Corley was about to run out of something to say and was beginning to wonder how he was going to get out of the conversation.

"I'll come over one day soon and we'll go for a swim if it's OK," he said, as they got up to go.

"You come over and we will talk about it," she answered. She gave a little four finger wave as she went into the building.

Corley was strutting down the hallway, feeling pretty good about things when he spotted old Sam coming toward him. When they met, Corley cocked his right hand and unleashed a blow to Sam's shoulder that sent him sprawling into the lockers. Just as Sam was about to recover and retaliate, Corley felt a hand on his shoulder. He turned and looked Henry Holt, the principal, square in the eye.

"Let's go," was all Mr. Holt said.

Corley followed him to the office with Sam pointing and laughing the whole time. Mr. Holt sat him down in his outer office and started in on him.

"It's not like you to be disruptive in the hall, Corley," he said. "What is it? You got some kind of problem?"

Corley did not really want to talk to Henry Holt so he started looking out the door.

"Answer me," he yelled. And, just as he yelled, Corley saw Julie go by and look in the door. If this is not the damned living end, he thought. One minute he was approaching being an international lover, and the next minute he was sitting in here being humiliated by a high school principal. He figured that he had better say something because old Henry was getting pretty hot.

"I didn't have a reason for hitting Sam, I just felt like it," Corley said.

"Do you realize someone could have been hurt?" replied Mr. Holt.

"Yes Sir," Corley said. "It was a dumb thing to do."

"Well, school is nearly out so I am going to let this go," said the principal. "From now on you keep this stuff outside. You got that?"

"Yes Sir," said Corley.

He thought that he was going to be dismissed but Mr. Holt kept looking at him.

"Corley, I'm expecting better things out of you next year. You have been sliding along for two years and your teachers think that you could do better. I think so, too. You realize that next year is your last chance to prepare yourself for something don't you?"

"Yes sir," said Corley. "I'll do better."

"Best you do," he said. "Now go to class."

Corley did not even look at Julie that evening on the bus. She respected his silence, but smiled as she got off the bus at the swinging bridge. Corley noticed that old Sam had been looking at him from the back of the bus all the way home. When they were getting off at their stop and Corley started down the steps of the bus, he felt Sam pile him from behind. They hit the ground and went over the hill and into the field, each trying to gain the advantage.

"You son-of-a-bitch," Sam said as they struggled. "Knocking the hell out of me when I'm not looking"

They were up and down two or three times before Corley finally landed on top of him and tried to hold him. Sam was stronger than he thought and he could not keep him down. Sam got a hammer lock on Corley's neck and held him a moment or two before he managed to break free. Just as he got loose and started to stand, Sam flattened him with a right to the chest. As Corley was getting up Sam spoke through heavy breathing.

"OK, let's call it even."

"That's fine with me. You started this and I'm tired as hell."

They dusted themselves off and went their separate ways. When they had gotten about fifty yards between them, Corley picked up a throwing rock and whizzed it by Sam's head."

"Goddamn you, Corley," he shouted.

Corley threw him the high sign and said, "Don't worry, Sam, you know I could have hit you if I had wanted to."

Corley walked on and wondered if he really could whip old Sam if he had to. Sam was a hell of a lot stronger than he thought he was, no doubt about that.

IV

Corley was glad that school was over. It wasn't that he minded school so much, he just enjoyed the freedom that the summer offered. School often got in the way of the things that he really enjoyed doing. He was very aware of the fact that this might be his last real summer of being irresponsible and he intended to make the most of it. He had quite a bit of work to do around the farm, but there was always time to pursue his interests. He spent time with his guitar every day during the summer.

Music had been a part of his life since he could remember. It seemed that everyone that he knew played some kind of stringed instrument, or at the very least sang a little. His dad played the banjo, his mom played the fiddle, and uncles and aunts on both sides of the family were musically inclined.

There was a pick'n session down at the local store at least once a month. Summers would find them out on the front porch, winters in around the fire. The songs that they played were little known and they sang with accents that would have been unappreciated on the commercial music market. Yet the thrill to Corley was real. And, God how he listened. Memories of those banjo breaks with a Martin guitar barking out bass runs in the background would be with him forever. And, neither would he forget the shuffle of feet as the fiddle inspired some of the pickers to get up and dance. Old tunes such as "Soldier's Joy" and "Old Joe Clark" always brought some of them to their feet. There were some excellent flatfoot dancers in the crowd, and Corley could hold his own with most of them. He was also beginning to play a little fiddle in addition to the guitar.

Some evenings, depending on their mood, they would sing fine harmony on old hymns or old country standards. They always laughed as each song ended, the expression of sheer delight with themselves. None of them ever gave a thought to performing for money. It was just something that they did together.

Corley was just arriving at the point where he was not afraid to move into some of the sessions with his guitar. The local pickers played well and did not have much tolerance for beginners. Young folks had to learn on their own time and earn their way into the sessions by playing respectably. Anyone who lost time or missed a lick, got disapproving looks from the veteran pickers. But lately, Corley had been gathering smiles of approval when he played guitar. He was definitely not ready to move in with the fiddle.

He had spent hours on his back porch, looking out over the Vandalia River and working on the old guitar. The one that he had learned on was not much of a guitar. It was one that he had dug out of the closet, put a set of strings on, and made it work the best that he could. A cousin and an uncle had shown him a few chords, but mostly he just found his own way. Then, last fall, his dad had shown up with an old Gibson. It was not a new one, had a few scratches on the front, but it was a Gibson. It rang like a church bell and Corley could not believe how easily it noted. It had helped him considerably.

Among his classmates at Bolton High, the guitar had not yet gained respectability, especially among the town kids who considered themselves urbane and sophisticated. And, many of the rural kids, who thought that they needed the respect of the town kids, kept their love for country music a closely guarded secret. To Corley, music was music, and he enjoyed just about all of it that he had ever heard. The high school band played some pretty heavy stuff such as "From The New World Symphony" and "The Overture From The Barber of Seville." Corley enjoyed that and he also liked the tunes from the Broadway shows that they sang in the school choir. "There is Nothing Like a Dame" was one of his favorites. Yet, he never let it be known around school that he was a guitar player, and certainly not a fiddle player, for he was afraid it would damage his already shaky image as a regular guy. He often wondered about Julie's taste in music because she was a very talented musician.

On the other hand, some strange things were beginning to happen on the popular music scene. Radio stations which only a year ago had been strictly country or popular with no crossing over were beginning to switch around a little. "The Ballad of Davy Crockett" which sounded pretty country was being played widely. The guitar sound was very dominant throughout the entire record. But more significantly, the new sound that was being labeled rock'n roll was being played on both kinds of stations, and the electric guitar was pretty much the main instrument in most groups who were playing it. Someone by the name of Elvis Presley was beginning to be the most talked about individual of the new sound and he played a guitar. The young sophisticates at Bolton High seemed to like him.

Dancing was definitely on the threshold of a revolution. The jitterbug step did not quite fit the new rock beat, but the young folks were modifying it so that it would. Corley was beginning to fool around with all of these styles on the guitar, but not where anyone could hear him. Down at the store, or anywhere else that he played with a group, he stuck with the traditional music of the area.

The day after school was out Corley was sitting on the back porch with his guitar when he looked across the river and saw Julie Meadows walking up the railroad track, probably going home from the store. He watched her go and let his fingers run to the C position and sung a verse to an old song that Blackie had been humming the day he and Sam had approached his porch.

>Just because you think you are something
>Just because you think you're so hot
>Just because you think you've got something
>That nobody else ain't got.

Then it occurred to him that those were probably the very reasons that he was so terribly attracted to her. He decided right then and there that he was going to have to look into the Julie situation before too long.

The rest of the week went by and he still did not manage to muster up the courage to make the trip across the river. When Saturday night came, he decided that he would hitchhike to town. He had already been driving for some time, but every now and then he just liked to hitchhike to town. It was something to do. He caught a ride with a neighbor, got out on Main Street and walked around town. He talked to a couple of locals, and checked out the movies to see what was playing. The marquee read: DADDY LONGLEGS LESLIE CARON BARES HER FOREHEAD. That did not seem terribly exciting to Corley so he concluded that the evening was a bust. He drank a cup of coffee at the diner and decided it was time to make it back home.

He walked over to the road leading back up the river and was standing there waiting for a car when he saw Denny Lewis' black Chevy come up the road and turn over towards town. He started to wave as the Chevy drew near, then noticed that there was a girl with him. He tried to tell himself that he was wrong, but it was Julie Meadows.

His mind went on a rampage. How the hell could she do this to him? Here he thought that she was a babe in the woods, tied to her mother's apron strings, then she shows up sitting nearly on top of the slickest talking bastard in three counties. Corley was numb and experienced hate, jealousy, depression, and outright rage all in one breath. A passing car responded to his gesture and Corley climbed into a '51 Ford with two guys who were passing a bottle back and forth.

"How far you going, Slick?" one of them asked.

"About ten miles," Corley responded.

"Want a drink?" the other one asked.

"No," Corley said softly, "but thanks for the offer.

He had tasted liquor before a time or two. His older brothers passed it around pretty frequently when they were in town. It tasted like hell. That was about all that Corley knew about it. He had never been high. After they had gone a couple of miles one of the guys looked back at Corley.

"Look kid, we will be going on up the river later on, but we are going to stop at The Beeches for awhile."

"Oh that will be fine," Corley said. "I'll just hitch another ride from there."

"Suit yourself," he answered

The Beeches was a better than average roadside beerhall. It usually drew a decent crowd and there was rarely any trouble. On Saturday nights there was always a square dance with a live band. Corley had been there before and watched the dancing and while he was a good flatfoot dancer, he had not yet gotten the hang of the square dance figures that they danced. Troy Carr owned and operated The Beeches and he welcomed teenagers because many of the older teenaged girls were good square dancers. They usually just drank cokes. The word was though that old Troy was not above selling a beer to a minor. Eighteen was the legal age in West Virginia, eighteen for beer, twenty one for hard stuff.

On this particular night the crowd looked to be pretty good so Corley decided that he just might go in for awhile and enjoy the band. He knew that Red Hanshaw would be playing fiddle. As he was getting out of the car he said, "I'll take that drink now if you still have some."

"Sure," the driver of the car said, "have a good pull."

Corley took three hard swallows and choked back a cough. His eyes watered but he held it down. When he got inside the place was buzzing. The band was on break and people were slow dancing to the juke box. Corley sat down at the bar where it was kind of dark.

"Give me a Falls City," he said to the girl behind the bar.

She looked at him kind of funny, but she sat the beer on the bar. He took a drink and spun around on his stool to survey the crowd. The beer tasted good, much better than whatever those two guys had in the brown bag. He drank it slowly.

As he looked around the dimly lit room, he saw Lucy O'Brannon smiling at him. Lucy had graduated from Bolton High a year ago and was working for the electric company. Corley had talked with her only a couple of days ago. She was a pretty, yet plain girl with long, light brown hair. She had taught Corley to dance at T-Club at school when he was in the ninth grade. He was always uncomfortable at T-Club but everyone told him that a man had to learn to dance if he was going to get along in the world. Lucy had been very helpful. She was taller than Corley in those days, but she made him feel comfortable and told him that he had a smooth step. He was a natural dancer, she had told him.

The juke box played mostly slow, cuddling, country songs. It was the best music in the world for slow dancing and Vandalia County girls were the best slow dancers that ever was. Corley had never danced in a beerhall but god how he wanted to right then. He looked at Lucy and she smiled again. His heart was beating too damned fast, but when the juke box started playing Ernest Tubb's "Waltz Across Texas," he made his way toward her. She eased the pain by meeting him on the floor, and boy did she feel good against him. No longer taller than he, she fit right into his grasp.

"You have grown some since T-Club," she said, "but you are still pretty smooth."

"Actually, I guess I haven't practiced much," Corley answered, "but it seems to be coming back to me."

They moved about the floor easily until the song ended and, bad as he hated to, he let her go and returned to his stool.

Troy Carr unplugged the juke box because it was time to square dance again. Corley saw Red Hanshaw moving back onto the band stand. He had a guitar player, a banjo player, and a standup bass player with him. Red played really well but he had a pretty serious drinking problem. He drank Falls City and the management kept one where he could reach it between tunes. During his breaks he would go to his car and take a couple of long pulls from a bottle of hard stuff. If anyone went out with him he would always offer them the bottle first, and if they did not take a drink, he was offended. The fact is, Red had no idea how well he played.

The tunes he played were mostly old traditional square dance tunes, "reels" is what Red called them. "Soldier's Joy" and "Blue Eyed Girl" were two of his favorites. There were plenty of fiddlers around who played those tunes, but Red had that special quality that was most assuredly a gift from the Gods.

The community at large viewed him as generally no good. He never worked at a steady job that anyone knew about. He had gone off to Ohio and Michigan and worked a stint or two in the factories, but he had never gotten serious about it. He had remarked to Corley once that "I'm too small for heavy work and I ain't got no education." Corley supposed that was his way of saying that he never intended to do much work.

He loved the ladies and he loved to watch them dance to his fiddle. The dance step that they did during the square dance routines made their bosoms bounce just right and Red could look without missing a lick on the fiddle. He loved them all and did not discriminate between those who were married and those who were not. He usually made his moves during the times between the square dance sets. After Red had gone for his drink of liquor, he would cruise the crowd and dance with the ladies who had returned his glances during the square dance. He was a slick slow dancer and usually left with a woman when the evening ended.

As the sets were forming on the floor Corley saw Lucy coming his way with her hand extended.

"I can't do this stuff," Corley said.

"Sure you can," she said. "You just go the way I push and pull you and you will do fine."

The caller moved to the mike and said, "Take a Little Peek."

Corley had seen it done plenty of times and thought that he could get through it with Lucy's help. She was an expert. He recognized the tune that Red began playing as "Uncle Joe" and he felt the rhythm immediately as they joined hands and circled left. When the caller called the grand right and left, Corley panicked because he knew that this was the hard part. But with Lucy pulling him and pointing out which direction to go, he was soon into the dance. Before the set was over Corley was practically the star of the floor because he had a really good step. He really hated to see the set end.

"Where have you been all these years?" Lucy exclaimed. "You are pretty good."

"It was my first time in a set," said Corley, "and you made it easy."

As he returned to his stool and was thinking about ordering another beer, his friends from the '51 Ford nodded to him.

"We're going up the river, Slick. Want to go?"

"Yes, I guess I'd better," Corley answered.

He definitely wanted to dance some more with Lucy but he could picture himself out there along the road at midnight trying to catch a ride, and he did not like that picture. He stole a glance at Lucy as he went out the door but she was busy talking with her friends and did not observe his exit. Corley thought to himself that she would not be interested in him anyway. She was older and experienced. But, she did feel good in his arms, no doubt about that.

They all got back into the Ford and motored up the river. The two guys were still passing the bottle, but Corley passed this time. When they let him out he walked toward his house with a very confused mind. He felt many things, but mostly he hated Denny Lewis and he could not get over that goddamned fickle Julie Meadows. He made up his mind right then that he would go over to her house tomorrow and ask her just what the hell was going on. As he crawled in bed he could still smell Lucy O'Brannon's hair. He turned out the light and concluded that he was a poor excuse for a lover.

Next morning was Sunday and the world always seemed different on Sunday morning than it did on Saturday night. It was a beautiful morning. Fog was rising from the river, but the sun was shining brightly above it. Birds were singing everywhere. It was the kind of morning that made Corley glad to be where he was on the earth. After morning chores he sat down to a breakfast of sausage which had been canned the previous fall, eggs which were gathered yesterday, home made apple butter, and biscuits baked as only his mother could bake them. The coffee, made from spring water, was delicious. Corley had been drinking coffee since he could remember.

As soon as the dew dried on the grass, he got him a straight back chair from the porch, his guitar, and found him a place out in the backyard where he could watch the river flow. He got in a couple of good hours of practice and decided that he was getting pretty slick. And, as he ran through his songs he decided that he would cross the river that afternoon and make his way up to the Meadows' place.

After Sunday dinner was over, he put on a clean pair of jeans and a good shirt. He wanted to look presentable since he had not met Julie's parents. He did not want them to think that he was some barefoot kid. He carried his boots as he waded the shoals. The water was warm and shallow, and once across, he put on his boots and struggled up through the brush to the railroad track. There was a trestle that had to be crossed right before you turned up the hollow to the Meadows' place and Corley could not pass up the challenge of walking across it on the rail. He walked the rail without breaking stride and thought to himself that he would ride a bicycle across that rail one day. Everyone said that only one person had ever done it and that was years ago. Someday he would give it a try.

The Meadows' place was impressive, a big two story house setting back in a grove of white oaks. Corley had admired it from the hill across the river, but had never been close to it. As he approached the house he heard a piano playing something classical, but he could not identify it. Julie's father was sitting on the front porch smoking a pipe. Corley boldly approached the porch.

"I'm Corley Malone, your neighbor across the river."

"Come on up and sit down," he replied. "What brings you over this way?"

With all of the courage in him and making his voice as strong as he could, Corley managed a reply.

"I wanted to speak to Julie for a moment."

"That's her playing the piano," he gestured. "I'll get her."

He went inside, the playing stopped, and Julie came through the door.

"Well, hello Corley," she said as here blue eyes penetrated to the depths of his soul. "What brings you across the river?"

He forgot all of the anger that he had pent up inside him and everything that he had planned to say suddenly left him.

"Well, I told you that I would come over and we would go down for a swim."

"I had just about given up on you," she said. "I went down one day last week, but it looked so brushy that I did not risk going down to the river."

"Today would be a good day to learn your way down," Corley said. "Get ready and I will introduce you to the world's best swimming hole."

"I'll have to speak to my mother," she replied.

Corley wondered if she had asked her mother if she could go out with that sorry assed Denny Lewis, but he did not say anything to that effect. She went inside and returned with her Mother.

"Mother, this is Corley Malone. He lives just across the river."

"Hello Corley," she said, condescendingly, Corley thought.

He immediately did not like Julie's Mother and it appeared that the feeling was mutual.

"Are you a good swimmer?" she asked.

"Yes," Corley answered. "It is one of the things that I do really well."

"Julie swims, but not that well," she said. "You two be careful."

As Corley waited for her, her father returned to the porch.

"Pretty good looking day," he commented.

"Mighty fine," Corley answered.

"What you say your name was?"

"Malone, Corley Malone."

"I think that just about everyone across the river is named Malone," he said.

"Just about," Corley responded. "I guess we are quite a clan."

Julie appeared in her swimsuit under one of her dad's white shirts. But Corley could see her plenty good and was again reassured that Julie Meadows was a quality woman.

By the time they got back to the river the sand bar was full of people. There must have been a hundred or so. When they broke into the clearing across the river from the crowd they really got some stares. The boys that he usually roughhoused with during swimming hours were all watching. Sam Somerville was grinning from ear to ear.

Corley had to remove his boots and roll up his pants in order to get back across the shoal. As they started to wade he caught hold of Julie's hand to steady her as they walked the rocky bottom. He had never touched her before. She squeezed his hand tightly.

Corley found them a good place in the sand. She drew plenty of stares when she removed the white shirt and sat down on her blanket. Corley hurried to his house to change. When he returned he pulled her up.

"Let's get wet," he said. "That's what we came for."

She did not pause, just got up and walked to the river's edge with him.

"Can you make it across?" Corley asked.

"I think so," she answered.

She swam smoothly, but never broke her hands above the water. Corley showed his best overhand stroke and they made it across easily. It was about a forty yard swim. They rested briefly on the other side and made the return trip without much conversation. Corley was not real comfortable. As they settled down to sun, the roughhouse gang was beginning to organize for the afternoon games.

"Come on Corley," Sam yelled. "We are going to have a little capture the flag in the old John boat here. We need you."

"Not today," Corley answered.

"Come on you fink," he persisted.

"Go ahead," Julie suggested. "I'll just get some sun."

It looked like there was going to be six on a side. Six would be in the boat with the flag, and six would attack the boat and try to take possession of the flag. The flag was actually a dirty old rag. The six with the flag got into the boat and rowed upstream and began to drift back down, taking a position about mid-stream where the water was ten to twelve feet deep. The flag forces were led by Sam Somerville himself. Corley was among the attackers, and they began to swim toward the boat. The object was to get the flag away from the defenders in the boat and return it to a designated spot on the sand bar.

Corley and his crew approached the boat and the battle began. At first it was fairly calm and harmless play with the defenders pushing the attacking forces gently away as they tried to get into the boat. But the struggle got more intense and violent with each passing moment. If one of the attackers got into the boat the blows to dislodge them were pretty hard and kicking was common. As one of Corley's team drew a crowd in the front of the boat, Corley managed to get into the stern and was making his way toward Sam when he felt a terrific smash to his back and ribs. Someone had hit him with a boat oar and sent him into the water on his head. He might have been stunned had it not been for the cool water reviving him. As he recovered and moved back to the battle he could see a bloody nose and several bleeding scratches. The strategy of the attackers then turned to overturning the boat.

When the boat capsized, Sam, a strong swimmer, dived away with the flag in his teeth and was headed for shore. Attackers and defenders pursued. When Sam reached shore he ran full stride toward the wooded part of the sand bar, out of sight of the people. Corley was not really that far behind him and when Sam realized that he was closing the gap, he charged back toward the river and was tackled and overcome by Corley's teammates. Corley wrestled the flag away and made for the goal. All of the players, exhausted and grimy from the battle, lay in the water and washed away the sand and the blood from their scratches.

Corley had nearly forgotten Julie and she was not looking especially happy as he returned to her side.

"Do you all do this often?" she asked.

"Just about every day," Corley answered, "in one form or another."

"It looks dangerous to me," she said. "I thought you were hurt when you got hit with the oar."

"It still hurts," Corley said, "but I don't think that there is any permanent damage."

"I suppose that I should be thinking about going home," she said.

"Let's swim again," Corley suggested.

They played awhile close to shore and Corley was awkward as hell. He was afraid he would touch her in the wrong place, touch something that he shouldn't. She had him psyched out, no question about it.

"I suppose I should be going," she said.

"OK, I'll help you get your things back across the river."

As they walked back up the railroad, Corley could not think of a thing to say. Finally, he managed an apology of sorts.

"Look," he said. "I guess I haven't been very good company, but at least you know where to swim. I'll cut you a path down from the tracks to the river and you can come swimming whenever you feel like it.

"That would be nice," she answered.

They walked a bit farther and she stopped him and looked him in the eye.

"You don't need to apologize. I've had a good time."

Corley was comforted some by the remark but when they got back to her house he could not bring himself to ask if he could come back over, but he tried to leave himself an opening.

"Look, I'll drive around some evening. Maybe we can do something."

"I'll think about that," she answered. "Thank you for a nice afternoon."

Corley watched her go into the house with a sinking feeling and turned to go home. It suddenly occurred to him that he and Julie Meadows might live in two different worlds. The atmosphere of her household was completely different from his. They were not farmers and the inside of their house reminded him of a scene from a movie. Everything looked orderly and expensive. Her dad was some kind on an engineer and was gone a lot. Other than that, Corley really knew nothing about them.

As he walked back to the river it also occurred to him that he had just completed his first date. It was a pretty sorry excuse for a date, he thought, but now if anyone asked him if he had ever had a date, he could say, "hell yes". If they asked him what he did on his first date he would tell them that he took a girl swimming, sat her down on a blanket, then went off to play capture the flag with a bunch of half civilized morons. Pretty damned racy stuff, he thought.

That evening he felt the need to be alone, so he got him a blanket and told his mother that he would be sleeping down at the river. He went down to the sand bar and began to build a fire. One of the strange phenomenons of the Vandalia River was that there was a lot of coal in it. The river cut through veins of coal as it meandered its way through the mountains. There were always lumps of coal ranging from the size of a marble to chunks as big as a bowling ball lying around everywhere. It made an excellent fire, and if banked properly, would burn all night.

The trick was to get a good hot wood fire going, then begin to add a few lumps of coal. Once the coal got going, you had yourself a fine camp fire with fine aroma. Some folks did not like the smell of coal smoke, but Corley always liked it.

There was a lot of good therapy in just building the fire. It gave a person a sense of accomplishment. Then, once the fire began to burn good, you could just sit and enjoy it, listen to the night birds, and sort out all of your problems. Corley decided on this particular evening that he just had one basic problem and it was spelled JULIE. He thought about her from every possible angle and more and more convinced himself that Sam was probably right. She was out of their league. Perhaps he should set his sights lower, he thought. He should just put her out of his mind and enjoy the summer.

Corley rolled into his blanket in the soft, warm sand. He usually slept better in that sand than any other place, but he did not sleep worth a damn this night. In fact, he really wasn't sure he slept at all.

V

Corley's dad had cut the first cutting of hay on the previous Saturday so the next day was a day of hard work. The hayfield was something that the men dreaded in conversation, but once they got into it, they loved it. It was something that they could all share, neighbors helped neighbors, and it was something of a social occasion. Corley did not mind the work at all.

That afternoon, as they were all out in the hayfield, a stroke of good fortune came along for Corley in the form of a man by the name of Porter Belk. He was a real estate man of sorts who lived in Charleston during the winter and spent his summers about four miles on up the river from the Malone place. He also had several small camps along the river which he rented out for a week or two at a time. He was a right jolly man, a little heavy, and he breathed too hard from chain smoking. He puffed up to the sled where the men were working.

"Hey, Mr. Malone," he hailed Corley's father. "Looks like you fellas are into it today."

"We got an extra pitchfork," his dad replied.

"No, hell no, I don't need one of those sons-a-bitches. Damned hayfield always made me sick."

"What can we do for you?" Corley's father asked.

"Well, I'm looking for a couple of boys to do some work for me around the camps, mow lawns, cut filth, do a little painting, that kind of thing. Thought maybe your boy here would be interested."

Corley's father looked at him and said, "speak for yourself."

"Yes sir, Mr. Belk, I sure would be interested. Of course, I couldn't work every day because there are things that I have to do around here."

"Well, it wouldn't be every day. Most times just two or three days a week. I'll pay you six dollars a day and your lunch. That sound fair?"

"Sounds fair to me," said Corley.

"You know anyone else who might want to work?" he asked.

"The Somerville boy on the hill here probably would," Corley replied. "He's my age."

"You talk with him. I'll pick you up on Monday."

Corley was very excited by the development. He could always use money and now that he was driving more, it meant gas money. Gas money meant that he could run around on weekends with a lot more class. So as soon as they got the hay in, Corley walked up and hollered out Sam.

"Hey, Sam, want to make some money next week?" Corley asked.

"Doing what," he answered. "We going to steal something?"

"No, goddamn it, were going to work."

Corley went through the details with him and Sam decided that it sounded pretty good to him.

"Listen," Corley said, "if we are going to work next week, we had better get in a little camping trip. What do you say we pack up and spend a couple of days back in the hills?"

"Sounds like a good idea to me," said Sam.

Next morning, Corley was up early and about his chores. He had to talk his mom into doing the milking while he was gone. She was not too crazy about it, but agreed to do it. Sam and Corley walked down to the local store and secured some necessary supplies. They got pork and beans, hash, and some peanut butter. The cellar at Corley's house provided the other provisions that was needed.

The boys distributed their packs until each had about thirty pounds including their poncho and blanket. Each carried a canteen of water and Corley packed his most prized possession, a .38 caliber pistol with a four-inch barrel. Sam carried a .22 rifle. They were both very experienced with guns and treated them with respect. The guns were not really necessary, they just made them feel more comfortable.

They were underway by mid-morning and began the long hard pull up the first hill. The initial hill was the worst part for once they topped it, they could follow the ridgelines. There were also several old haul roads left behind from logging projects that made walking easier. The pre-planned camping spot was about four miles away so they could take their time.

The West Virginia woods during the summer were not really a very inviting place. The underbrush and weeds were nearly as heavy as a tropical rain forest. Chiggers and ticks were a constant threat, not to mention rattlesnakes and copperheads. And, when camping without a tent, as they were, there was always the threat of a sudden summer thunderstorm. Such storms could be a harrowing experience if you were caught out in the open woods. But all of the hazards were really the reason for their trip. It was a challenge, an adventure to be sure, for two seventeen year old boys.

As they made their way along the ridgeline Corley could see the Meadows place off in the distance. Julie was probably playing her piano and waiting for Denny Lewis to call, Corley figured. Telephones were not yet common along the river valley and Corley viewed that as a general disadvantage to his love life. He had to do all of his talking face to face. He had a momentary urge to curse Julie under his breath, but remembered his decision to put her out of his mind.

"You know, Sam, since we are in no hurry, we ought to swing out by the old Briney Horton place."

"Who the hell is Briney Horton?" Sam asked.

"Well, if you have never met him, we definitely need to go by there," Corley answered.

It was a steep climb to the top of the hill where he lived, but once you saw him standing in front of his shop you knew that the walk was worth it. The uniqueness of the man was evident at first glance. The shoulder length grey hair and the look in his eye told you immediately that you were not dealing with an ordinary man.

The area surrounding his house was a junk yard. Old cars were everywhere. Some of them had been driven over an embankment and left to rust away. Some sat in clusters for inexplicable reasons. There were two or three that had been stripped except for the frame, motor, running gears, seat, and wheels. Briney called them "skeeters." He used them to run the dirt roads back on top of the hills.

His shop was in absolute disarray. But among all the apparent nothingness, there was some rhyme and reason to the place. Working power tools were hidden among the clutter. Pieces of paper with diagrams that he had drawn were scattered everywhere. Products of his efforts were strewn about, some of which he had forgotten about for years. He seemed to be able to find what he was looking for among all the confusion and always had a new project underway.

Briney had a terrible stuttering problem which caused area children, and adults who had not met him, to erupt in laughter. And, those who had known him for years delighted in his conversations because he had a tremendous wit and sense of humor. Folks laughed both at him and with him because he was an absolute delight and was not at all self-conscious about his speaking problem.

Briney did not come down from his mountain retreat very often, but when he did, it was a happening. He always came to the one room schoolhouse on election day and entertained the loafers who faithfully gathered outside the polling place. And, when he made an appearance at the local store, word would travel fast and the place would soon be filled with listeners. He would talk about the state of the nation, tell old hunting stories, and preview things that he was going to invent. It made no difference what he was saying because the humor was in his wit and delivery of the words. He was basically against everything in society, even the Indians. They had not been around for a couple of hundred years but he continued to blame them for local problems.

He always seemed to have money when he needed it. It was said that during his younger days he had worked around the coal mines and made a decent living. He never dug coal, but invented, installed, and repaired the various mechanical devices that were used to extract the black stuff. Local mine owners had recognized his talents and had rewarded him handsomely. Folks who remembered his early life remarked that he worked for the mines when he wanted to, loafed some, but mostly amused himself with his own projects.

As Corley and Sam entered the clearing that surrounded his place, they saw him working on something underneath a big white oak tree that stood in his yard.

"What you up to Briney?" Corley greeted him.

"You're one of them damned Malone boys," Briney answered. "Don't know which one, but I know you are one of them. How's your old daddy?"

"He's fine," said Corley.

"You tell him he can't rabbit hunt worth a shit next time you see him," Briney said with a laugh.

"I'll be sure to tell him," said Corley. "This here is my friend, Sam Somerville, Briney. We are headed back into the hills to camp a few days."

Sam was biting his lip to keep from laughing but he was enjoying the visit.

"You boys come on in the house a minute, I want to show you what I'm building," said Briney. "It's a thhhhhhing of beauty." He really got hung up on thing.

He took the boys into his living room and there on a table was a coffin, made of beautiful cherry wood. It was nearly done except for a few carvings that he was working on.

"I've been working on this soooon-of-a-bitch for yeeeears." Briney said. "When I die they can plant myyyyyyyy ass in style."

His living room was filled with pieces of wood, sawdust, and shavings where he had been working, but Briney didn't even notice the mess.

When they got back outside, they enjoyed a good drink of cold water from Briney's well. The boys listened to a few more of his stories and were on their way.

"Wasn't that worth the stop?" Corley said to Sam.

"I'll say it was," replied Sam. "He is one of the most colorful people that I have ever met. Is he crazy or what?"

"He's not crazy," replied Corley. "He's just different."

They arrived at their destination about four in the afternoon and began making camp. The boys had chosen the spot for two reasons really. There was a good spring there, and also a fairly good sized rock cliff that would provide shelter if it did happen to come a storm. The big rock protruded out from the hill providing a shelf effect and the old timers in the area called it "shelf rock." If it did rain, they would have a dry place to sleep, but otherwise they would sleep out in the open. They cleared away some undergrowth and began to put things in order.

The big job was firewood. It takes a lot of firewood to keep a fire burning all night. Very little chopping was required for there was a good supply of dead limbs lying around on the ground. They dragged in a couple of good sized dead chestnut logs for late night burning. A blight had killed all of the chestnut trees in West Virginia in the 1920's, but the dead trees were still a good source of firewood. They worked hard for a couple of hours then feasted on fried potatoes, pork and beans, and hash. The coffee brewed on the open fire was always good and the unusually cool evening made it taste even better. As the night closed in, the boys enjoyed the fire.

"You ever had any?" Sam said almost suddenly. "Tell me the truth now, you bastard."

"No, I've never had any," Corley answered truthfully. "I've never even been close. The other day when I was with Julie is the only time I have ever fooled around at all."

"You acted like you were afraid of her."

"Hell, I guess I was," Corley said. "There is something about her that scares me."

"Like I said before, she might be out of your class."

"You might be right," Corley answered.

After a long pause and some flame gazing, Sam got back to the original point.

"Well, it's about damned time we got some, don't you think?"

"Past time, I'd say," Corley answered. "But, hell, I don't know how to go about it. My brothers used to tell me that you had to pry around with your hands and get them hot and ready, then get their clothes off. The rest will come natural."

"What if they cool off while they are getting their clothes off?"

"I don't think they cool quite that fast," said Corley.

"You know anyone who is putting out?" Sam asked.

"Well, if you believe everything that you hear, everybody's putting out. But frankly, I think there are a lot of liars around when it comes to that kind of stuff."

"I think that you are right," Sam agreed. "I think that a man is just going to have to find his own way. Ain't nobody going to do it for you."

"I danced with Lucy O'Brannon the other night down at The Beeches," Corley interjected. "She did get me excited."

"Well, I'll be damned," said Sam. "You sit there telling me about everyone lying about their love life, then you start lying like hell to me."

"I'm not lying," Corley said. "I did dance with her."

"What the hell you doing in The Beeches?" Sam asked.

"Dancing with Lucy O'Brannon, goddamn it," Corley answered.

"Bullshit," Sam said softly.

Corley related the story to him and he listened so quietly that it was funny. He was green with envy whether he believed the story or not.

"And they sold you a beer?"

"They sure to hell did," Corley said.

"Well, we are going to have to check that place out some Saturday night and that's for sure," said Sam.

"We'll do it," Corley concluded. "Meantime, you want the first watch?"

"Hell no," said Sam. "I'm tired as hell, you take the first one."

It was a tradition that someone would stay awake all night during camping trips. There really wasn't any reason for it, but it was good to keep the fire burning, and it added to the adventure. Whoever was awake kept the coffee pot going and the watch usually rotated about every three hours. Corley rolled old Sam out about one a.m. and he came out of his blanket shaking.

"No one but a damned fool would come out here and live like an Indian unless he had to," he said.

"Stop your damned crying," Corley said, as he rolled into his blanket.

Sam woke Corley about four a.m. and he sat and stared into the fire until it started to break day. Dew was starting to drop from the trees almost like rain so Corley broke out the ponchos. He threw Sam's over him, pulled his own up over him, and turned in for some early morning snoozing. He awoke to the smell of bacon frying, and the sun was well up into the sky. Sam had breakfast underway and was scolding Corley for being lazy. Afterwards, they straightened up camp a bit and set up some cans on a log for target practice. Sam was interested in the .38 as he had not fired a pistol. Neither of them was a Wyatt Earp but they had great fun trying to be.

Corley suggested that they get in another night's supply of firewood before it got too hot, so they busied themselves with that for the rest of the morning. They had just settled down for a short break prior to getting lunch when the first rock came crashing into the camp. It was not a big rock, just a throwing rock, and it really buzzed in there. It hit a white oak tree and glanced off through the brush. The next one came from another direction and hit the ground in front of the fire.

"What the hell?" Sam cried as they looked at each other.

Before Corley could answer him another rock came in and caught him in the back and it hurt like hell.

"It's those goddamn Dudley boys," Corley yelled as he and Sam stumbled and bumped into each other, trying to dodge the rocks. They were coming in pretty steady now. The Dudley boys were all around them, but they could not see a one of them for the underbrush. There were no rocks to throw back anyway, so the boys were defenseless unless they wanted to shoot someone.

"What are we going to do?" Sam asked.

"There isn't but one thing left to do," answered Corley, "and that is to get the hell out of here before one of us gets beaned."

They grabbed their guns and ran toward a nearby creek, jumped down into the creekbed and ran low until they didn't hear any more rocks whizzing over their heads. They stopped to catch their breath.

"We did just what those sons-a-bitches wanted," Corley said. "They wanted us out of there so they could ransack our camp."

"We ought to shoot the bastards," Sam retorted.

"They ain't worth shooting," Corley replied, "but we can now become the attackers."

They stashed their guns, began gathering up some throwing rocks from the creek, and made their way slowly back toward the camp. They could hear the Dudley boys talking and when they could see them they realized just how right Corley had been. They were going through their things. Corley saw Paul, the oldest, Alex, Tom, and David. He knew them all. They were the adult male part of what the local people called the Dudley set. They were a worthless, shiftless breed of people who seemed to live to break the law. They hunted out of season, stole from gardens, stole gasoline from parked cars, dynamited fish, and reaped all of the possible benefits of the government relief system.

Sam Somerville had a rifle arm. He could outthrow anyone who challenged him down at the sand bar, and he could knock you down with a baseball one hundred feet away. When he started throwing, the

Dudleys scattered fast. A squall from old Tom told Corley that Sam had connected at least once. But when they returned to camp, they discovered that the damage had been done. They had made off with most of their food, and with Corley's good hatchet. Sam looked around worriedly and shook his head.

"How did they know we were here?" he asked.

"Probably heard us shooting this morning," said Corley. "And, they have a nose for food."

"Do you suppose that they will be back?" Sam asked.

"Not before dark, but I suspect that we had better head back. I would hate to try to defend this place after dark."

They gathered what few thing they had left together. They had even taken one of Corley's blankets. Sam went to retrieve the guns and Corley could hear him swearing to himself as he returned. This had been his first encounter with the Dudleys.

As they started for home it occurred to Corley that they could swing around the ridge and go by the Dudley place on the way home. They lived in an old place down in a deep hollow, accessible only by dirt road. They always had two or three old junk cars sitting around, and usually one that would run well enough so that they could cruise the roads at night. If they could not steal any regular gasoline, they burned the drip gasoline that accumulated in the natural gas wells that were scattered around the hills. A car would knock and bang and smoke on the stuff, but it would work.

When Sam and Corley came out on the ridge above the Dudley place there was no one in sight.

"Can you throw that far," Corley asked.

"Hell yes, and so can you," Sam answered.

Each of them picked two good rocks and let go right toward the house. Just about time the first one hit the tin roof and made one hell of a noise, they let the other one go and ran like hell out the ridge, down into the next hollow, laughing like hell as they ran.

"That ought to rattle their ass a little," Sam said.

"At least it rattled their roof," Corley quipped.

After they caught their breath, they headed home at a leisurely pace and talked about how they would get back at the Dudley boys one of these days.

That evening at the supper table, Corley related a watered down version of the incident to his parents. He told them that someone had raided their camp while they were out hiking and stole all of their goods.

"It was probably some of that Dudley outfit," his mother said.

"Probably," said Corley.

That night when he took of his shirt and looked into the mirror, Corley saw a big blue bruise on his back where the rock had hit him. It was sore as hell. He would have to hide that from the folks for a few days. He did not want them to know that he had been at war with the Dudley clan.

VI

The mid summer weeks were busy for Corley. The job at the Belk place provided about three full days of work per week, and with his chores at home, he had little time for recreation. By the time he got to the sand bar in the evenings the crowd had left. He had not seen Julie Meadows for quite some time, but he had thought about her often. He had heard that she had been coming swimming often and he was sure that she wasn't sitting home nights. He and Sam had not been burning the streets with a hot night life. They had been out cruising around a few times, nothing exciting, just fooling around the drive-in restaurants and drinking coffee. They mostly drove Corley's dad's old pick-up. It was a '40 Ford. It wasn't beautiful, just transportation. They talked about girls all the time but did very little about it.

Then, one evening while loafing at the store, Corley saw a sign announcing a revival meeting over at a place called Sarvis. There was to be a guest evangelist by the name of "Freed" Jones. Corley had been to that church several times when he was a kid.

Revivals were common in the summer around Vandalia County. They usually ran for two weeks and would attract people from a pretty wide area. In addition to the religious service, the revival provided a social opportunity. Folks went for many reasons, a few of them religious. It was a place where the women could discuss how the canning and pickle making was going, and to gossip in general. The men would stand around outside before the service started and smoke Camels and Lucky Strikes while they talked about getting the hay up. They often discussed whether or not smoking was a sin. Most thought that it was not.

The young girls came to be looked at and the young men came to look. The small children came because there was nothing else to do with them and they were a general nuisance most of the time. Some of the ruffians of the area came to fight. A group from one part of the county would come and stand around somewhere near the church, daring another group to challenge them. This segment never went inside the church, and rarely fought. It was mostly a show of force. Corley was very familiar with the structure. He had grown up with it.

That evening, remembering the sign, he walked up to Sam's house and hollered him out. It was a Friday evening and they definitely needed to do something.

"Sam, we ought to drive over to Sarvis this evening and take in that revival meeting," Corley said.

"What the hell do we want to go to church for?" Sam asked.

"You just never know what might be going on over there," said Corley, "and besides, I can probably get the Buick if I say I'm going to church."

"Might as well," Sam said. "Beats the hell out of standing around on the street corner downtown."

Sarvis was about nine miles away and they started just as soon as Corley washed up after evening chores. Milking always made a person smell like cow shit whether you stepped in any or not, so Corley always washed very carefully. They got to the Sarvis Methodist Church about 7:00 p.m. and the sun was still fairly high in the sky. The church was situated in a grove of white oaks and folks were already gathering to talk. People leaned against cars and sat on the benches which were provided out under the trees. Someone was handing out literature on the evangelist who was conducting the revival. Corley did not need the literature because he spotted him immediately, standing among a group of men out behind the church. A glance told anyone that he was not of the same cut as those with whom he talked.

He was a pretty man. His facial features were nearly perfect, especially his teeth. You saw them before anything else because he flashed his smile with nearly every word he spoke. His suit was not expensive but it fit him well and he definitely got the most out of it.

Those who stood around him were plain men, many of them overweight, and all of their faces were weather-beaten. They dressed in the best that they had but it was obvious that they did not have much. Most of them wore white shirts with the sleeves rolled above the elbow, and they were generally tieless.

The church bell rang signaling the beginning of the meeting and everyone moved toward the door. As the evangelist approached Corley and Sam, he flashed his smile.

"How you doing, boys?" he said. "Glad to see you out this evening."

It was warm inside as the faithful and the unfaithful settled into their seats. The paper fans with wooden handles provided by the local funeral home immediately went to work. The women sort of gravitated to the right front of the church. The men, who considered themselves the backbone of the congregation, sat proudly on the front rows of the center section. Casual attendees and visitors from other churches tended to choose the seats to the left of center. The young men who represented major sin in the community filled the back rows. They would be the victims of the evening's activity. Corley and Sam joined this group.

"I hope you know what you are getting us into," Sam said as they sat down.

"Just be cool," said Corley. "I've been to a million of these things."

Sam was pretty uneasy because his family had never attended church.

All eyes in the congregation were on "Freed" Jones. He sat motionless in the back of the pulpit. There was no printed program and it appeared that old "Deacon" Bartley would be the leader of the evening's activity and would introduce the speaker. "Deacon" was a ubiquitous church-goer and loved the limelight. He put a short blessing on everyone in a fashion that would have made the Pope green with envy. Then, he asked everyone to stand and sing hymn number 145. It was "Standing on the Promises," one of Corley's favorites. The piano player jolted them into the mood with a rousing introduction. The singing was superb. Vandalia County congregational singing was second to none and Corley always enjoyed being a part of it. Sam looked at him like he was crazy.

"You're a regular choir boy," he said softly.

"And you're a damned heathen," Corley replied.

After the hymn, "Deacon" went into the introduction. Every eye was glued on "Freed" as he told the story. It seemed that the Reverend Jones, from out in Indiana, had been imprisoned for armed robbery in his youth, and while doing hard time, his mother had sent him a Bible. He read the Bible each night and soon began to share his readings with his fellow prisoners. He had gotten on his knees in his cell and had repented all of his sins. Soon, he had converted the entire cell block. "Freed" then cut a deal with the warden. He would spend the rest of his entire life converting sinners if he could only be set free. With God's help the warden had seen fit to let him go, and he had now been at his work for two years.

When "Freed" moved toward the podium, Bible in his hand (the one his mother had sent him), a faint gasp emanated from the right front of the church. The women of the church were not accustomed to such a man. When he flashed his smile, some of the younger ones could not conceal their excitement.

It was immediately evident that he was the master of his trade. He began quietly, speaking intently but without raising his voice. But he slowly increased the pace of his sermon. He began to walk slowly, back and forth across the pulpit, Bible always in his right hand. All of his words came from the heart because he had no prepared text. As he gradually worked himself into a frenzy, the congregation was in the palm of his hand. The ladies were in a trance and the men contributed verbal gestures of approval. Even the sinners were very attentive. Toward the end of his message he began to gradually lower his voice, and when he finished, his voice was nearly a whisper. He concluded with the alter call. In typical evangelical style he raised his right hand and made his plea. "While every head is bowed, is there one among you here tonight who would come forth and commit his life to Christ? Would there be any of you ladies who would like to recommit your life?

A few young folks came forward and Corley noticed the extra long stare that "Freed" gave the good women of the church as he scanned the audience. The evangelist then sat down and old "Deacon" took over. He asked everyone to shake hands with their neighbors and move toward the front of the church so that they could all pray with the sinners. As the singing got underway the pace quickened. There was hand clapping, shouting, and outright hollering in progress. Sam looked at Corley with concern in his eye. When they finally knelt and began the group prayer, Corley nudged Sam.

"This is where we get out. They will be back here trying to drag us to the alter soon."

Sam quickly consented and they exited quietly.

"Some of those people are crazy," said Sam, shaking his head.

"They're just having a good time," said Corley. "They won't hurt anything nor anybody. They will be perfectly normal tomorrow."

Corley did observe the Reverend "Freed" Jones embracing the good looking women during the frenzy, and he saw some pretty prolonged stares between him and some married women of the church.

"Thought we came here to pick up women," Sam said, almost to himself.

"Hell, I had a good time in there, didn't you?" asked Corley.

"No, I was half scared to tell you the truth," answered Sam.

"Just wait till the service ends, we might do some good yet," said Corley.

"Horseshit," Sam said disgustedly.

Corley had exchanged glances with the Phillips girls several times during the service and had gotten some pretty responsive smiles. He had know the girls since they were children. They were not sisters, maybe first cousins, Corley thought. But, they had matured since he had talked to them last. They were in his Sunday school class during his church- going years and he had always spoken to them at school.

When they came out of the church, he made his move.

"What are you girls doing this summer?" he asked.

"Oh, just staying around home," Brenda Phillips, the older one, answered.

"I'll bet," said Corley. "You girls probably have a date seven nights a week."

"Not hardly," the youngest one, Sue, replied.

"Now old Sam and I have thought about asking you girls out a dozen times, but we have been pretty busy working, and you know how it goes. We just never got around to it."

They both blushed a little and Sam was standing there not saying a word.

"How'd you girls get to church?" Corley inquired.

"We walked. It's only about a mile," Brenda said.

"Well, the least we could do is to give you a ride home," said Corley. "Better yet, why don't we drive into town for a coke? It's still early, not even ten o'clock yet."

"Oh, we couldn't do that without asking our parents," Brenda said quickly.

"Well, get in the Buick here and we will just drive over and ask them," said Corley. "Come on, we'll drive you home and if your parents don't want you running around with the likes of us, we'll just forget it."

"OK", said Brenda softly.

Sam pulled Corley back. "Now just which one of these lovelies is supposed to be mine?" he inquired.

"Take your pick," Corley answered.

Both the girls were getting into the back seat of the Buick as they turned around. Sam got up front with Corley and they started up the road. Once in the car, the girls seemed more at ease. They visited both sets of parents and secured the needed permission. They were given an eleven o'clock curfew which did not give them much time.

"Why don't you get up here with me, Brenda?" Corley said, as they came out of her house.

"Sure," she answered, and bounced right into the front seat.

Sam and Sue got into the back without words. Brenda did not sit on top of Corley, but she did not sit against the door either. What really got Corley was that he felt completely at ease with her. Yet when he was around Julie, or even Lucy, he was nervous. He could not look Julie in the eye for nothing, not those eyes of hers. He looked in the mirror at Sam and he was sitting in the corner of the seat with his arms folded. He had not said a word to Sue.

They cruised through Bolton a time or two, made sure that everyone saw them. Then, Corley decided to motor over to the drive-in restaurant where he and Sam loafed all the time so they could have some cokes. Anabell Stricker, the carhop, looked at the boys strangely before coming to the car. She had never seen them with girls in the car before.

"You are out late for a couple of country boys," she flirted.

"Well, I'm just driving these other people around," Corley answered.

As she walked away to get the orders, Brenda smiled. "You just flirt with all the girls, don't you."

"Oh, he's a regular international lover," Sam broke in.

"I thought you had died back there, Sam," Corley said.

"I was beginning to think the same thing," Brenda teased.

Sam looked sick and uncomfortable but he managed a few more comments during the evening.

They took Sue home first and Brenda and Corley watched as Sam walked Sue about halfway to the door and turned around and came back. When they got to Brenda's house Corley walked her to the door then stepped inside to say something to her parents. Brenda came back out on the porch with Corley and thanked him for the evening. He thought about kissing her but had a sudden impulse to hit her lightly on the shoulder and said goodnight. There just wasn't any fire there. Back in the car, Sam looked straight ahead.

"Well, how did it go?" he asked.

"I laid her on the couch in front of her mother," Corley said.

"You dumb bastard," was all Sam could muster as they drove away.

That night in bed it occurred to Corley that he was fully grown, seventeen years old, driving a car, and not only had he never made love to a girl, he had never even kissed one. A pretty poor start for someone who wanted to be an international lover, he thought.

VII

The next evening Corley was faced with Saturday night anxieties. He lay around in the back yard for an hour or two after he got his chores done trying to decide what do with himself. He thought some of going over to see Julie but he figured she wasn't home. He hadn't seen Sam all day. Sam was probably afraid that Corley was going to ride him about all of those moves he put on Sue Phillips. He was laying low, Corley figured. He fooled around with his old fiddle for awhile and learned a new lick or two.

As darkness began to fall he asked his dad if he could have the Buick to drive to town.

"You can drive that Buick anytime you need to, just as long as I am not using it and you buy your own gas. Just remember that it's the only car we have and if you wreck it, you will be walking or driving the old pickup. Take care of that car and you will have good transportation anytime you want it. You wait here and I'll give you a set of keys."

Corley was a little stunned by the speech and the set of keys. Feeling pretty good about himself, he climbed into the Buick and headed down the river. It was a five year old Buick, but it looked good. It sparkled like a new one and rode like a Packard. Corley was proud to drive it. When he got down to The Beeches he pulled down into the parking lot and parked under a big sycamore tree. He could hear the fiddle already as the square dance band was warming up for the evening. The crowd was still small and Corley knew that he was going to be conspicuous. He ordered himself a coke from the bar and walked back near the band. The band this particular evening consisted of Red on the fiddle, backed up by a banjo and guitar player. They played damned good square dance music. Since there wasn't anything going on, Corley asked the guitar player if he could sit in on a tune or two. He gladly consented because playing a guitar behind a fiddle can get a little old. The guitar player went for a fresh beer. Red looked at Corley skeptically.

"You ever second for a fiddle before?" he asked.
"A time or two." said Corley.

Red began playing "Old Joe Clark" without saying another word and Corley picked it up. It was in the key of A. After Corley had whipped two or three slick runs on him, Red turned and smiled approvingly to the banjo player. Red was far better than anyone Corley had ever played with and it was a definite thrill for him. He also gained the approval of Troy Carr, the owner, and that took some pressure off him. The regular guitar player returned with two beers in his hand and sat down on the apron of the platform where the band stood when they played.

"A man that plays guitar like you deserves a beer," he said as he handed Corley a Falls City.

Corley looked toward the bar.

"It's alright," the guitar player said. "Troy said to tell you to be careful and if the State Police happened to come in, just walk away from it. You come back later in the evening and give me another break."

"I'll do it," Corley said proudly.

The crowd was picking up and Corley settled in at a table near the band. A chill went up his spine when he saw Lucy O'Brannon come in with two other girls. Corley waved and smiled and they came back to his table.

"You all sit down with me," he said. "I feel kind of funny holding down this entire table by myself."

They sat down and Lucy introduced him to the other two, both of whom he knew by sight. Hell, everyone knew everyone in Vandalia County. Lucy looked absolutely delicious and she and Corley talked easily.

"When did you start drinking beer in the open?" she asked with teasing eyes.

"Just about ten minutes ago," Corley answered.

"You going to square dance with me again tonight?" she asked.

"Why not," Corley said. "I got through it the last time."

He was a little surprised to see Lucy order a beer. When it came, she poured herself a glass and shoved the bottle over in front of Corley. Then she smiled the prettiest damned smile that Corley had ever seen. He wondered deep inside if he could handle the situation that was beginning to develop. One thing for sure, he was going to have to go easy on the beer because he was not a big boozer in any sense of the word. The caller was calling the first set to the floor.

"Four couples," he said. "Four couples to a set and we'll dance one."

One set had already formed before Corley and Lucy got on the floor and they made the second set complete.

"You sure you know how to do this?" she teased as she squeezed his hand.

"As long as we are not the first couple, I'll do fine," said Corley.

In the old traditional square dance, the first couple does the routine first after the grand right and left so Corley knew that he would be able to watch the routine three times before it got to him. He felt confident. The couple with their backs to the band was always the first couple. The music started and the set went smooth. Lucy and Corley made their round like professionals and Corley was having a great time. Lucy had a great sense of rhythm and Corley's flatfoot step was catching everyone's attention. When the music stopped and they sat back down, the beer tasted better.

Troy Carr plugged in the juke box so the band could rest and folks began to slow dance. Lucy and Corley danced every dance and he held her tighter than he had ever held any girl in his life. As she snuggled against him he wondered why the hell he had been running around in the hills all of these years playing games with a bunch of boys when he could have been dancing with pretty girls. Occasionally, one of the new rock and roll tunes would play on the juke box and people were trying to figure out how to dance to it. The older folks tried to jitterbug, but it did not quite fit. The new beat required a little more head nodding and body movement. Lucy and Corley tried one, and while Lucy did fine, Corley felt a little awkward. She was encouraging with her comments as they sat down. She knew how to make a person feel good. She kept putting her hand on Corley's arm as they talked. She was looking better with each passing moment. The band was moving back into position and Corley saw the guitar player coming his way.

"Want to play this round?" he asked.

Corley did not really want to play. He was enjoying Lucy too much, but he took the guitar and headed for the bandstand. Lucy watched him curiously as the music started. Corley did not look at her for fear of forgetting what he was doing. Old Red locked his eyes on Corley and leaned the fiddle right down onto his guitar so he could hear it good. Corley looked him right back in the eye and began to whip it on him, note for note. They forgot that anyone else was in the room as they got lost in the contagious singing of the fiddle. When the dancing stopped, they played for a couple of more minutes and ended in a burst of laughter. They had a damned good time and had not even noticed the people dancing.

"Aren't you something?" Lucy exclaimed as he returned to the table.

"I'm learning," said Corley. "Some day, I'll be good."

She held on to his arm when he sat down. They remained close the remainder of the evening, square danced another round and the hour was nearing twelve. West Virginia beer halls closed at midnight in 1955.

"Are you driving tonight?" Corley asked.

"Yes," she answered. "But, one of the girls can take my car if you want to go somewhere."

Corley could not believe how easy things were going. As it turned out, the other girls were going with some boys, so they each had a car. She bought a six pack of Falls City and they got into her car, leaving the Buick under the sycamore. Lucy had a '49 Chevy, black, with a torpedo back.

"You drive," she said.

They drove up the river until they came to Sugar Creek Hollow where a dirt road turned off to nowhere. Corley drove out of sight of the highway. He turned around, parked, and turned off the lights. Christ, it was dark up that hollow, Corley thought. He couldn't see anything but her teeth.

Lucy was all over him before he hardly had the lights off. Her first kiss damned near smothered him. He was just holding on and enjoying every second of it. He did not know a damned thing about snaps, zippers, nor left handed buttons, but he managed to get her blouse open and the back of her bra unfastened. He buried his head into her breast and tasted the warmth that had pressed against him all evening on the dance floor.

"Let's get in the back," she said. "We are going to get hurt on this steering wheel."

By the time they got into the back seat, her top was gone, and Corley began to work on her skirt. With her help, he soon had her nude on his lap. She was helping him with his clothes and Corley was shaking like a leaf.

"You got any rubbers?" she asked.

"Yes," Corley answered.

He had been carrying the things for years and it was hard to tell what condition they were in. By the time they got situated in the seat, Corley was wild as a bull. He lost all control of what little cool he had managed up to that point. He went absolutely wild and very shortly, became unaware of everything in the universe except Lucy O'Brannon beneath him in the seat of that '49 Chevy.

His head went limp on her shoulder.

"You are in too big a hurry, Corley Malone," she said.

There was a blanket over her back seat for a seat cover and she pulled it over them.

"You just wait awhile," she said.

Corley really wanted to get up and get the hell out of there. Suddenly, he didn't like her at all and didn't want to be near her. More than anything, he was embarrassed. He suffered through the first few kisses she was putting on him. She comforted him with encouraging remarks. She was a terribly good teacher. Finally, Corley felt himself beginning to rally and became the aggressor.

"You just take it easy and let me do some of the work this time," she said.

Corley did not resist and did as he was told. He learned about women right there in that dark hollow on Sugar Creek.

He got home about 2:00 a.m. and went to bed aware of the fact that he had just accomplished something that had been on his mind since he was twelve years old. He had dreamed about it, wondered about it, and talked about it. Now it was done. And Lucy O'Brannon had been great. She had known that it was his first time, but she had not mentioned it. He would not forget her, even in the years after he finally became an international lover, he thought as he went to sleep.

He was by nature an early riser, so he was up as usual next morning and about his chores. His dad had always told him that a man who lies around in bed all day would never amount to anything. At breakfast, Corley fully expected someone to ask him where he had been so late, but no one said a word.

"Your grandfather sent word that he would like to have some help with his hay this week," his mother said. "You going to be able to help him this year?"

"Well, I don't know. I'll have to see," Corley said.

He had spent a week on Chestnut Run where his maternal grandparents lived since his early childhood. As he became older, he had helped his grandfather for a week or so each summer during his peak work time. It was an experience that he sort of enjoyed and it put him in good stead with the family.

"I think Sam can handle the work at the Belk place for a week if you and dad can cover the chores here. I'll talk with Sam."

By evening he had everything worked out and was headed for Chestnut Run with a change of clothes and his guitar. It was about a two mile walk because there was not a road into the Fletcher farm. Once you passed through the low gap to where you could see down in the valley, the farm was visible. This was Grandpa Fletcher's domain, his slice of paradise. He did not clear this land in the first place. He was the second, or perhaps third user. But there would be no more users of this piece of Vandalia County. Corley's grandpa was the last who would know how to use it, or more precisely, who would have any desire to use it. Corley admired the independent life that his grandpa lived, but he knew that modern folks wanted too many things. There would not be any kind of life like this once his grandfather's generation passed from the scene. Corley was sure of that.

Grandpa Fletcher was up every morning before dawn. Saturday and Sunday made no difference. His routine was exactly the same. He got up and dressed according to the weather and went to the barn. He fed the stock and milked the cow. When he got back to the house, his breakfast was ready. Eggs, ham or bacon, fried potatoes, hot biscuits, and coffee awaited him every single morning. There were no exceptions.

He was one of the few remaining folks who lived from the land. He raised all of his own food except for a few staples such as sugar, salt, and coffee. Money did not mean a thing to him. He told Corley once that he had never had a hundred dollars all at one time.

He was quiet, but always happy. He never once doubted his faith in God and lived the way that he thought God intended. While he had no money, Corley figured he was the richest man that he knew.

When Corley reached the top of the hill and looked down on the place, it looked like something you would see in a story book. There was the neat, white frame house with a picket fence around, a good barn, a chicken house, a blacksmith shop, and a shed or two. He could see the milk cow and work horse grazing on the hill above the house and a new calf bouncing around the calf lot near the barn. He could see his grandmother in her bonnet, fooling around with her flowers along the fence. Grandpa Fletcher was sitting on the front porch with a flyswatter. Sunday afternoons was the only time the old man ever sat down and relaxed. He got up to meet Corley when he saw him coming.

"Sure glad you could come," he smiled. "I sure can use a good man."

"I'm not near as good a man as you, Grandpa, but I'll do what I can. I'm looking forward to some of Grandma's cooking."

The conversation was a little awkward at times, but Corley did pretty well, talking mostly about the hay.

Most of it was down and Grandpa was worried about rain. His grandmother kept talking about how much he had grown.

"His shoulders are as broad as yours," she said.

"Yes, we'll be lucky if we have him around another year or two. He's all growed up and he'll be wanting to go off somewhere like his older brothers."

"Maybe not," Corley said. "I might just stay around and aggravate everyone. Is old Dwight home this evening or has he gone to church?"

"Don't believe they're having service tonight," Grandpa answered. "I expect he is up there."

"I think I'll walk up and see if I can get him in a checker game."

Grandpa nodded his head. "He'll like that."

"I'll not be gone long," Corley said as he departed.

Dwight Darrow was a man not quite forty who had the adjoining farm. He was a brute of a man, strong as an ox, and quite a worker. He, like most other Vandalia County men, held a full time job in addition to maintaining a farm. He loved to play checkers in the evening if he could find a partner. Corley knew that he would be glad to see him. He and his wife were childless and they were sitting on the porch alone. Dwight raised his hand in a low salute when he saw Corley coming.

"Hello, Corley," he said. "You looking for work?"

"No, I think Grandpa already has mine cut out for me," Corley answered.

"I expect," Dwight said. "Come on up and sit down. Had your supper?"

"Yes, I ate an awfully big dinner and had a snack before I left home."

"How's your folks?" his wife inquired.

"Oh, they're fine. Thought I might get Dwight in a checker game."

Old Dwight smiled and went after the board.

He always insisted that Corley make the first move. He would study several minutes before he made his move but it was always the right one. He won four straight games but Corley was not in the least surprised. He knew that Dwight was way out of his class but he just liked to watch him play and listen to his comments. Dwight's wife served them a piece of cake and some milk after the fourth game and Corley headed back to his grandpa's place before dark.

There was no electricity and no running water on Chestnut Run and it was always kind of exciting for Corley to live in the old ways. There was free natural gas on the place because one of the gas companies had a well on the hill above the house. So they had gas lights and gas stoves for heat. By the time Corley got back to the house it was nearly dark. His grandparents were both in the sitting room reading the Bible as they did nightly. Corley sat down and tried to read, but could hardly see. His grandfather's evening prayer closed out the evening.

Corley took full advantage of his grandmother's breakfast because he knew it was going to be a long, hard day. The morning was not too bad. They worked at some general repairs around the barn and fixed some fence. It was a bright, hot day and the hay was dry by noon. They ate another full meal, harnessed the horse, and went about haying. His grandfather raked the hay into windrows with a horse-drawn rake and Corley made the windrows into shocks. They would then wrap a chain around the bottom of the shocks and use the horse to pull them over to where they were stacking the hay. They both put the hay on the stack until it got about head high, then Corley got up on the stack. He would then move the hay snugly around the pole as his grandfather threw it up to him. His grandfather did not know the meaning of the word rest and they worked endlessly, or so it seemed to Corley. Finally, he saw his grandmother coming with a jug of water. Red with heat, they started for the shade. They rested and talked.

"You've done a lot of hard work in your time, haven't you Grandpa?"

"I guess I have, but the main thing is, there was no one around telling me how to do it. I tried to work on some public jobs, but there was always someone who thought he ought to tell me what to do. I never liked that. I always figured that I wanted to be my own man. Lots of folks don't agree with that, I know. But, I always figured that if you can't be your own man and live your life the way you want, there isn't much use in living."

Soon they were back at it. They worked until six o'clock and headed for the house for supper. They washed up at the outside washstand and sat under the big box elder tree in the yard for a half hour or so. The evening meal was a feast, as always, at his grandmother's table. Every meal was practically a ceremony. His grandfather always said grace and Corley could never understand what he was saying. It was something about the "blessings of life". He always wondered what the hell the "blessings of life" were. The men always said that when they prayed at church. "We thank you for the blessings of life," they would say. One of his older brothers had told Corley that they were talking about sex, but Corley had not taken that too seriously because that was all that his older brothers ever thought about.

After supper they were right back into the hay and they worked until nearly dark. By the time they got the horse put away, the day time was definitely over. They cleaned up a little and was soon out for the night. Next day they got the remainder of the hay that was cut down all stacked, and his grandfather mowed the rest of it. Most of it he could get with the horse drawn mowing machine but some of it had to be cut with a mowing scythe. The mowing scythe part was tough and required skill which Corley had not yet mastered.

His grandfather made it look easy. He kept his blade close to the ground and maintained a smooth rocking motion with the scythe. Very frequently, he would stop and hit his blade a few times with his whet rock. The part that he mowed was cut as closely and as neatly as if the machine had mowed it. Corley's part looked a little chewed up.

They spent the remainder of the day trimming around the fences, creek banks, and rocky places. Most of what they were cutting then could not be used for hay, but Grandpa Fletcher would not tolerate anything standing that might make his place look bad. That evening, Corley ached all over and again was in bed just after dark.

Wednesday was easier as they let the hay cure. They stirred it around a little with pitchforks, but generally just let nature do its part. There was plenty to do elsewhere on the farm, but the work was more leisurely while the hay was curing. Corley wasn't so tired when the sun started to go down, so he got his old guitar and started for the Keefer place. The Keefer boys had been on his mind all week and he was hoping that he would get an opportunity to visit with them. The Keefer brothers lived together out around the ridge from the Fletcher farm, and they were about the best old time musicians around. Frank Keefer played the fiddle and his brother, Albert, played the drop thumb banjo. They were both in their sixties and they played some tunes that no one else played. Corley loved to hear them play and he had not seen them since the past fall.

The Keefer place was less attractive than the average place around the area. It was run down some, but still remained presentable. Frank was married and his wife maintained a tidy household. Albert was not married and he stayed with Frank most of the time. He had a case of wanderlust and on occasion would bum around for a few weeks. Neither of them ever held a steady job and just did what they had to do to survive. Corley found them sitting on the front porch as he approached the house.

"That you, Corley?" Frank said, squinting a little.

"Yes, it's me," Corley answered.

"What brings you over here in the scrub pine country?" Albert asked.

"I'm trying to find some pickers good enough to play with me," Corley joked.

They both laughed.

"We hardly ever get to pick with a good guitar man," Frank remarked as they went for their instruments.

Albert put in a fresh chew as they all tuned together.

"What you want to play?" Frank asked.

"I just want you boys to play and I'll find you," Corley answered.

They played and they played and they played. Hornpipes, jigs, reels, and waltzes came in a never ending line. Corley could identify a few of them by name, was lost a good part of the time, but was having an awfully good time. Some of the tunes would drop into a minor key, sending a chill down Corley's spine. As he watched the rapport between the old men as they played, he got a little emotional and felt some moisture in his eyes. They were a joy to behold. When they finally stopped, Corley bragged on them, and they just went on and on about how he had improved. They shared a terribly good laugh. They started in on "Hop Light Ladies" and Corley could not resist getting up and doing a little flatfoot step. They smiled but never missed a note. After about three hours of unadulterated joy, Corley made his departure.

"We sure enjoyed it," Frank said. "Looks like you would come over more often."

"I will, I will," Corley said. "I forget how good you boys play."

Corley walked back around he hill to the light of a full moon with that old fiddle ringing in his ears and Julie Meadows on his mind. Life would surely be a joy if he could just include her in his rounds, or else get her out of his mind. Damn her to hell, he thought to himself, and damn her snobby mother to hell with her. Then he had an afterthought that he just ought to go over where she lived and knock her mother's ass right in the goddamned creek.

Morning came too soon and they were back into the hay. There wasn't really all that much left and they soon had it in the barn. He had one more of his grandmother's meals and started for home.

"How much do I owe you?" his grandfather asked.

"You don't owe me anything," Corley answered. "I just enjoyed working with a good man."

His grandfather just smiled and went into the house.

VIII

Saturday morning found Corley up and at his usual chores, but there was something different going on inside him. Somewhere, sometime, during the week on Chestnut Run, he had decided that no one on God's green earth was out of his class, and that if it was Julie Meadows that he wanted, then he best go after her.

He said nothing to no one, just went down to the river at mid-morning and crossed over in the boat. When he got to the Meadows place he didn't see anyone around, so he walked up to the door and hit it with authority. I ought to knock the son-of-a-bitch down, he thought to himself. Julie came to the door looking just like always, like some misplaced goddess.

"Well, Corley Malone," she said. "I thought you had left the country."

"Not yet," he answered, his confidence fading a little as she threw the blue eyes on him. "Let's you and I go for a little walk down by the river. I want to talk with you."

She looked at him with teasing eyes and said, "What to do you want to talk about?"

"You just come on," he said, feeling bolder.

She came out the door without hesitating and they started toward the river. He grabbed her hand. She did not resist nor respond. He took her down to the river and they sat down on a big flat rock at the head of the shoal. It was a pretty spot and Julie enhanced it considerably, Corley thought.

"You want to go out with me tonight?" he asked without looking at her.

"Out where?" she asked in return.

"Hell, I don't know, the movies, to Charleston, any damned where."

"Don't you swear at me." she said.

"I'm not swearing at you, I'm just swearing."

"Well, you ought to clean up your talk," she said firmly.

"What is it with you? I ask you for a date and you lecture me about my language."

He pulled her to him and kissed her hard on the lips. Again, she did not respond, but did not resist.

"Was that supposed to convince me to go out with you?" she asked.

"No, that's just something that I have wanted to do since April."

"You look disappointed."

"Well, you must admit, you really didn't put your heart into it."

"Just who do you think you are? You speak to me once a week, ignore me most of the time, tell me that you will see me soon, and then I don't see nor hear from you for two weeks. Then you come over here acting like you own me. Meanwhile, you cruise around with other girls."

His defenses shattered, Corley made an attempt to recover.

"Look, let's start fresh right here. Julie, will you go out with me tonight? We'll go to Charleston and take in a movie."

"Alright," she answered.

"I'll pick you up about seven."

They walked back to her house in silence. She smiled pleasantly and waved as she went inside. Somehow things still did not seem right. She seemed reluctant to accept and he could not read what was going on behind those blue eyes. He felt like kicking her ass right up between her shoulders on the one hand, but was thrilled at the thought of going out with her on the other. He also felt like he ought to go kick the shit out of Denny Lewis. Yet, he had a notion that old Denny might whip him in a fair fight. Corley didn't figure that he was much of a fighter. He was rough enough at play, but he had heard the sickening sound of a fist to the teeth in a beer hall or two, and he had decided that he did not want any part of that. He figured that he was too good looking to fight. That's what it was.

He went home and cleaned on the Buick the rest of the day. He had it sparkling inside and out. This was going to be a big night in his life and he wanted everything to be right. He even decided to wear his pegged black slacks and a pink shirt. All of the so-called cool cats were wearing them and he had bought his in a moment of weakness, then decided that he would never wear them in public. He had worn blue jeans and a chambray shirt for too long to change, he figured. Yet, he feared some change was inevitable if he was going to make any time with Julie. He felt like a damned moron when he got into the Buick that evening and his mother looked at him like she wasn't believing what she was seeing.

"I'm taking Julie Meadows to Charleston," he said. "Be back late."

"Be careful," she said. That's what mothers always said.

He drove down river to the bridge, then across the mountain to the dirt road that led down to her house. He never did understand why the hell her dad built such a nice house in a place so damned hard to get to in a car. He had his reasons, he supposed, probably looking for privacy. If so, he sure to hell had it, Corley thought. He had some dust on the Buick before he got to her house and he was not too happy about that.

She was sitting on the front porch, pretty as a rosebud. She was wearing that white dress that he liked so much and she had a red ribbon in her hair.

"Well, look at you," she said as he approached the porch. "I've never seen you looking quite like this."

"Take a good look. It may be the last time," he smiled. "I can hardly walk in these stupid pants."

"You look fine," she said. "I'll tell Mother we're leaving."

When they got into the car Corley was nervous. He did not know what she thought of the car. It was a four door sedan, a family car, nothing like that job that Denny Lewis sported around. But it was a quality automobile and he was proud of it.

"Speaking of looking good," he finally got around to saying, "you look awfully good this evening. A lot of girls are pretty, but you are kind of beautiful, I suppose."

"Well, thank you, Corley, I never expected that from you."

"What did you expect from me?" he asked.

"I don't really know. You are a different breed from what I am used to. I can't quite figure you out."

Boy if that wasn't the all time turn around of the century, Corley thought. He would have given anything to figure out what the hell was going on inside her head. One thing for sure, she tore his nerves all to hell and he was sweating through his shirt. When they got to Bolton, he dragged Main Street twice before he drove on to Charleston. He wanted to make sure that every son-of-a-bitch in Vandalia County saw Julie in his car, and he wanted to make damned sure that someone told Denny Lewis. There was little doubt in his mind that someone would tell him.

He wondered what the hell they were going to talk about all evening. Talking with her did not come easy. He just could not figure out what the hell it was about her that bugged him so and made him so uncomfortable. Yet, having her there in the car with him was one of the greatest joys that he had ever experienced.

"How long have you played the piano?" he asked.

"I don't really know, since about the second grade, I suppose. It's something that I really enjoy."

"You play really well," Corley said. "You play more than notes. I could hear the feeling in your playing the day I came to take you swimming. I know a lot of people who have taken lessons all their lives. They play all the notes, but they don't really play the music."

"Why, you said that well, Corley, and that is a nice compliment."

"It's not a compliment, really, it's just the truth."

"I have heard that you play the guitar," she said. Any truth to that?"

"Oh, I play a little, but not the kind of music that you would like. I play mostly old fiddle tunes and old folk songs that I have learned around here. I just play for myself."

"I would really like to hear you some time," she said. "I'll bet you are better than you say."

Boy, that would be the day, Corley thought. He could hardly talk in front of her. The very thought of playing for her made his hands sweat on the steering wheel.

Charleston was a good town for taking a girl out. There were several movie houses, and a couple of really hot drive-in restaurants where all the "cats" rich and poor, came to show off their cars. On a warm clear night, there was a constant parade of wheels rolling through those places. Cadillacs with continental kits, long as a city block, sort of knocked everyone else out. But the '55 Chevys and Fords were also the rage. The old Buick sparkled in the light and Corley was not ashamed of her. And, he certainly was proud to have Julie sitting next to him. She was second to no one in the whole damned town as far as he was concerned, plenty damned good for a country boy in a '50 Buick. They buzzed both places twice and then headed for a movie.

Julie was very poised and almost distant during the early part of the evening and Corley could not bring himself to touch her. They walked down the street to the movie house like a brother and sister act, or like they were going to Sunday school with her mother walking behind them. But, when they got inside and were settled, she took hold of his arm with both hands and held on all during the movie. Corley maintained his poise through it all. He never did like to see teenagers fooling around in a movie house. He always figured that if people wanted to mess round, they ought to go to the car, the front porch, or out in the woods somewhere. He figured that no one wanted to watch a couple of horny people claw at each other in a movie. Some of the people that he knew would do that kind of stuff, then stand around and brag about it the next day. As far as he was concerned that kind of activity showed a definite lack of class. He didn't figure Julie would go for that stuff either because she was a pretty classy girl.

The movie was pretty typical fare, some girl trying to break into Broadway, falling in love with a singer, and experiencing the old marriage/career struggle. Julie really liked it, but Corley was so wrapped up in being with her that he hardly noticed the movie.

When they got back in the car Julie scooted over very close to him. He wasn't even sure that he could drive with her sitting so close. Then, to make it worse, she put her left hand on the back of his neck. He cruised through the drive-in restaurants again like Caesar back from Gaul, or MacArthur back from the Far East. It was getting time to start home in order to meet her twelve o'clock curfew, so they left the big city and drove back up the Vandalia River. They soaked up the music from the car radio, and again, Corley noticed the dominance of rock and roll music.

When they got to the dirt road that led down toward her house, one part of Corley wanted to stop the old Buick, pull over in the brush, tear off that white dress, and make love to her. But a stronger part of him wanted to take her home and preserve her for motherhood. The Meadows place was dark as they pulled up in front of the house. He walked her to the porch and held her for a moment.

"I hope you had a good time," he said.

"I did," she answered softly.

This time when he kissed her, she came alive and responded in a fashion that made his maleness all too evident so he had to pull away so that he would not be embarrassed. When he let her go, she turned quickly and went inside.

"I'll be in touch," he said.

When he got home and put the Buick away he noticed a fire down by the river. He wondered who the hell would be down there this time of night so he decided to investigate. He walked quietly until he could see who it was. It was Sam, sitting there looking into the fire like some old Indian. He jumped when he saw Corley.

"Might have known it was you," he said. "Anyone who had any brains in his head would be in bed."

"What the hell you doing down here?" Corley asked.

"Oh, just sort of thinking things out. I came down to your house this evening to see if we could get something going and your mom said that you had a big date with Julie. How did it go?"

"Not too bad I guess."

"I stopped down at The Beeches this evening," he said casually. "Lucy O'Brannon asked about you. I told her that I didn't know where you were, but that I had heard that you had some kind of a heavy date. She looked kind of strange when I said that, Corley. You and Lucy got something going?"

"No, I just dance with her some down there, that's about all."

"She looked pretty damned serious to me," Sam said.

Corley had not said a word to Sam about Lucy, and he wouldn't say anything. Some guys just couldn't wait to go out and tell everyone in the world and the *New York Times* who they had just laid. Corley couldn't see any point in that. The fact that he knew was enough for him. Why should he go around putting a girl down because she did what she was designed to do? But the mention of her name gave him a chill down his spine.

"You find anything there?" Corley asked.

"No, I didn't stay long. Drove over and talked with Sue Phillips awhile. She is a cute kid, don't you think?"

"No doubt about that, Sam."

"Guess I'll take her out tomorrow night," Sam said casually.

"You are a slick operator, Sam," Corley teased, "a regular Rock Hudson."

Sam did not respond to the comment, just stared into the fire awhile. Then he took a long look at Corley.

"You know what's wrong with us, Corley?"

"No, Sam, what's wrong with us?"

"Well, we need some excitement. You know, something besides girls. First thing you know, we'll be just like those punks in town. We'll be pussy whipped, sucking around some girl all the time. You and that goddamned pink shirt there are pretty good evidence of what is happening to us."

"You might have something there," Corley admitted. "What you got in mind?"

"Tell you later," he said.

IX

Corley and Sam were busy the next week as the work at the Belk place picked up. They were painting all of the porch floors on the camps. It wasn't hard work and it was quiet. It gave them lots of time to talk and Sam began laying his plan on Corley about the excitement to which he had alluded when they had talked down on the river bank. He sort of broke it to him a little at a time to see how it would take.

"Would you be willing to do something that was outside the law?" Sam asked.

"That would depend on how far outside the law you want to go," Corley answered. "I've been outside the law before as you well know. I'll do about anything as long as it is under the heading of raising hell, but I don't want to get involved in robbing or stealing or anything like that."

Sam studied him for a moment before he spoke.

"Well, it ain't exactly stealing, I don't suppose. What we are going to take is not of much value. We just need it to make the hell raising proper."

"What in God's name are you talking about?"

"Dynamite," Sam whispered.

"You are out of your mind," Corley said. "I don't know anything about dynamite and I sure to hell don't want to steal any."

"I know about it," Sam said. "You just wait until you've heard my plan. Don't be so damned self-righteous until you have heard me out."

"Let's hear it," Corley said.

"You know that old house that sets back there on the mountain that's about to fall down. Everyone around here calls it the Shanty Field. You know where I mean?"

"Yeah, I know, it's the old Cummings place. No one has lived there for years."

"You have to admit the old house is no good," Sam said.

"I couldn't argue with that," Corley agreed.

"Let's blow that son-of-a-bitch to smithereens," Sam said, his eyes wide with excitement.

"Where are we going to get the dynamite?" Corley asked.

"That's where the outside the law comes in. We have to steal it. Not only steal it, but break and enter and steal it."

"Where?" Corley asked.

"When you and I were camping earlier this summer, I noticed a little wildcat mine over on Sycamore Run. There was a little building there. I'd bet anything that there is dynamite in that building. I have been around enough mines till I know how they store it. Those little wildcat outfits never have a night watchman. We just need about a dozen sticks and they probably would never miss it. We could take a crowbar and a hammer, take a couple of boards off, get the stuff, and nail the boards back on. It would be a piece of cake. What do you think?"

"I think that you are crazy as hell, but I got to admit, it sounds exciting."

"Remember what I said down at the river the other night. We have to do something to set ourselves apart from that bunch of punks in town. You want to follow some girl around all the time looking like a horny foxhound?"

He had a point, Corley thought. It did bother him some to see boys knuckle under completely to girls. Just like rock and roll. It was the girls who brought the stuff around. The boys just went along with it. Corley could already see that men would put up with a lot just for a little loving once in a while. Sam was right. A man ought to strike out for adventure on occasion. Yet, the breaking and entering bothered him some.

"Sam, I think that you are on to something. When do you want to do it?"

"Saturday night," he said. "It wouldn't be right if we didn't do it on Saturday night when all of those punks in town are out smelling around the girls like a bunch of mongrel dogs."

"OK, Sam, you're on. I just hope you know how to handle dynamite. I don't know a damned thing about it."

"Never fear," Sam said confidently. "I'm an expert. I've helped my dad set it off plenty of times."

Saturday night came quickly, too quickly for Corley. He and Sam told everyone that they were going to Charleston. They both put on their best jeans and a nice shirt and left home looking like they were going out for a night in the big city. They took the Buick. Corley sneaked some tools into the trunk as he washed it that afternoon. Sam secured wire and batteries somewhere.

They cruised around Bolton until it was dark, then drove back up the river and up the dirt road that led to the mine. They hid the Buick in the brush, took off their shirts, and moved out on foot. It was a warm, almost hot night. The mine was a thirty minute walk from where they left the car.

Securing the dynamite was easier than Corley had imagined. The building was made of rough oak boards with a crack between each board. They popped three boards off easily. They quickly found a case of dynamite that had been opened and took fifteen sticks and some caps. Sam held the light while Corley nailed the boards back onto the building.

"I hope no one hears that hammer," Corley said.

"No one but a damned fool would be up this holler tonight," Sam said.

Corley looked him in the eye and they broke into laughter. Sam was dead right about that.

The Shanty Field was a good little walk from where they were, but there was an old haul road left over from a timbering project most of the way. It was easy walking. Corley had stuck the old .38 down in his pants when he left home and he was glad it was there as they walked through all of the dark woods. It was spooky as hell and there was no moon. They did not risk a light. Corley knew all of that country like the back of his hand. He had played on it since he was ten years old.

Corley noticed that his hands were not shaking, but he was shaking inside. Sometimes a person can seem perfectly calm outwardly, but inside, his liver, his lungs, and everything else is shaking like hell. That's the way Corley was.

Sam was right, he thought. It was high excitement. If they ever got caught it was going to be hell to pay. That was for sure. It was nearly midnight before they got to the old house and got organized. The house stood out in the middle of a field. Brush and briars had grown up all around it, but there were no big trees.

It was a very typical situation in Vandalia County during the 1950's. A man had lived off the land, raised his children on a place like this, but as soon as the children grew up, they all left the farm to find work in the cities. Then, when the old folks died, the place just sort of went back to nature. If no one looked after the house, it would just rot down in a few years. The Cummings place was in pretty bad shape, but was still standing. People had shot most of the windows out and there were no doors remaining. About all it was fit for was a haven for rattlesnakes and copperheads. Some kind of varmint ran out of the house as they approached. They guessed it to be a raccoon.

Sam was the demolitions expert so Corley let him do all the wiring. He held the light and helped Sam string the wire out of the house and over into the woods.

"We'll lay down behind that big white oak," Sam said.

"Is fifteen sticks enough?" Corley asked.

"It's enough," Sam smiled.

It was ready to go according to Sam. They positioned themselves flat on the ground and behind the white oak. They were about three hundred feet from the house. Corley was expecting a big bang, but he was not prepared for what happened. Sam touched the wires together and there was a blinding flash followed by a bang to end all bangs. Pieces of debris, rocks, dirt, and limbs flew over their heads from the initial blast. Then, they were showered with objects that had been blown high into the air. The tree probably saved them from being injured.

"Holy Christ," Sam murmured. "It's a wonder we are still alive."

"The thing we have to do is to get the hell out of here," said Corley.

They made off through the woods at a dead run, and as they were getting close to where they had left the car, fear began to subside and they began to brag on themselves.

"Did we blow that son-of-a-bitch up or not?" Sam said, laughing as they slowed to a walk.

"I couldn't argue with that," said Corley. "We sure to hell blew it up."

Back at the car they put on their dress shirts and eased the Buick out of the hollow in the dark. When they got back on the highway they drove a couple of miles toward Bolton, still without headlights. They were into the morning hours when they got to Bolton, but they spotted some boys that they knew standing around some cars and talking. They stopped and dropped the word that they had been to Charleston.

When they got home everything was quiet. It was about 2:00 a.m. when Corley turned in, but he was up early because he had to do the milking. At breakfast, he got his first test of displaying his innocence.

"Did you hear the big boom last night?" his mother asked.

"No, I didn't hear any boom. What time?"

"Must have been about midnight. It jarred the house until I was afraid the windows were going to break."

"I guess I was still in Charleston," Corley said.

"I got up," his dad chimed in, "but I couldn't tell anything about where it came from. It may have been a pipeline explosion. They do blow up you know."

"We'll find out soon enough, I guess," said Corley, hoping to hell no one ever found out.

Someone did make the discovery though. A few days later, Corley's dad remarked at the supper table that someone had dynamited the old Cummings place and that there was going to be an investigation. There was some fear that there was a maniac among us. The word investigation chilled Corley a bit, but he maintained his cool. There was no way that an investigation was going to lead to him and Sam.

X

The summer was coming to a close and the workload for Corley had been extremely heavy. He and Sam were getting the camps at the Belk place ready to close for the season and they had been working nearly every day. Porter Belk would rent a few of them out on weekends during the fall, but the season for the camps was pretty much over when school started. He had asked Corley to look after them during the winter also, had given him keys to all of them. There really wasn't much to do during the fall and winter months, but Porter just wanted someone to keep an eye on them, make sure none of them were leaking, or that no one had broken into them. He offered Corley twenty dollars a month as the winter caretaker and he was not about to turn that down. He might even share some of it with Sam, he thought.

The last week in August had been extra busy because there was a lot to do around the farm in addition to his little job at the Belk place. Corley had gotten in very little swimming and he had not seen Julie for quite a while. She was pressing heavy on his mind though. No matter how hard he tried, he could not seem to shake her from his thoughts. He did not go out on Saturday night. He was pretty much exhausted so he just stayed around home and turned in early. He had lain awake most of the night thinking about the two times that he had kissed Julie, especially that second time. He decided that he would cross the river next morning and head her off as she was going to church.

He was sitting on the rail about 9:30 a.m. when he saw her coming down the track looking disgustingly beautiful.

"Well, hello stranger," she greeted him. "Where have you been keeping yourself?"

"Working mostly, I guess," he answered.

"You work all day and all night?" she asked.

"Well, no, I have just been staying pretty close to home lately. I've been meaning to come over, but something always came up."

"You going to church with me?" she asked slyly.

"Hadn't planned on it, not dressed for it," he answered.

"You look fine," she said. "Come on and go with me."

He thought about it for a minute and decided that just maybe he would. He hadn't been to Sunday school for ages so it might improve his image in the community. Folks were always asking him why he didn't come anymore. Maybe if he went they would shut the hell up. Besides, it was a nice morning for a walk. He ran all of those thoughts through his head but the truth was he just wanted to be with her and he would have gone anywhere she asked him to at that moment.

"Might as well," he said.

She took hold of his arm and they started down the track. Then Corley did a really stupid thing. He got sexually excited. He didn't want to and he wasn't even thinking about sex, but he had to walk like a moron to conceal the bulge in his pants. He was very embarrassed. Fortunately, things were back to normal by the time they got to church.

Julie had to sit at the piano for most of the service, so Corley sat with the late teen group during Sunday school. They had a big discussion about what was a sin and what wasn't. Someone said that it was a sin to dance, another thought using playing cards was pretty sinful, and most agreed that smoking and drinking were major sins. One boy thought it was a sin to kill game and leave it. His statement brought strange stares from some quarters but Corley kind of agreed with him. Corley commented that he thought it was a sin to be unkind to the less fortunate. It always irritated the hell out of him to see people ridiculing or taking advantage of the less fortunate. The Sunday school teacher, old Sly Fuller, loved that. He preached a regular sermon about how we should treat everyone right, regardless of their station in life. Little Frankie Bower, a red-headed kid with a mass of freckles, said that it was a sin to rock the cows. Everyone agreed with that. All told, the class was not terribly intellectually stimulating, but Corley sort of enjoyed it.

After Sunday school, they sang a couple of good hymns during which Corley admired Julie's talent at the piano. She could play, not doubt about it. Most church piano players that Corley had heard just played straight chords, but Julie slipped in some pretty hot runs, notes that were not on the paper. Corley decided that she was a very, very talented girl.

Finally, there was a message from the minister for those who wanted to stay. Most of the young folks left, but since Julie had to play the piano, Corley had to stick it out. It wasn't really too bad. The minister, Reverend Bonar, just told everyone what a rotten bunch they had been all week and that they had better shape up their act if they expected to collect any of the rewards God had promised. Corley always thought that it was good for a preacher to tell everyone how worthless they were. It toned down their vanity and made them less nauseating, at least for a few hours after church.

The service finally over, Corley shook hands with all of the elders, got his back slapped a few times, and they were on their way. Julie seemed especially happy. She bounced along and rattled about how terrific it was that he had gone to church with her. When they got back to where the boat was tied they stopped and talked awhile.

"Why don't you come back down for a swim after you have had dinner? You want me to come and get you?"

"No, I'll meet you right here about two o'clock."

"Great," Corley said. He gave her a quickie kiss and headed for the Sunday dinner which he knew was going to be cold.

It was a great afternoon. Julie was playful and Corley coached her with her overhand stroke. She learned rapidly and was developing a pretty style of swimming. Corley even behaved himself and did not join in the usual roughhouse games. He wanted to, but he had a feeling that the games had strained their relationship some the last time they were there. He figured that Sam would be along soon, giving him grief about being with Julie. But, it wasn't long before Corley saw him coming up the sand bar with Sue Phillips in tow. Corley was relieved to see that because now he would not have to listen to Sam's lecture that evening about giving into the girls all the time. He and Sue looked like Antony and Cleopatra as they frolicked around in the water. Later, as the girls sunned, Sam and Corley met out in mid-stream.

"Getting any on you?" Sam asked.

"Maybe," Corley answered.

"You ain't never been no farther than your goddamned hand," he said.

"Could be," Corley answered, "but I doubt if you have found yours yet."

Corley helped Julie back across the river about five o'clock and walked her up to the track.

"You know what I would like to do to make this a perfect day?" she said.

"No, what?"

"I would like for you to come over and get me and take me for a boat ride about twilight. And I want you to bring your guitar and sing to me." Then she looked right through him with those blue eyes.

"Christ, I can't do that," he said.

"You most certainly can," she replied, "and stop swearing. I played the piano in church for you today, so you can play for me tonight."

"That's a little different isn't it? I mean you were going to play anyway and besides, you didn't have to look at me."

"It doesn't matter," she said. She was so damned excited and full of herself, and so disgustingly pretty, that Corley could not contain her.

"I'll come over and take you for a boat ride, but I don't know about the guitar," he said firmly.

"I don't want to go unless you will play for me."

"OK, OK, I'll be up about eight."

She blinked her eyes and faded into the brush.

Corley tried to leave the house that evening without anyone seeing him with his guitar, but his mother saw him and asked where he was going. He told her that he was going down to the river and build a fire. She smiled a smile as if she did not believe him.

Corley got Julie into the boat and began rowing up stream. He was facing her as she sat on the back seat of the boat. She had on pedal pushers and a white top. The ever present ribbon was in her hair. Corley thought he would row upstream a mile or so, then let the boat drift back with the current. There wasn't much of a current in the eddy.

"Let me row," she insisted.

He moved to the back and gave her the rowing seat. She fooled around, splashed water all over the place, and generally went around in circles.

"You have never rowed a boat in your damned life," Corley exclaimed.

"You just stop swearing and help me."

Just then Corley heard the roar of a motor. The sound was coming from up stream and it sounded like a very small motor. He knew who it was almost as soon as he heard it. He got Julie back in her seat and began pulling hard on the oars. As the small motor boat approached, Corley confirmed that it was old George Camp and his fishing buddy Howard Dobbs. George cut the engine when he recognized Corley.

Corley had known George Camp since he could remember. He was a big man and fairly decent looking. He kept himself neat and clean but he had never worked at a job in his life. During the spring and summer months when respectable folks spent every spare moment in their gardens, George would be asleep in the front porch swing, or sometimes he would lay on a blanket out under a big box elder tree which shaded most of his front yard. He had always lived with his mother.

He drove a pretty decent looking Ford and always had money for cigarettes or whatever else he wanted to buy for himself. Everyone who lived in the area pretty well knew that George made and sold a little shine, but no one got excited about it.

"Evening Corley," he said with his deep resonant voice. His voice really carried across the water.

"Catching any fish?" Corley asked.

"Gee Gawd, ain't doing no good at all," was the answer. Corley knew what the answer would be because he always said the same thing.

The truth was George Camp was a major league fisherman. He had caught some record muskie in his time, and his buddy Howard practically lived off the catfish that they caught.

"What you doing on the river?" George asked. "Going to do some fishing?"

"No, I was just taking Julie for a ride here," Corley said sheepishly. He hoped George had not noticed the guitar.

"Who is that girl?" George asked. "Don't believe I know her."

"This is Julie. Her folks moved in over across from our place. You have probably seen the new house there."

"Well, I'll be damned. She sure is a pretty one."

Julie was too embarrassed to look up and Corley thoroughly enjoyed seeing someone get the best of her. She did manage a faint smile. Corley noticed that George was taking a few drinks from a quart jar of clear liquid. It looked like water but Corley knew what it was. Suddenly, George turned around to his motor, removed the cap, and poured some of the same liquid that he was drinking into the tank. He replaced the cap and turned and smiled.

"You two enjoy the evening," he said as he cranked the motor. It fired easily and he was under way.

"Did he pour water into his gas tank?" Julie asked.

"That wasn't water, Julie, it was shine, moon shine."

"Are you telling me that he drinks what he runs in that motor?"

"You saw it same as I did," said Corley

The sound of the little motor was soon gone and Corley continued rowing up stream. When he arrived at where he wanted to be, he pulled in the oars and let the boat begin to drift. The river was beautiful in late summer. Big sycamores, willows, and water birches hung out from the bank and the water in the eddies was still and deep. As darkness began to fall, frogs and night birds began their endless chanting along the shore. But, Corley was painfully aware of the fact that the moment of truth had arrived for him.

He was a pretty good singer but he had never sung for anyone except his family and a few musicians like the Keefer boys. He figured this was a poor place to start. Julie made a nervous wreck out of him anyway, so how was he going to sing to her. Yet, there wasn't but one thing to do. He reached for the old Gibson and gave her a little bit of "Bouquet of Roses," an old country standard. He did alright but he never looked at Julie all through the first song. He just looked at the neck of the guitar like he was really searching for the chords.

It was getting dark and his courage increased as the light faded. It was a clear night but the moon was still behind the hills. He managed four or five songs for her. Julie went on and on about how great he was but he was still having trouble looking at her. When he did manage a glance, she was sitting there looking like she had conquered the world. It occurred to him that she had conquered a part of it. He had been eating out of her goddamned hand all day and now he was out in the middle of the Vandalia River making an ass of himself. The worst part of it was that he had been enjoying himself all day long.

Finally, the boat had drifted back downstream to where they had started, so he laid the guitar aside and rowed over to the path that led to her house. Then, the strangest thing happened. When they got out of the boat she was all over him, kissing his breath away and caressing the back of his neck with her hands. Corley did not quite know how to respond, but was soon under the control of Mother Nature herself. They were both afire almost immediately, and before he knew it, he had his hands under her top and was pushing up against her bra. Suddenly, she broke from him and ran a few steps up the hill.

"You just slow down, Corley."

"Me slow down, what about you?"

"I know I got a little carried away, but you just never mind. I'm fine now."

"Look, I'm sorry," Corley said awkwardly.

"It's alright, it was as much my fault as yours. Let's go."

The walk to her house was conducted in silence. The moon was high now and they could see almost is if it were day. He was embarrassed and didn't know quite what to say, so they just walked. When they got to her house, she turned, gave him a long look, and smiled.

"I had a terrific day and I loved this evening. Come over one evening this week. I plan to be home all week." With that she put a very gentle kiss on his lips and whirled away.

Corley went back down the railroad track taking three ties at a time, bursting with pride in himself and thinking about going to Nashville and becoming a star. He thought that he might buy him a Cadillac about five blocks long, bring it back to Vandalia County, set Julie on the front fender, and parade her right through downtown Bolton. She might be out of Sam Somerville's class, he thought, but she sure to hell is not out of mine.

XI

Corley did not work at the Belk place that Monday. The summer was winding down and most of the general work around the camps was completed. About all that was left was mowing the grass, and he and Sam could knock that out in a day or so. The day turned warm early and Corley just fooled around the farm after the morning chores were over. He didn't start any big jobs. It was a hot, muggy, and generally miserable type of day, the sort of day that usually ended with a thundershower. He thought it would be a good day to stay in the shade and read. He was into some Hemingway short stories. He had especially enjoyed "Big Two Hearted River" and "Soldier's Home."

He was lying in the front porch swing, taking an in-between stories snooze when he heard a car coming up their driveway. It was a '51 Ford and he thought he recognized the car. When the man got out his suspicions were confirmed. It was Red Hanshaw, the fiddler. He saw Corley get up and he walked toward the porch.

"Hey, Corley."

"Red," he answered. "What brings you up this way?"

"Just wanted to talk a little if you have time."

"I've got plenty of that. Come on up and sit down."

"Hot as hell ain't it," Red commented as he found the glider.

"Hot I reckon," Corley responded.

"I want to talk a little music with you," he began. "I've lost my guitar man and I need someone to take his place. You've got good time and I really enjoyed playing with you that night down at The Beeches. You're a fine picker for your age. You interested at all?"

"Well, I don't really know. I've never thought about playing regular or anything, and I'm not eighteen."

"I know," he said, "but I don't see that as a problem. I don't think anyone around here gives a damn how old you are. Besides, you could pass for eighteen."

Corley was flattered, but he did not know quite what to say. He didn't know how his mother would react to all of this. She was not much on beerhalls. The whole proposition kind of scared him a little.

"I'm interested, but I don't know if I'll be able to swing it. School will be starting soon and I'll have a lot to do."

"We just play Saturday nights most usually. Once in awhile we will catch a gig in Charleston on Friday night, but not often," Red explained. "I'll give you five bucks a gig and, of course, all the beer you want. I hear that you sing pretty good too and we could use a singer. People like to slow dance between square dance sets, and we have never been able to play much for that. Do you think you could sing some slow stuff?"

"I've never sung in public," Corley answered. "I don't know if I am ready for that or not."

"Tell you what," Red continued, "you come down to my house tomorrow night and we'll run through a few and see what it sounds like. Want to give it a shot?"

"I'll have to talk it over with my folks."

What he had not noticed was that his mother had been standing in the doorway and had heard most of the conversation. She came out onto the porch looking pleasant enough.

"Mother, this is Red Hanshaw. He's a musician."

"Yes, I've heard of him," she smiled as she extended her hand.

"Your son is a good guitar man, Mrs. Malone, and I would like to use him some in my band."

"He'll have to talk that over with his father," his mother said.

Corley was surprised to hear that. That was the same as a yes because he knew that his father wouldn't mind. He would probably be kind of proud to hear that his son was going to be playing for money. Red got up and made his departure and Corley wished his face wasn't so red from the booze. He showed the wear of the liquor pretty bad. Corley was pretty excited and didn't want his mother to change her mind.

The next day was about the same, hot and muggy, so Corley sort of cooled it in the shade all day. He made sure that he hadn't lost anything on the guitar because he wanted to make a good impression. He sang several of the old standards to himself. He made it down to Red's house about sundown and was a little surprised at what he found. They were all drinking and fooling around which he expected, but what surprised him was that Red was putting together a bigger sound. He had picked up an electric guitar man and a Dobro player. With Red on fiddle and the bass player there would be five of them. Corley immediately figured out that he was the rhythm guitar man.

"I want you to sing something, Corley, something slow."

"Bouquet of Roses?" Corley asked.

"That's fine. Just start singing and we'll find you."

Corley took off and he felt a rush when they started coming in behind him. These guys were slick and Corley never imagined that he could sound so good. He could already see his name up in lights in Nashville. They ran through several songs and by ten o'clock Red figured that they were ready.

"You're hired, kid. We're going to make you a goddamned star."

They all laughed and Corley shared the laughter. He left them drinking and generally raising hell with the understanding that he would meet them at The Beeches Saturday night about seven.

Corley drove into Bolton before he went home, parked the Buick on Main Street, and walked down in front of the pool hall. He stood around out front for awhile and talked to a few boys that he knew. As he was walking back to his car he noticed that the theater was turning out and he thought that his eyes were deceiving him. But, a long look took away any doubt. Julie was coming out of the theater holding onto Denny's arm like he was going to get away. Corley stopped and stepped in behind a pick-up so that they wouldn't see him. They got into the hot Chevy and buzzed out of town. She was sitting nearly on top of him.

Corley's stomach turned upside down and he was nearly nauseated. Of all the goddamned fickle females on earth, she took the prize, he thought to himself. Only two nights ago, she was smooching the breath out of him, then here she turns up hanging on to that sorry excuse for a son-of-a-bitch. Corley had never experienced such a feeling before and did not quite know how to handle it. He got into the Buick and started for home. It was beginning to thunder pretty loud and before he got home he was in the midst of a driving rain. His eyes were moist and there was one hell of a knot in his throat. He put the car away and went into the house. He knew he would never sleep.

    He went into his room, got a flashlight and his .38, and went down to the river. He wasn't going to shoot anybody, he didn't think, he just took the pistol for comfort. It was kind of spooky along the railroad at night. The rain had let up some. The thunderstorm had passed, but there was still an occasional roar off in the distance. It made sort of a rolling sound through the hills. He got into the boat, paddled across the river, and made it up the track. He didn't know what it was, but something within him was driving him toward the Meadows place. He guessed he just had to see for himself what the hell was going on.

    By the time that he got to where he could see her house, he was soaked to the bone. Water was running down into his eyes and dripping off his nose and chin. He walked up against the hill, found some shelter under a big beech tree, and waited. The Chevy was not there yet. Corley could see them in his mind locked together in a clinch somewhere up an off road.

    But, it wasn't long before he saw the lights of the Chevy coming down the dirt road. Julie's mother turned on the porch light when she saw the car coming. Corley was standing there feeling even more foolish than he looked, but he was not about to leave. He watched them embrace in the car for a minute or two, then get out and run toward the house, laughing at the rain. He watched her kiss him with everything in her, knowing exactly what it felt like. He felt like he would never eat again. She went inside and Corley watched the Chevy head back up the road.

He stood there a moment or two, then made his way back toward the boat. The rain was warm, but the breeze that usually follows an evening shower in the mountains had a chill to it. His soaked condition made it seem even colder. He shivered a little and quickened his pace. Back in his room, he dried himself and retired. It was the longest night of his life.

It wasn't often that he heard the 2:00 a.m. run of the freight train. Most of the time he was dead to the world. But that night he heard the old train go through all of its routines. The engineer stopped to take on water not far up the river, and he heard the old steam whistle blow five haunting longs, letting the flagman know to light the flare and get back aboard the caboose. He heard every chug as the old engine struggled to get the long train underway. He listened as the chugs grew into a smooth roar. Finally, he heard the engineer blow the highball as he passed the station below Corley's house where they sometimes offloaded coal. It was a beautiful sound really, and he was kind of glad that he was awake to hear it. He damned Julie Meadows all night as he tossed and turned, wondering if this was how all international lovers got their start.

Next morning turned clear and beautiful and the ground was dry by noon. It was time to put the second cutting of hay in the barn and all of the folks up and down the valley set about the task. It appeared that the weather was going to be cool and dry for a few days after the thunderstorms had moved through. Late summer had been kind of dry and the hay crop was pretty thin. There wasn't much of it, but it was a job that had to be done.

The Malone farm was sort of semi-mechanized. The hay was cut down with a two horse mowing machine, but they used the old pick-up to haul the hay to the barn. The barn loft held most of the second cutting usually. Someone had to get up in the loft and throw the hay back as the others threw it up with pitchforks. That job usually fell to Corley. It was awful up there, hot as hell under the tin roof, and the wasps always got stirred up and would sting the hell out of him. His dad and the other men below would just laugh about it and made comments like, "stay right with it, Corley."

Despite the hard work and suffering that came with haying, Corley always enjoyed the fellowship that went with it. Neighbors would usually help one another and there would be all sorts of teasing and arguments about who was the strongest. Physical strength was very high on the value scale among Vandalia County men because most of them made their living at hard work. Often, as they rested around the barn, they would engage in lifting contests. They would see who could lift an anvil the highest, or who could throw a sixteen pound sledge hammer the farthest. Corley's dad was usually among the winners. Pound for pound, he was as strong as anyone around. Corley was usually somewhere in the middle.

He also got a kick out of listening to the men talk about the women. They would ask one another how much they were getting and the answers would run from "not getting any" to "more than I can stand." Old Charlie Cook, in his seventies, said one day while they were working that he couldn't decide anymore which was best, the sex, or scratching his ass afterwards. They all cracked up over that. Corley wondered if a man his age really did still have an active sex life.

He spent the entire week in the hayfield, some of it on their own place, the rest of it on one of the neighboring farms. He was really kind of glad to be there. It kept Julie Meadows off his mind and made him so damned tired that he slept good at night. And eat, christ, did he eat. He had put on about ten pounds over the summer and was in better physical shape than he had ever been in his life.

When Saturday night finally arrived, he got the old Gibson and headed for The Beeches. It was a pretty evening, cool and comfortable. He figured that there would be a good crowd out on such a night. The band was setting up when he arrived. Red had acquired a public address system somewhere and the thought of singing through a mike made Corley just a little more nervous. He went over and had a little discussion with Troy Carr, the owner, because he wanted to make sure that everything was alright with him.

"I don't think we will have any problems," Troy said, "just don't stand there and drink in the open like Red does."

"I don't really plan to do much drinking," Corley said. "I need my head about me to play with these guys, and I have to drive home."

The band warmed up a little while the place was still pretty empty. The electric guitar man doubled on banjo when they played fiddle tunes. It sounded good.

It was obvious that Red really loved the old fiddle tunes and just tolerated the other music. When they got ready to play the first set the place was about half full. Red made a little speech about his new band, about how they were going to play some tunes for round dancing. No one paid much attention to him and when he introduced Corley, no one applauded except Troy Carr. He was a real big hit.

They opened with "I Can't Help It If I'm Still In Love With You," a Hank Williams tune. Corley was pretty stiff at first. Then, when he noticed that no one was paying any attention to him he got more relaxed. He just pretended that he was singing to Julie. The words really fit well. He did not look at anyone's wife or girlfriend while he was singing for fear of getting his head knocked off. He had been around beer halls enough to know better than that. Actually, he wasn't very comfortable, but he was enjoying every minute of it.

After a song or two people started to dance and that really took a lot of pressure off Corley. It gave him a pretty good feeling to see people dancing to his music. The place really came alive when they called the first square dance. The band was really cooking and people hollered, stomped their feet, and generally got with it. Corley really kept his eye on old Marshall Wilson. He was the undisputed flatfoot dance king in the area. Many times, during the dance, he would break into the middle of the set and just dance alone while the others watched. Corley was very interested in polishing his own flatfoot step, and it always helped to watch the old timers do it.

During the band's first break, Corley was standing behind the bandstand trying to get better acquainted with the bass player when he saw Lucy O'Brannon step in the door. Just as he was about to get excited, his hopes sank because right behind her was the biggest pipeliner that he had ever seen. Corley immediately looked away because he could imagine himself being stomped in the gravels out front for flirting with Lucy.

He generally ignored her for awhile, but as he was singing "Cold, Cold Heart," he noticed that Lucy's big friend was not at her table so he locked his eyes on her and sang right to her. Her eyes told him that she liked it and he wanted to hold her so bad that it was awful. She smiled and nodded as he finished. She was lost in the crowd for the remainder of the evening, but Corley noticed that she and her big friend left about eleven o'clock. Corley figured that her date was probably one of the Oklahoma immigrants who had come into the area to work on the pipelines. He hated him, he knew that, and he didn't even know him.

By closing time the place was pretty rowdy. Everyone had enough beer to make them prime and Corley was glad to see them go out the door. Most everyone took at least a six pack with them and headed off somewhere. Many times, a group of young men would just go somewhere and park along the road and talk and drink beer for an hour or two before they went home. If a man had a girl, he usually headed for a dark hollow somewhere.

The band fooled around for a little while after closing. Corley got to play a fiddle tune on Red's fiddle. He could get through "Liberty" and "Soldier's Joy" pretty good. Red bragged on him but Corley knew that he had a long way to go on the fiddle. Red gave him some good pointers. Corley collected the first five dollars he ever made playing music and they all agreed to meet at Red's house on Tuesday evening for some practice.

When Corley got out into the parking lot, he saw Lucy's '49 Chevy backed right against the Buick.

"What the hell you doing out here?" Corley asked.

"Waiting for you," she answered. "You would hardly look at me inside so I thought I would see if I could do any better out here. There is just no end to you is there? I couldn't believe you were up there singing like a professional."

"I'm a big star," Corley said sarcastically. "Didn't you notice how everyone applauded after each song?"

"They were all drunk and not listening," she said.

"So I noticed."

She had gotten out of her car while they were talking and had put her arms around his waist. The minute she touched him the memory of her sweetness flashed back to him. He sat his guitar aside and kissed her. She was fine, no doubt about it.

"Why didn't you come over and talk to me tonight?"

"I didn't want that damned mountain that you were with to knock my head off."

"Oh, he's harmless, I think. He's kind of a dud, but likable."

"He looked pretty mean to me," Corley said.

They had an awkward moment when neither of them knew quite what to say. They looked at each other and said several things with their eyes.

"What is it you see in me?" he finally said.

"Oh, you're different. You're quiet and kind. You just don't know how some boys are. They bore the hell out of you talking about how great they are, about how cool they are, then try to manhandle you. They have no idea how to be gentle. You are a very gentle person, Corley Malone."

"I'm just inexperienced," he answered.

"No, you won't change," she said. "It's not in you."

He took a good long look at her. There was not a thing wrong with Lucy O'Brannon. She was pretty as she could be. She had a perfect smile, a fair complexion, and her long, light brown hair set her off just right. He held her against him for a moment trying to control his natural drives when a car came roaring through the parking lot. It was a bunch of boys in a '46 Ford. They were yelling and throwing beer cans out the windows. They slowed down as they approached Corley and Lucy and one of them yelled.

"Get your finger out of it, buddy!"

The others hollered with delight. Lucy stiffened in his arms.

"See what I mean," she said, "see how awful boys can be."

"Get in my car," Corley said, "I hope they are not looking for trouble."

The old Ford stopped just beyond them, but no one got out. Corley started the Buick and drove off up the river. He wondered what the hell anyone got out of riding around all night in a car with a bunch of boys. Yet it was a common practice around the county. They would gather up in bunches of four or five, usually on Saturday nights, get them a case of beer, and drive around from one little town to another. They yelled at all the girls and harassed all the old men driving pick-up trucks. Then, they would get together Sunday evening and go over every detail and laugh and laugh about it.

It was very late, and after a short drive, Corley took Lucy back to her car. She was worried about getting home late because she still lived with her parents. Corley was also thinking about the morning chores. The cow was always there the next morning, no matter how late he got home at night. He put Lucy into the Chevy after a couple of lingering kisses.

"You like to swim?" he asked as she started her engine.

"Sure do," she answered.

"Why don't I come and get you tomorrow afternoon and we'll go up to the swimming hole for awhile."

"I'd love it," she smiled.

XII

Sunday dawned bright and beautiful and Corley spent the morning in the shade. Sam came down and they talked awhile. Sam was a little concerned about the big explosion. His father had asked him about it and was, of course, aware of the fact that Sam could handle dynamite.

"We ought to go and blow up something else so the investigators can get some more clues," Corley said.

"I think that we had just better lay low for awhile," Sam replied.

Corley also gathered from the conversation that Sam and Sue Phillips were getting pretty serious. In fact, he was worried about him.

"Remember what you said about letting girls dominate our lives, Sam. You are not getting in too deep are you?"

"Don't worry," said Sam. "I'm alright."

That afternoon the sand bar was crowded. It was probably going to be the last big weekend for swimming. School would be starting in another week, and even though it often remained warm enough to swim in September, most people didn't bother. There were just too many other things going on.

By the time Lucy and Corley made their appearance, there must have been a hundred or so people gathered along the river. They drew stares of surprise from every direction. Lucy was well endowed and Corley felt pretty good about being seen with her. They found a spot near the river and sat down to sun.

Just as they got settled, Corley spotted Julie coming out of the brush across the river looking like she needed help with her things. She scanned the crowd for Corley, waved and smiled, but Corley looked at her helplessly. She read the situation and came on her own. Lucy was totally unaware of any relationship between Corley and Julie, but that did not relieve any of the pain for Corley. He asked himself why the hell he had brought Lucy here. He asked himself why he wanted to go help Julie. He asked himself a bunch of stupid questions, then he just put the classic cool treatment on Julie. She sat down a few yards away, but Corley pretended that she was in Rome. He took Lucy to the water.

"I don't swim very well," she confessed.

That was the understatement of the year. She sank like a rock. As a result, they stayed close to the shore and she clung to Corley like a leech. They did it up right for Julie. Lucy had her arms around him one too many times and Corley knew that he could not come out without advertising his credential. He sent her to the blanket and went for a swim across the river.

As he neared the opposite shore he heard the water splash behind him. He turned in the water and saw Sam picking up another piece of coal to throw at him. He really burned the next one in there and Corley had to duck under to avoid it. It was the oldest game on the river. It was never safe to swim very far from shore alone when there was a good rock thrower around.

"You'd better stay over there," Sam yelled, "or I'll knock your damned head off."

"You couldn't hit the side of a barn," Corley replied.

He went under and came nearly all the way back across under the water. When he came up, Sam cocked to throw but didn't. That's the way the game was played. They would never throw at you if you were too near to dodge.

"He was trying to hit you," Lucy said as Corley returned.

"No, he wouldn't really try to hit me unless he got a chance. It's just a game we all play. Next time I get him isolated like that, I'll bean him."

"Has anyone ever been hit?" she asked.

"Oh, a time or two, but no one has ever died from it that I know of."

The afternoon was a real strain on Corley. He tried to ignore Julie, but they exchanged some pretty harsh glances. She could go to hell and take Denny Lewis with her as far as Corley was concerned. It occurred to him that she was probably having the same thoughts about him and Lucy. Old Sam decided he would help Julie back across the river. He carried her things for her as they waded the shoals. He looked at Corley and laughed like hell as he was swimming back. Corley promised himself that he would kick his ass later.

Lucy and Corley spent the late evening on the farm. She was not a farm girl and enjoyed seeing the animals up close and was fascinated by the blacksmith shop. They fired up the old pick-up and roared around the dirt roads for an hour or so. She loved that and squealed with delight if they slid a little in the curves.

That night, on the way to her house, Corley turned the Buick up Sugar Creek. When he came to their spot, he cut the engine. Lucy sat motionless and did not say a word. They were both tense with excitement. They wasted no words and were immediately helping each other with their clothes. He could not help but wonder if all women were as aggressive once they got started. She was a tiger and seemingly uninhibited. Corley performed much better. He was much more comfortable with her.

"I hope that you don't think that I'm the county whore," she said afterwards.

"Why would I think that?"

"Well, I've been very easy for you, but I want you to understand that I like you. I liked you from the start. I've liked other boys too, but I want you to know that I'm not this easy for everyone."

He did not know quite what to say but after some awkward silence, he managed a response.

"I've never really thought of you as being easy. It just seemed to come natural for us. I certainly don't think any less of you for letting me do what I wanted to do."

"Do you like me, Corley?"

"Of course I like you. You are a fine person and God knows you are far too pretty to be fooling around with me. I'm flattered that you ever noticed me at all."

"See how sweet you are," she said. "Some boys get right disgusting once it's over and never say anything nice. That's why I like you, Corley."

As he drove home that night he was not thinking about Lucy. He was thinking about Julie and wondering what he was going to say to her the next time he saw her. He would see her. There was no way to avoid that and he would have to say something. He wanted to think about Lucy and how sweet she was, but all he could think about was that aggravating Julie Meadows.

He wondered how anyone so beautiful could be such a goddamned pain in the ass.

Actually, he did not see much of anyone until the opening day of school. He had mixed feelings about the approaching senior year. He mostly dreaded it because he saw school as something that was going to get in his way. He did not have much sentiment for the old high school. He had never been a part of the *esprit de corps* of the place. Athletics he could take or leave, and cheerleaders gave him a real pain. He had decided not to continue with the high school band because it demanded so much time, and besides, it meant too much exposure to Julie. He entered his senior year mainly with the thought of getting it over with and enjoying it as much as possible.

It was a pretty typical first day of school in Vandalia County. The air reeked of new denim material as they gathered in the gym for the general organization meeting. They had the usual welcome speech and they had to suffer through the introduction of the football team. The band played a couple of numbers and Corley enjoyed that. When they divided up for scheduling, Corley remained in the gym with those who were following the general curriculum. He was about to sit down when he saw Henry Holt, the principal, motion for him to come. He wondered what the hell was on old Henry's mind. He looked awfully grim about something. When they got to his office, Frank Kerns, the band director, was sitting there. Henry closed the door.

"Sit down, Corley," he said mildly.

"Am I in trouble already?" Corley asked.

"Well, no, Mr. Kerns and I just want to talk to you a little about some things. First off, we wondered why you have quit the band?"

"It's just a time factor, I suppose," Corley answered truthfully. "I lead a pretty hectic life with the farm chores and all, and I value my own time pretty highly."

"You always had time before," Mr Kerns said.

Then he went into a regular lecture about what an asset Corley was to the band, how the other members looked to him for leadership, and about how he was depending on him to be his military drum major this year. He was really laying it on pretty heavy.

"You want to reconsider quitting?" he asked finally.

"I don't know. I'll have to think about it. I didn't realize that I was such an asset."

Then it was Henry's turn. He repeated his lecture from the previous spring about not living up to potential. Corley heard him out in silence.

"You ought to be thinking about college instead of singing in beer halls," he said in conclusion.

That line caught Corley off guard. He did not know that his fame had spread into the upper social circles. He was pretty damned uncomfortable and didn't know quite what to say next, but he was rarely speechless.

"Listen, I appreciate you gentleman taking an interest in me and I'll give all of this some thought."

He got up to leave, but Frank Kerns wasn't finished.

"You come to practice this afternoon, now, you hear!"

Corley left the office without answering. Old Frank Kerns had always done right by Corley and he really felt kind of bad about deserting him if he really did need him. He was a damned good man, a man for whom Corley had a great deal of respect. He knew that he would not have said a word to him if he hadn't really been interested. So, after school, Corley showed up for band practice still not quite sure that he was going to go through with it.

The band had been practicing for a week before school started so they were organized. They were forming out beside the building. Corley walked over to Mr. Kerns to ask what he wanted him to do and he responded by announcing to the band that Corley was going to be the military drum major. That's what he called the person who actually led the band through its paces. Having made his announcement, he handed Corley a whistle.

Corley was pretty shaken by all of this for several reasons. He never asked for the job and really did not want it. Worse than that, Julie was a majorette and would be right behind him all the time, watching every move that he made. Finally, he was not sure that he was up to the job. He made that comment to Mr. Kerns, but he just ignored him.

"You'll learn quickly," he said. "Go ahead up front and march them to the football field and back."

It was a mile to the field and several corners to go around. It was going to be a challenge. As he walked to the front of the band he felt Julie's eyes go right through him. Actually, he felt fairly confident. He had been in the marching band for four years, had conducted some close order drill, and knew all the commands. Mr. Kerns took a very military approach to the band and spent several hours each year drilling without instruments.

Corley got them to the field with no major blunders and told them to take five before the return trip. Julie Meadows headed straight for him.

"You did well, Corley," she said.

"Did you think that I wouldn't?"

"No, not at all, I knew you could do it. Have you given up talking to me?"

"No, I just haven't seen you," Corley replied.

"You have made an effort not to see me it seems to me," she answered.

That's the way it was with her. Corley would try to leave her alone, to stay away from her, then, she would come around with those damned eyes of hers and erase all of his good intentions with one flash. God, she was a pain.

"Listen, Julie, why don't I come over this evening. I want to talk to you."

"Sure, come on over. I'll talk to you anytime."

"I'll come over after supper and chores, maybe about seven."

Corley took the band back to the high school building and Mr. Kerns who had been marching alongside the band came over as Corley dismissed them.

"You did fine," he said. "I think that you are just what we need. You have an air of authority about you."

"I have never thought of myself as an authoritative person, but I suppose that I can do the job," Corley replied.

"You are not one of the crowd, Corley, and that is important. The leader must remain aloof."

"I've never thought of myself as aloof either," Corley said.

"Well, you are," he said, "and you'll do the job for me."

"Thank you, sir, I appreciate your confidence in me," Corley said. "I'll do my best."

That evening Corley found himself crossing the river again, almost hating himself for doing it. He used the boat and made the walk up the track. It was a cool September evening, a harbinger of the beautiful October evenings that would be coming soon. It was dry and crisp and the sunset was going to be beautiful. He stopped for awhile to watch as the sun settled on the ridgeline.

Julie's mother answered the door so Corley figured that he was off to a great start.

"Is Julie home?" he asked politely.

"She just drove up the rode with her father," she said. "I'm sure she won't be long. Do come in and wait."

This was just what he needed, Corley thought. There was going to be a very uncomfortable conversation between him and Mrs. Meadows.

"Julie speaks of you often, Corley. I'd like to know more about you."

"What do you want to know?" Corley asked.

"Oh, what your plans are for the future, what college you are looking toward, that kind of thing."

"Well, I'm afraid that my future is pretty foggy. I have no earthly idea what I'm going to do with my life and I'm not planning college."

"Oh," was her only response.

They sat in silence for a long moment and then she looked right through him. He was miserable to say the least.

"We have such high hopes for Julie. We hope that she will continue with her music and we want to get her into the right college."

"She is a very talented girl, Mrs. Meadows, and I'm sure that she will make you very proud of her."

And, Corley was very sincere about that. Julie Meadows was a very talented person. And, he understood what her mother was saying. She was saying that she did not want her daughter getting too involved with the likes of Corley Malone. She was asking him to be noble. She was about to say something else when Julie and her father came in, and Corley was very glad about that. He exchanged greetings with her father and Julie pulled him outside. He felt like he had just gotten out of prison.

"Let's walk down to the river," Julie said. "It should be beautiful down there this evening." Everything that he had planned to say to her just faded away. He wanted to tell her that they shouldn't see each other anymore. He had a big speech planned about how they lived in two different worlds, and that they did not need to spend time together. But she seemed so happy to be with him that he never really got around to his planned conversation.

"I hear that you have been singing down at The Beeches."

"Yes, I have and I kind of enjoy it."

"Do you also sing to that girl you were parading around at the sand bar?"

"Now, goddamn it, Julie, don't you start that stuff with me. I have never said a damned word about your friend Denny Lewis. So, just get off it."

"Why must you always swear at me when we are talking?"

"Because you make me so damned mad, that's why."

"Denny is nice and I like him. He has been a perfect gentleman to me."

"Well, if you like him so damned much, take him and go with him."

"Corley Malone, you are not being fair. You don't own me. You've never even asked me to be your steady girl. What am I supposed to do, sit around and hope that you will come and see me once a month?"

"Alright, then you stop jabbing me about Lucy O'Brannon."

"Oh, is that her name?"

"Yes, and she is a nice girl. She's good company."

They were yelling at each as usual and not settling a thing. He grabbed her and kissed her with everything he had and did she ever respond.

"Why do we fight so?" she said quietly. "You must like me a little or you wouldn't get so mad."

He did not answer, just pulled on her and started for her house. They walked back in silence in the late twilight, stopping to smooch a little every ten or fifteen yards. By the time they reached her house, he was destroyed. When she turned to go into the house he saw the sparkle in her eye and thought what a failure he was. He was right back where he started when he went over there, wanting her so bad that he could hardly stand it, yet knowing full well that it would be better for both of them if he left her alone.

XIII

"You are getting better all the time, Corley," Red said.

It was early evening at The Beeches and the band was fooling round with some new songs. A few people had come in but they expected the crowd to be small because early November was usually a pretty slow time. It was sort of the in between time in Vandalia County. The beauty of the fall had faded, but there was no snow yet. Everything was brown and ugly. Worse than that, it had been raining quite a bit and everything was muddy. It was the kind of night that folks tended to stay home. Corley sort of liked the slow nights because they did not have to work too hard, and they tended to play the songs that they liked as opposed to what the crowd wanted to hear. And, he got to dance with Lucy during break time. She was a great dancer, so light in his arms that he could hardly feel her sometimes. He was about to get the hang of the rock and roll step. It played more and more on the juke box.

Later in the evening the band was fooling around with a tune called "Bill Bailey". Red loved to play the old ragtime tunes on the fiddle and was really pleased that Corley could sing some of them. No one could really dance to that kind of music so they only did it during slow evenings. Corley was feeling especially good and during one of Red's fiddle breaks he had put his guitar aside and was doing a little shuffle on the bandstand. He was having a good time and not really paying much attention to the crowd. Red was pretty high and was thoroughly enjoying Corley's dancing. Suddenly, Corley thought his eyes were deceiving him, because right through the door came Julie and Denny Lewis, big as life. Denny had never been in the place in his life, and Julie's mother would have had heart failure if she could have seen her daughter. They came to a table just to the right of the bandstand. Corley cleaned up his act quickly, picked up his guitar, and sang another verse of "Bill Bailey". He got really nervous and looked at Lucy. As far as he knew she was not aware of any kind of relationship between him and Julie. But, he did not know what Denny Lewis knew. All he knew about Denny was that he gave him a general pain in the ass. But, there they sat, looking right at him. He waved and smiled after he finished the song. He did not know what else to do.

    The crowd had picked up some and old Marshall Wilson was trying to get a square dance organized. He yelled at Red and asked for a little fiddle music to get the people inspired. Red jarred down on "Old Joe Clark" and the band came in behind him. Marshall danced all over the place by himself and eventually coaxed a set onto the floor. He chose Lucy for his partner because she was one of the best female square dancers around. Julie Meadows was really getting an education. She had obviously never seen anything like the free wheeling square dancers at The Beeches. Her eyes were sparkling and she was smiling broadly as she watched them. Denny looked miserable.

    Corley could hardly keep his eyes off Julie, and he was not the only one looking. She had on a tight red dress and was certainly an eyeful. It occurred to him that Denny was liable to get knocked on his ass before he got out of there. They made an attractive couple, but Corley had come to realize that Denny was a simple son-of-a-bitch. He could tell by talking with him that he was pretty narrow. He figured that he bored the hell out of Julie talking to her about his overhead cam and his twin exhaust system. He was definitely simple and Corley liked him less all the time. Julie could do better, he knew that.

When the square dance ended, Corley figured that he was going to have to go over and speak to her. After all, she was his neighbor.

"You folks are out of your element tonight aren't you?"

"Maybe so," Denny ventured. "Your friend here wanted to hear her neighbor sing. It sure wasn't my idea."

"Why, I'm disappointed, Denny. I thought sure that you had dragged her in here."

He smiled, but it was more of a smirk.

"You'll have to dance with me before you leave, Julie," Corley said as he moved back over to sit down with Lucy.

"You know Julie don't you Lucy? She lives out near me."

"I know who she is, but I don't know her," Lucy answered.

Corley felt better because Lucy did not appear to make any connection between him and Julie. He hoped to hell it stayed that way. The two girls gave each other the once over. Corley figured it was safe to go dance with Julie so when the juke box played a slow song he made his way to their table and asked Denny if he could dance with his neighbor.

"Sure," he said, "just bring her back."

The juke box was playing "Please Release Me Let Me Go" by Ray Price. It was a decent tune to dance to.

As they began to move about the floor Corley looked her in the eye.

"What the hell you doing in here?"

"I came to hear you sing."

"Why? You have heard me sing already."

"I know, but I've heard that you were singing here with this band and my curiosity was killing me."

"If your mother knew you were in here, you'd get murdered."

"You going to tell her?"

"Hell no, I'm not going to tell her, but someone might."

"I'll take my chances," she said. "You dance like you have done it all your life."

"I'm the best dancer you'll ever dance with," he said.

"Modest too," she answered.

When the song ended he took her back to Denny and thought what a crime it was for such a girl to be going around with such an asshole. Corley smiled a phoney thank you and returned to Lucy.

"I didn't like the way you danced with her," she said.

"Well, you dance with people all the time when I'm on the bandstand," he answered. "Besides she doesn't dance as well as you anyway."

"You remember that," she replied.

Red was nodding for Corley to come back to work.

"What do you want to do, Corley?" he asked. He was always asking Corley that.

"Let's do some Hank Williams. I feel like 'I Can't Help it'."

"OK," he replied. "Do it."

Corley sang better than he had ever sung in his life and it got kind of spooky quiet. When he got to the line that said "I Can't Help It If I'm Still In Love With You," he turned and looked Julie Meadows right in the eye. She dropped her head and it occurred to Corley that for once he had gotten the best of her. She never looked back, and when the song ended, she and Denny were out the door. Corley even got a little round of applause from those who were dancing.

"You sounded good on that one Corley," Red commented. "You sounded like you were singing from the heart. Good job."

It was the first time that he felt like people were really listening to him sing and it definitely felt pretty good. He started to wonder if he really could sing, if he really could make a living singing.

As he and Lucy were getting into the car at midnight Lucy stunned him with a remark that he thought was totally out of character.

"I'd like to try a bed sometime, wouldn't you?"

He looked at her for a long moment and said, "I know where there is one if you want to risk it. I have a key to all of Porter Belk's camps and a couple of them are out of sight of the road. Want to take a chance on it?"

"We'll be so late getting home," she replied.

"I'm game if you are," Corley said.

She consented in silence and Corley drove up the river. He picked the camp farthest from the road. They went inside and Corley got some heat going. He had a sobering thought that old Porter would have a conniption if he ever found out about this little incident. But his passion and desire overrode all of his common sense and he and Lucy found the bed.

He got her home at 5:00 a.m. He hoped that she did not have any difficulty with her parents. She was nineteen but still a part of the household. He figured that there wasn't much he could do to help her. It was beginning to break day when he pulled the Buick into the garage at home. He went out like a light and was awakened by his mother's voice.

"It's dinner time," she said, "you going to sleep all day?"

Holy Christ, he thought. I have slept all morning, didn't do the milking, nor any of the chores.

His dad was busy with the fire when he came into the room.

"You are getting more like a foxhound all the time," he said, "run around all night and sleep all day. I hope you had a good time."

"Well, I guess I did. I didn't mean to sleep through the chores."

"Hell, you nearly missed the whole day," he replied.

"Guess I did at that," Corley confessed.

"You ain't never going to amount to anything running around all night and sleeping all day," he concluded.

Corley could tell by the tone of his voice and his general attitude that he was not really too upset. His mother was silent through it all. He hoped Lucy got by as easily as he did.

XIV

Corley was not looking forward to the next Monday morning at school. Football season was over and he was going to have to talk to Frank Kerns about getting out of the band. He had agreed to stay on through marching season, but he knew that Mr. Kerns was expecting him to stay on with the concert band. He felt sort of bad about it all because he knew that Mr. Kerns had spent a lot of time the previous year teaching Corley to be the school's first timpani player. And, he had enjoyed the hell out of playing them, but he just wanted to be free from all of the after school rehearsals. So, he was going to do battle with old Frank Kerns and see what happened.

He went to talk with him at noon. He found him sitting out on the fire escape smoking a cigarette. That's what Corley liked about Mr. Kerns. It was against the rules to smoke on school property, but he didn't give a damn. If he wanted a cigarette, he went and had one.

"Want a smoke?" he asked, shoving a pack of Lucky Strikes at Corley.

"Don't mind if I do," Corley replied. He wasn't a regular smoker but he figured that if Mr. Kerns were good enough to offer him one he should take it. He lit the cigarette for Corley and looked him in the eye.

"What's on your mind, Corley?" he asked.

"Not much, I was just wondering about the concert band."

"What about it?"

Corley looked at him for a moment and just sort of couldn't bring himself to discuss it with him. He was just a hell of a nice guy, and he decided right then and there that he would be a real horse's ass if he would quit on him.

"Well, I haven't fooled around with the timpani since last spring. Thought I ought to get them out and brush up a little."

"Good idea," he said. "You have a study hall this afternoon?"

"Yes, at two o'clock."

"I'll write you an excuse to get out and you can come on up and practice."

"Sounds good," Corley replied.

They crushed their cigarettes and Corley walked away a little disgusted with himself for not going through with his plans to quit. But yet he felt kind of warm inside about the whole thing. Frank Kerns was about the only teacher that he ever had who could talk to him on human terms. He liked the man and felt fortunate to know him.

That evening at after school practice, he noticed Julie looking over her flute at him several times. Actually, it was a kind of a strange look and he did not quite know what to make of it. And, as soon as practice was over, she came at him in a straight line.

"You have a way home this evening, Corley?"

"I'm hitchhiking, I guess."

"I have Mother's car. Why don't you let me drive you home."

"Sure, if you don't mind. I'm kind of out of your way though."

"I don't mind at all," she said.

They got into her mother's Dodge and rode in silence for a mile or two. Finally, she spoke.

"I was really impressed with your singing Saturday night. Have you ever thought of doing anything with it?"

"No, I haven't thought about doing anything with it. I just do it for fun. I'm not that good, and if I started trying to do it for a living it would turn into work."

"Do you plan on just having fun all your life?" she asked.

"Just as long as I possibly can. I'm in no damned hurry to take life seriously."

"Is that why you shy away from me? I know you like me, but you pretend that you don't."

That was the thing about old Julie Meadows, thought Corley. She was too goddamned smart for her own good. She had him all figured out but he was not about to admit that to her. He looked at her sitting behind the wheel of the Dodge. She was something. The truth was he was afraid of her, afraid that she would put a ring in his nose and make him want to go to work in some factory for the rest of his short life so that he could support her economic wants. As badly as he wanted her, he had an almost haunting fear about losing his freedom and never getting a chance to become an international lover. But he took another approach.

"Hell, I don't know Julie. It's just that it's never seemed right with you and me. I mean we always quarrel. You won't let me swear, and besides, you are too damned good looking to fool around with me. You are also too bright and talented. Hell, you will be able to get any man you want in a year or two. Or, if you don't want a man, you will be able to accomplish what you want."

"Why don't you just preach me a sermon?" she said.

They were approaching the little dirt drive that led to the Malone place and as she turned in, it occurred to him that it might do her some good to meet his parents, to get a glimpse of the life that he led.

"Why don't you come in and meet my folks?" he asked.

"I don't know," she replied, "I might feel awkward."

"Hell, if I were as pretty as you I would not feel awkward any damned place," Corley said as he pulled her from the car.

They went in through the back door that led to the kitchen. His mother had supper ready for the table and his dad was getting in the way as usual, looking into the pots on the stove.

"Folks, this is Julie Meadows, our neighbor from over the river."

"Oh, so you're the reason that Corley has been crossing the river all the time," his dad said. "I can see why."

"Corley talks of you all the time," his mother chimed in.

Corley gave her a shut up look and Julie gave him the look that she always gave when she had conquered him.

Julie unleashed all of her charm and when she let it go, it was considerable. She went on and on about how talented Corley was, and what a pretty place that they had, and how she was so glad to finally get to meet them.

"You and Corley wash up for supper," his dad said.

"Oh, I can't stay. My mother will be expecting me."

"You have time to eat with us. It's ready and it will only take you a few minutes."

"I really can't," she said.

But she did not know how Corley's dad was when it came to having people eat. If there was someone there, and it was supper time, he insisted that they eat.

"You get over there and sit down," he ordered.

Julie looked almost scared as she moved in behind the table. Corley was enjoying the hell out of seeing her being ordered around. As they ate, Corley's parents asked her all about her family, where they came from, where they'd been, and why they moved over across the river. They did not miss much. Corley learned more about her in fifteen minutes than he had all summer and fall. It seemed that her father was a native of the area, just a county away. He had traveled around a great deal, married a Connecticut girl, had always wanted to come back and settle near his native home, and had finally managed to do so. He had to travel some but he was mostly able to stay around. Corley found himself wishing that Mr. Meadows had found somewhere else to settle.

Afterwards, Corley walked her out to the car and they talked a minute or two.

"Corley, I would like to learn more about you and your world. You seem to find so much to do and you move in such different circles. Would you take me out on the same kind of date that you would take your friend, Lucy O'Brannon?"

Boy, if she knew what she was saying, thought Corley. He had a feeling that she had a somewhat inaccurate view of his relationship with Lucy. He looked at her a long time, thought of all the reasons that he shouldn't take her out, and finally told her that they would do something one night very soon.

"I really want to," she said.

"What will your friend Denny think of all of this?"

"Denny Lewis does not own me, and what he doesn't know won't hurt him."

"I'll talk to you about it at school one day," Corley said. "Lucy and I do not have an understanding or anything, but I really don't know if I should go out on her."

"That does not say much for me," she replied. "You talk to me about being afraid of getting tied down, then you allow yourself to be just that with someone else."

"I am not tied down," he shouted. "I am just trying to be considerate which is more than I can say for you."

She put her finger over his lips and said softly, "Let's don't fight, Corley, we have done so well all evening. I don't want to spoil it."

She drove away and he stood there feeling defeated again, knowing full well that he would take her out just like she wanted and at the same time, knowing damned good and well that it was the wrong thing to do. But, on the other hand, it might cause her to see him in a different light. She might decide that Denny Lewis was more her style. He began thinking about Friday night and where he could take her.

When he went to pick her up, her mother met him at the door and asked him in.

"What are you kids doing this evening?" she asked.

"I thought we would take in a movie, probably in Charleston," he lied.

Julie came down the stairs in a full skirt with six or eight petticoats under it and a white blouse that fit her just right. She had a white ribbon in her hair and it was just about more than Corley could stand. She did not ask where they were going until they were in the car.

"Are you willing to be a little bold and take a few risks?" Corley asked.

"Yes," she answered.

Corley had decided to drive over to Blair County and hit a few of the spots that he used to hit with his older brothers. Blair County culture was a little different. There was a little more poverty, and, if there was such a thing as a class system, many folks there would have been considered low class. It was a very rural county and had a reputation for being a little rough. It was full of roadhouse beer halls, most of which Corley had at least made a stop or two in at one time or another. His older brothers always went to Blair County to chase women and they had dragged him along a few times. Most of the beer halls were less than respectable, but they all had a good juke box for dancing, and if a person minded his own business, they were safe enough-- usually. Corley figured if they went to Blair County where no one would know Julie, it would decrease the risk of someone telling her mother that they saw her in a beer hall with one of the Malone boys.

His first stop was in a place called the Riverside Inn. It was out in the middle of nowhere, a very typical location for a West Virginia beer hall. There were several cars out front. Some of them were occupied with men sitting in them drinking liquor out of the bottle, usually chasing it with Coke or Seven-up. They would eventually end up inside the place, but liquor by the drink was not permitted in West Virginia and the State Police usually cruised the beer halls on a pretty regular basis. Yet, for some reason, the police respected the custom of folks passing a bottle in a car.

The Riverside had a fairly good crowd for early evening. It was about eight o'clock. Corley chose a table in a dark corner and when the bar maid came he ordered them both a Coke. The juke box was loud and playing one slow, country cuddling song after another. Corley pulled Julie up to dance and she came willingly. He held her as tight as he could and she danced like she had been dancing to country music all her life. They were soon joined by another couple who were older, perhaps in their thirties. The man immediately put his hand on the girl's ass and really began putting a feel on her. She pulled his hand up a time or two, but she let him pretty much do what he wanted. Corley did not know if Julie was watching or not. He could not see her eyes, but he could feel the tenseness in her as they danced. She was less than comfortable for some reason. It could have been that she saw the same two guys come through the door that Corley saw. They were big, unkempt, and very drunk. They stood at the bar and weaved around a bit, then ordered a beer. One of them turned and addressed the room.

"I can turn a back flip off the bar," he said.

"You can hardly stand up," his friend said laughing.

"I got five dollars says I can," he said. "Anyone want to bet?"

There were no takers but the place got deathly quiet in anticipation of what might be coming. Julie was about to squeeze Corley's arm off right above the elbow. The man pushed his way to the bar and climbed upon it. He was a well proportioned man, perhaps in his early twenties. He got up on the bar and steadied himself, yelled like a damned Indian, and lunged backwards. To Corley's utter surprise the son-of-a-bitch turned a perfect back flip and nearly jarred the place down when he hit the floor. He then turned back toward the bar, smiled, and held out his hand.

"Who wants to put that five right there?" he asked.

Everyone tried to ignore him and the bar maid hurried over and put money in the juke box. Corley figured that it was time to make an exit so he hurried Julie out the door. He didn't know for sure what was going to happen next, and he knew that they were not going to top that act at the Riverside that evening.

As they drove on up the road, Julie rattled on and on about how scared she was, but admitted that it was pretty exciting. Corley was not about to tell her how scared he was. Those two guys would have been a handful, drunk or not.

His next stop was a place called the Crossroads. It was bigger and slightly more respectable than the Riverside and tended to attract more teenaged kids. It was about the only place in Blair County where there was a good dance floor, and the teens came to dance. They mixed right in with the beer drinkers and some of the late teenaged girls provided possible targets for the men who came to drink and all that went with the drinking.

Corley was recognized by a few of the Blair County teens and got a few mild waves. The owner of the Crossroads was very strict about selling beer to minors, and he ran a pretty tight ship. The dance floor was full with every song that played. They sat down, ordered a Coke, and just observed for awhile. The kids were just starting to get the hang of dancing to rock and roll and some of them looked awkward as hell, especially the boys. But Blair County was famous for dancing so they were all out there trying. When "Rock Around the Clock" played, Corley pulled Julie toward the floor.

"Can you dance to this?" she asked timidly.

"I can sure try," he answered. "Lucy and I have been working on it some."

"If she can do it, I can," she said smugly.

Corley thought that they looked pretty good. His step was somewhere between the old mountain flatfoot and the boogie, but he made it fit the music. Julie probably danced better than anyone on the floor. They enjoyed an hour or so of the Crossroads culture and they left on a natural high. Julie had the time of her life showing off on the dance floor. Corley did not want to admit it but he was in absolute ecstacy. Being with her and being seen with her was even better than he ever imagined. When they got back in the car they went into a clinch and got involved in a kiss than went on too long. She was so warm and so alive and had a very sensuous mouth. You talk about burning kisses, Julie could put a scorcher on a person.. Corley thought that he was going to bust the crotch right out of his pants. He pulled her over on him and sent his knee into those full skirts searching for the magic spot. Julie bounced back into the seat and began to straighten herself up.

"Where do we go next?" she asked happily.

"We have one more stop to make, then I'm going to have to get you home."

The last stop was the Ice Cube Inn. It was on the way home and near the Vandalia County line. It was probably the worst of what Blair County had to offer. It was small and attracted a very low class clientele. Many of those who were getting government assistance spent their relief checks right there in the Ice Cube while their kids went hungry. Corley was repulsed by the place but he wanted Julie to see it. She wanted to know how the other half lived so he was going to show her. The place was pretty full, but they found a booth in the corner. Julie got stares as they crossed the floor which made her very uncomfortable. Corley ordered a Falls City and Julie passed. The dance floor was crowded with fat women and men with rotten teeth. They pawed each other and made suggestive, vulgar movements. The language was terrible. A man coming from the bathroom approached a woman on a barstool and grabbed the cheeks of her ass with both hands.

"You'd better move your hands or I'll shit them full," she said.

Everybody at the bar laughed and Corley picked up his beer and pulled Julie toward the door. He thought that she had seen enough and he wished that he hadn't stopped. She did not say anything but when they got into the car she sort of shuddered.

"That's the other West Virginia," Corley said. "It's not very pretty and we try to pretend that it's not there, but it is. I have seen it all my life."

"I guess I have lived a pretty sheltered life," she said.

The drive back down the Vandalia River was beautiful. The moon was reflecting off the water and it seemed as if the whole valley was sparkling. Julie was sitting as close as she could get, squeezing the back of his neck. When he got down to the Sugar Creek road, he just turned the old Buick right up the hollow and drove right up to where he and Lucy sometimes parked. He did not know what Julie would think about parking with the Malone boy, but there wasn't but one way to find out. He turned the car around, pulled over into the spot and turned off the lights. Julie did not say a word. The moon was so bright that he could see her eyes and they told him that it was alright.

After about three of those long smoking kisses from Julie, he reminded himself of one of his dad's bulls around a cow that was ready. She tolerated his knee in her crotch, but the minute he put his hand under those petticoats, she struggled away and stiff-armed him.

"You don't know how bad I want to cooperate with you, Corley, but this is all happening too fast."

Corley did not press the issue, just started the Buick and drove back down the hollow.

"You're not mad at me are you Corley?" she asked.

"Not at all," he replied. "I wouldn't ever want you if you didn't want me."

"I want you alright," she said, "but I have a lot to think about".

They drove on in silence, but Corley couldn't help but wonder how far old Denny Lewis had made it with her. They had seen a lot of each other and he was a cockhound if there ever was one. And, he knew that

Denny would not give up as easily as he had. He thought to himself that if he ever did find out that he had made it with Julie, he would just get the old .38 out and shoot the hell out of him. She deserved better.

They pulled up in front of her house thirty minutes before her midnight curfew. He was not interested in getting into another session with her and going home with the stone aches, so he got out and pulled her out behind him.

"I've had such a terrific time, Corley. You're lots and lots of fun and we must do something together real soon. I'll tell you what, since I went with you tonight, I want you to go to church with me again Sunday morning. You owe me one."

"Now, just hold on," he replied. "I'll be out late Saturday and I won't feel like doing anything Sunday morning. I'm not going to go to church Sunday. I would feel like a hypocrite in church after playing The Beeches Saturday night. I wouldn't feel right about it."

"Oh, pooh," she said. "It won't hurt you one bit to go. You come over to get me about 9:30 and we'll walk."

"I'll think about it, but don't really expect me."

She planted another burner on him to remind him how good she was and while he was kissing her, he took the ribbon from her hair and stuck it in his pocket thinking that it might be the last time that he would ever kiss her.

XV

Julie came into the bandroom after school on Monday and walked right over to Corley.

"I waited for you yesterday morning, but you didn't come."

"I told you that I probably wouldn't come. I slept all morning"

Corley had enjoyed a great time at The Beeches Saturday night. He had decided once and for all that he was not going to fool around with Julie anymore, and that Lucy was the kind of girl that he needed. He had gone and picked her up on the way to The Beeches and told her that they were going to have a really good time, better than usual, because he really felt like dancing. As soon as he got there he began to search the audience for someone to play guitar during the square dancers. There was always a stray guitar player or two in the place. He found an older man who had played some with Red and coaxed him into playing some so he and Lucy could square dance. He had gotten into old Marshall Wilson's set once because he wanted to learn all that he could from him. He wanted to learn that mountain flatfoot style. He thought that he almost had it. And, when Marshall had broken from the set and started to freestyle, Corley had jumped right in with him and danced him step for step, flatfoot for flatfoot. When the set was finished, old Marshall had complimented him.

"You can do it boy, just keep it up and you can take my place one day."

Corley felt really good about it and decided that he was where he belonged, doing what he was born to do. He had no business in Julie Meadow's world, and she had no business in his. Afterwards, he and Lucy had spent too much time up in Sugar Creek, snuggling under an old Army blanket in the back seat of the Buick.

But Julie looked at him with that knowing look of hers and was not about to back off so easily.

"I'll bet that Lucy girl just made you forget all about me."

"Now damn it, Julie, don't start on me today."

She laughed and took hold of his hand. "I just wanted to tell you how much I enjoyed being with you Friday night. I really had a good time."

"I'm glad you did," he replied.

"Why don't you come over tonight" she asked.

He looked at her a long time and decided that he would just go over there and have things out with her. It had to be done, he thought.

"OK," he said, "I'll be over tonight. We need to talk."

The November nights sometimes got bitter and it was cold as hell when Corley crossed the river that evening. When he got up to the railroad, he heard a bobcat scream up against the hill. He caressed the butt of the .38 for comfort. He knew that bobcats would not bother a person, but they could sure put the fear in your body. He listened as it walked in the leaves parallel to him. He screamed back at it, trying to psyche it out. He did not hear it anymore, but he didn't know where it was so the hair on the back of his neck stood up during the rest of the walk. He was glad to see the lights at Julie's house.

Her mother answered the door. What a phoney smile she had, thought Corley. Julie came out of the kitchen looking like something on the cover of a teen magazine. Her mother left them in the living room. Corley hoped that she went upstairs and choked on something.

"Well, just what is this big talk that we are going to have?" Julie asked.

Corley went into his planned speech.

"Julie, I have been giving this a lot of thought, and I have decided that you and I are going to have to come to an understanding. You see, Julie, you are not an ordinary run of the mill girl, at least not in my eyes, and I can't take you or leave you the way you do me. And that kind of a one-sided relationship just won't do. Besides, I am never at ease with you. I always feel like that there is something wrong. Do you understand what I am saying?"

"No," she answered. "I feel very comfortable with you."

Corley wished that he were somewhere else, but he was there and he had to get out of this one way or another. He took another approach.

"Look, you're going to college next fall, right?"

"Yes, I hope to. I want to continue with my music. My parents have invested a great deal in getting me ready."

"You see, that's it. You know where you are going in life and you don't need to be getting involved with anyone like me who doesn't know where he is going. I have fooled around in high school until I couldn't go to college if I wanted to. Besides, I can't afford it. And here's the clincher, Julie, I can't fool around with you without getting serious."

She looked at him for a very long time and finally said, "That was quite a speech, Corley. I never quite know what's coming out of you next. But, I don't see why we can't enjoy each other's company without getting serious. And, I think that you are selling yourself a little short. You are a pretty talented guy and whether you will admit it or not, you are basically a good person. But I appreciate what you are saying, and I agree that we do not need to be getting serious. So are you saying that you don't want to see me anymore?"

"That's exactly what I am saying."

"Well, if that's what you want, I will certainly honor your wishes, but I think that I will still want to see you. I know that I will miss you."

"It's not like I'm leaving the world or anything," he said. "We'll see each other all the time. All I'm asking is that you just stop giving me those looks with those damned eyes of yours."

She smiled knowingly and put her hands in her lap.

"I want you to do something for me before I go," he said.

"Yes," she answered.

"I want you to go to the piano and play something for me, something pretty."

She shuffled through her music and placed a piece of sheet music in front of her. She began playing "Fur Elise" by Beethoven. Corley sat there and watched and listened and then got emotional as hell. For the first time in his life he thought that maybe he ought to try to amount to something. He pictured himself ages hence sitting on the patio of a big mansion in the hills, his temples getting grey, having a drink, and listening to Julie play the piano. He got up and started for the door. He wanted to leave while she as still playing, but she spotted him and followed him out.

"Maybe someday, we'll see things differently," she said.

"Maybe," he answered.

It was a lonely walk back down the railroad track. Even the bobcat had given up on him because he did not hear it anymore   He shivered against the damp air as he crossed the river and contemplated his place in the universe. He was sure that he had done the right thing. Or, had he? Here he was, a speck on the river which had provided him so many good times, about to feel sorry for himself. But, he decided that there was not going to be any days like that for Corley Malone. Julie Meadows was headed for a life of white shirts and afternoon teas. Corley Malone was headed for a life of good times up and down the Vandalia River. Or, was he? The image of Julie sitting in that living room playing the piano kept haunting him. He got almost a sickening feeling. Maybe he was getting on the wrong track or about to catch the wrong train. Maybe there was a better life out there somewhere. He thought about the doodle bugs and the little game that they used to play with them when he was a child.

The doodle bug was a little bug that lived in a hole in the ground. The hole was about the size of a hole that a ten penny nail would make if someone drove it into the ground. Corley's grandfather had taught all the children that if you yelled down into the hole and told the doodle bug that his house was on fire, he would come out and flee. So all the children would find a doodle bug hole and yell down into it "doodle bug, doodle bug, your house is on fire." And, sure enough, the little fella would come right out of his hole and flee.

Corley thought that maybe he was just like the doodle bug. He was fleeing at the first sign of danger, fleeing from the unknown. Maybe if he just let things take their natural course with Julie, it would all work out. Then, on the other hand, he might get burned, and he really wanted to avoid that.

It was still early when he got home. He went into his room, closed the door, got the old guitar down, and began to write a song that had been bouncing around in his mind. It was all about a pretty girl who was trapped and unappreciated in a dirty little river town with no hope of escape.

XVI

Corley Malone was soon preoccupied with his own world and all thoughts of girls, music, school, and careers were put aside. It was mid-November in Vandalia County and most of the male minds were concentrating on deer season. It changed everything, at least for a few days.

Deer season in West Virginia was more than just deer hunting. It was a happening of great significance. Schools closed, men neglected their jobs, farm chores, and their wives. West Virginians who lived out of state came home in droves. It was a time when families drew closer together and brothers felt a closeness that they did not feel at any other time of the year. Deer season made Thanksgiving an extra special time.

The November deer season brought many cars with Ohio and Michigan license plates back to Vandalia County. High powered rifles began to crack up and down the river valley as everyone zeroed in their sights. The local store became crowded during the evening hours and the talk was of nothing but whitetailed deer. Men would come into the store and make exaggerated reports about how many deer they had seen that day while scouting up some hollow that was familiar to all of them. Word of a sighting of a big buck would cause immediate silence. Liars would abound as the men swapped stories of previous hunts, and the younger men, like Corley, listened eagerly to every story.

During that particular time the favorite deer rifle in West Virginia was the Winchester 94, 30-30 caliber. It was a very adequate gun for West Virginia because it was rare that anyone saw a deer more than one hundred yards away. The hilly terrain and heavy cover made visibility very difficult much farther than that. Hunters had to be very alert because one look was about all that they got at the elusive buck. Does would sometimes walk out into an opening and stop, but in 1955, it was a strictly bucks only season.

Corley was the proud owner of a Winchester 94 but he had never killed a buck and he was approaching his fifth year of deer hunting. It was no disgrace because bucks were fairly scarce and many people hunted for years and never got a shot at one. That was why it was such a challenge. Corley had never gotten a shot at one so he could not be ridiculed for missing. If you missed and someone saw you, they would cut your shirttail off, or at least that was always the talk at the store. A cut-off shirttail would show the world that the shooter had choked in the clutch. Corley did not even want to think about missing one.

A few days before the season opened he got him a couple of boxes of 30-30 shells and began shooting at the bottom of a five gallon bucket. He fired twenty rounds into the bucket at one hundred yards, and the pattern was near perfect. He knew that it would be a different story when the moment of truth came, but he felt like that he was ready.

By Sunday evening prior to the Monday morning opening day, all of Corley's brothers were home and a tremendous feast had been prepared. Spirits were high as was family rivalry. Corley was the only one who had not made a kill and he was undergoing a great deal of pressure. His father was leading the charge, claiming that he was well past his time. Corley countered with the argument that he had not yet seen one to shoot at, but according to the criticism, that was part of the skill involved. You had to have the eye to spot one.

Late Sunday evening the wind began to blow from the northwest and by nightfall, snow was falling. Everyone was delighted because the snow made it easier to see the deer. Corley slept only occasionally during the night. His mother was up way before dawn and when the men got to the kitchen, the biscuits were piled high. They all ate like loggers. It was blue cold outside and Corley felt it bite into him as he loaded his gun and started up the first hill. No one had much to say at first, but soon Corley's dad was giving instructions. He loved to direct the hunt, and his sons loved to hear him do it. Corley heard his name.

"Corley, you go back the ridge, back past the old Cummings place, and find you a good spot where you can see in all directions. Get in above the pine thicket now, you hear. Stay there until you see me come through. Me and the boys will crisscross all of the country between here and there."

Corley realized that they were giving him the advantage. They all pretty well knew the pattern of the deer and it was obvious that they were going to try to put some toward him. Of course, there was always the chance that one of them would get a shot if they jumped some out. All Corley knew for sure was that it was cold as hell. He put his head down and started the mile or so walk back the ridge. The wind was whipping through the trees until he could not hear a damned thing. He walked as fast as he could in the cold darkness.

By the time he arrived at his designated spot it was light enough to see. He settled in at the edge of a pipeline right-of- way and began to watch. He stood for over an hour and never saw nor heard anything. The wind had settled some and he could hear better but the air was still bitter cold. Every part of him was cold and he struggled to keep from shaking. He contemplated his place in the universe. No one but a goddamned outright fool would be up here on this ridge freezing his ass off, he thought. He could be at the house, sitting by the fire, playing his guitar, and really enjoying life. But no, here he was, out here in zero weather watching for a bunch of deer which really probably did not exist.

He heard movement below him and shook from both the cold and excitement. Two does walked out into the open and stopped. Corley had heard literally thousands of stories about how there was usually a buck following doe, so he searched the brush behind them carefully. The does loped off, but no buck was forthcoming.

He pulled his thermos of coffee from his hunting coat and poured his first ration. It was hot and it sure tasted good. Folks who had never stood out on the top of a hill in zero weather and froze their ass off for two hours had never really appreciated coffee, he thought to himself. He had just finished the coffee and was putting his gloves back on when he heard a rifle crack. Two, three, four shots, and they were close. He looked toward where the shots came from and he heard brush cracking like a herd of cattle coming. He saw the deer about fifty yards before it got to the right of way, but he could not see any antlers. He was not sure, but he followed the deer in his sights until it hit the clearing. It was definitely a boy. He squeezed once and the buck went end over end down the hill, got back up and came right straight toward him. He fired again and it went down hard. The buck was kicking and struggling, but he was down to stay.

Corley charged toward it, watching closely. He had heard too many stories about deer getting up and running away after they were down. But this buck was down for good. It had nearly stopped moving before Corley got to it. He got out his knife, pulled the deer around and cut the scent glands off the inside of the legs, the way he had seen it done. He cut the throat, turned the head down hill, and let the brute bleed awhile. The next part he had never done and he was not looking forward to it. The fellow had to be "field dressed" as it was called. Corley tried to remember what he had been taught. He cut the deer from his breast bone back to his tail and reached inside and pulled out everything that he could find. It was hot in there and the odor grossed him out for a few seconds. He cleaned him out as best he could and stepped back to admire his kill. It was a six point, not a trophy, but a nice buck. Anyone would have been proud of him.

His father stepped into the clearing. He had observed the entire operation and was smiling broadly.

"You did good, Corley. I shot at him four times, but really did not have a clear shot. Did you miss him the first time you shot?"

"No, I knocked him down, hit him right at the top of the back above his front shoulder. He came straight at me then and I hit him right in the breast the second time."

"He's a nice one," his dad said. "Let's get him home."

"Where are the other boys?" Corley asked.

"They went off tracking a bunch toward the old Smith place. They'll be alright."

They each grabbed an antler and started the long pull back the ridge.

"Once you pull the trigger, the fun's over," his dad said. "The rest of it is work."

He was right about that, Corley thought. He was exhausted when they got to the house. His dad did not believe in resting. They put the deer in the back of the old pickup and took him down to the store to check him in. Corley checked him with a swollen chest and no comments, then took him back home for the real tough job.

They pulled him up on a chain hoist in the barn and skinned him out. His dad always argued that the sooner you got the skin off the better the meat. They quartered him and hung the quarters in the smoke house. Since the weather was good and cold, they would let him hang for about three days prior to cutting up the meat. Corley sawed off the top of the skull so as to keep the antlers in one piece. His father had told him that there would probably never be a thrill like the first one and Corley knew that he was probably right.

By the time Corley and his father had finished working with the deer it was too late to go out again. They spent the remainder of the afternoon at small chores. Shortly before dark, they spotted the brothers, bone tired, dragging one down the hill. It was a huge ten point and they had killed it well over a mile from the house. When they took it to the store to check it, there were deer everywhere. Men stood around trucks in freezing temperatures to admire one another's kill and to tell anyone who would listen how they had got their buck. Each time they told it, it got longer and more interesting. There would be great arguments about how much each one weighed before they finally put it on the scales. For those not familiar with deer, their weight can be very deceptive. They appear to weigh more than they do. The average West Virginia white tail runs between 130 and 160 pounds. But a man who has dragged one for a couple of hours usually guesses it to weight at least two hundred pounds. But a two hundred pounder was pretty unusual.

Corley and his brothers spent the next two days trying to jump out a deer for their dad. They jumped several doe, but failed to turn up another buck. Corley figured that he must have walked at least fifty miles during those two days, but he enjoyed it. In fact, that was his favorite part, crashing around through the brush and not having to worry about being quiet.

They spent Thanksgiving day at light hunting. Those who had already killed a deer carried a shotgun and searched for ruffled grouse or rabbits. Those not yet scoring a deer kill still carried their rifle. But the hunt was not so serious on that day. It was more for fellowship, and the big anticipation was for the great Thanksgiving dinner that they knew awaited them at the end of the hunt. Then after the meal, they all gathered around the fire and discussed the week's activity. For the Malone family, the hunting season ended with Thanksgiving. Deer season remained open for the remainder of the week and small game for the rest of the year, but for them it was over. The next day was hog killing day, and for them, it was as much of a tradition as hunting. And the last thing that Corley heard before he went to bed was his dad telling him to get out early in the morning and go get "Sparrow Hawk".

They called the place Camp Creek for reasons unknown to Corley. It was just a little hollow that branched off one of the main hollows which branched off the Vandalia River Valley. There were a million spots just like this one, most of them without names. But somewhere back in time, this spot had become Camp Creek. At any rate, this is where "Sparrow Hawk" made his home.

Home to "Hawk" consisted of two rooms constructed out of rough oak boards. It was what the locals called a "gentle end" house. There were no studs with an inner and outer wall. It was just a frame with one inch oak boards nailed vertically from the floor to the ceiling. Narrow oak strips were nailed over the cracks between the boards. There was a tin roof. "Hawk" had tacked cardboard on the inside of the walls to help keep out the cold. He had a coal heater in the center of the main room and a small wood cookstove in the corner of the same room. He dug what coal he needed out of the hill near his house. There was no heat in the small room where he slept. There was no electricity nor running water. He got his light from oil lamps and his water from a dug well out back. But it was a pretty cozy place, especially when the coal stove was roaring good in the winter. It served his needs.

He was a big man, perhaps six foot three. His hands were especially large. He was not too concerned about his personal hygiene and carried the odor of wood and coal smoke on his person. Corley never knew him to initiate a conversation. And, if spoken to, his answer was always as brief as possible. If there ever was a loner, it was "Hawk."

Compared to most folks in the area, he raised very little garden. Sweet potatoes were his favorite dish so he raised a long ridge of those, and he also cultivated a small patch of Irish potatoes. Mostly, he lived from the woods. He hunted constantly during the fall and canned all the meat that he killed. Grey squirrels, rabbits, and often illegal deer kept him going. He also picked all of the blackberries that he could find and canned them. He fished the river year around. But, of all of his attributes, he was first recognized by the local people for his skill with a .22 rifle. He was a dead shot.

It was because of this talent that he was a much sought after man at hog killing time. Nearly every family in the area slaughtered a hog or two when the weather cooled down in the fall of the year, and everyone called upon "Hawk" to help. They wanted him not only for his expert shooting ability but also because he knew all about the entire operation. He kept the sharpest bunch of knives in the country.

When it came time to shoot the hog everyone gathered to watch. "Hawk" was not only a dead shot, but he also knew just where to place the bullet. There was a spot between the eyes, perhaps just a little above the eyes, where the slug had to hit. He would sometimes aim for a full minute, then drop his aim and begin all over again. But once he squeezed the trigger, the hog would drop and die in a quiver. He never missed the spot.

Hog killing was a messy job and Corley hated it. He was very glad to have "Hawk" around because he performed many of the unpleasant tasks. Corley's job was to build a big fire out near the barn and to heat two or three washtubs full of water. He set about that task as soon as he got back. While the water was heating they all gathered to watch "Hawk" make the kill. Then they dragged the hog over to a temporary platform. The hot water was poured into a barrel near the platform and they would douse the hog into the hot water, snake him out, and scrape the hair off his hide. They would repeat this task until all the hair was gone. The smell was terrible and the work nauseating. Finally, they would hoist him up with a coffin horse and gut him.

Once the outside work was done, the job moved to the kitchen. The kitchen was always a mess for a week after the kill. Corley avoided it as much as he could. The truth was he hated the entire operation, but he really enjoyed the ham, the bacon, and the sausage for the rest of the winter. It was worth it, he supposed. He was just glad when it was over.

"Hawk" was given a generous portion of the meat for his labor along with a good meal. That's all he ever wanted. Corley took him home afterwards and enjoyed a few minutes sitting by the coal fire. "Hawk" never had much to say but he seemed to enjoy the company just the same.

On the way back home, Corley thought about The Beeches for the first time all week. He thought about the approaching Saturday night gig, Lucy O'Brannon, and all of the other things that had haunted his mind prior to the week of hunting. And, yes, he thought about Julie Meadows. When he got home he went to bed thinking that maybe he was not an international lover yet, but he was at least a great white hunter.

XVII

It was that very Saturday night at The Beeches that Corley finally became convinced that the world of music was going through a revolution. The term "rock and roll" had been around since 1951 and people had been gradually modifying dance steps to fit the new beat. But as Corley observed the crowd on the dance floor he concluded that the change was complete.

Everyone was well aware of Elvis Presley, and more and more the juke box at The Beeches was dominated by the new sounds. Some folks still enjoyed the square dance, but it was becoming more and more obvious to Corley that the music that he was singing between square dance sets was falling flat. People were looking forward to the breaks so that they could plug in the juke box. He kept thinking about it all evening, and he regretted seeing the music that he had known and loved slipping away.

Dress and hair styles were also changing. Boys were beginning to wear bright colors and let their hair grow longer. Pink shirts were everywhere. Corley had tried the new trends in dress some, but always reverted back to his jeans. He was not yet comfortable with the changes that were upon him, but he had to admit that he did like some of the new music. The music that some had branded as "rock-a-billy" sort of appealed to him. Carl Perkins had caught his attention.

"What's wrong with you this evening, Corley?" Lucy asked finally.

"I don't know. I've just been watching people dance to this rock and roll and it has sort of got me in a blue mood. Here I am, nearly eighteen years old, just getting interested in singing country music, and I see it dying right in front of my eyes."

"Maybe you ought to try to do some of the new music," Lucy suggested.

"I don't think I have it in me, and Red would have a shit hemorrhage if I mentioned it to him."

"Oh, I think that there will always be country music," Lucy said.

"I'm not so sure. When you watch this crowd, mostly young people, moving to the new beat, it makes you wonder. Maybe I ought to quit this shit. I sure don't want to stand up there and sing if no one wants to hear me, especially if people would really rather be dancing to something else."

Corley just sort of went through the motions the rest of the evening. The truth was his ego was suffering a little. He was pretty discouraged because no one was paying much attention to him when he was singing, and what was worse, few people were dancing. He got Red over in the corner at the end of the evening and gave him the word.

"I want to quit, Red. I think this is my last night."

"What you want to go and do a thing like that for, Corley? Don't you like us any more or what?"

"I like you fine, Red. You're a damned good fiddler and one of the finest fellows that I know. I'm just tired of it all, I suppose."

"If that's what you want to do, I wouldn't want to talk you out of it," Red said.

"I think it's what I want to do."

"Well don't ever give up playing and singing. You do a damned good job, and you show some promise on the fiddle. You're not quitting music altogether are you?"

"No, I don't think I could ever quit. I just need to think about it awhile."

"Well, you come around and play with us some. We'll always be glad to have you."

"Thanks, Red, I'll do that."

They shook hands and Corley got the old Gibson, and Lucy, and made his way out. Lucy was being very quiet. She was not sure that Corley was doing the right thing, but she was not the sort of girl who would say anything. Finally, she managed a sentence.

"What are we going to do on Saturday nights if we don't go to The Beeches?"

"We'll find plenty to do. We can take in some movies, maybe check out some of the night life over in Blair County. I just felt like I was boring people up there on the band stand and I don't want to do that."

He drove Lucy home and hardly kissed her goodnight. He just wasn't in the mood for girls, and wanted to be alone. He found some good music on the car radio and drove home slowly, trying to sort it all out in his mind. He concluded that there was no immediate solution.

The next morning after breakfast he got to thinking about old Frank and Albert Keefer. Maybe he would just go over and play some music with them because that was the music that he really loved. Those old, old fiddle tunes with that rapping banjo beat in the background gave him a feeling like no other music. Then, he had another thought that he just might go over and see if Julie Meadows would like to go with him. She might enjoy that, he thought, and he needed some company. He was well aware of the fact that he told her that he was not going to see her anymore, but this would not really be a date. This would just be a learning experience for her.

He got his fiddle and guitar, put them in the old pick-up, and took the dirt road over to the Meadows place. When he got to her house she wasn't even dressed yet. He heard her run upstairs when he knocked on the door. Her mother came to the door with her ever present phoney smile.

"Good morning, Corley. Julie just ran upstairs to dress. I'm afraid that you caught her a little early. She was out late last night."

Corley was aware of the fact that she intentionally got that statement in. She wanted to make sure that he knew that Julie did not have to depend on him for a date. But, he was well aware of that. They were probably standing in line to take her out.

"Come on in and have a seat. She'll be down soon."

Her father was reading the Sunday paper. He looked over it when Corley came in and nodded.

"Hey, Corley. How are you doing?"

"Alright, I suppose. I apologize for coming by so early without telling anyone. We don't have a phone you know, and I just decided what I wanted to do after breakfast."

"That's alright," he replied. "I'll share the paper with you."

Corley hardly got seated when Julie came flying down the stairs. She had on blue jeans, rolled up to the knees, and a red top. And, the thing that really got to

Corley was that she looked absolutely beautiful. Some girls looked awful in the morning, but not her. He was more convinced than ever that she was just a damned natural born beauty.

She was looking at him kind of funny as she came over to sit down, like she was wondering what the hell he was doing there. After all, it had just been a few days since he had told her that he didn't want to see her anymore. She sat down right against him.

"Listen Julie, there are a couple of old guys who live over near my Grandfather Fletcher and they are about the best old time musicians around. I am going over to play some music with them today and I thought maybe that you would like to tag along. We'll have dinner with my grandparents, then spend the afternoon with the Keefer boys."

"It sounds interesting, but I don't know," she said, looking at her father.

"It sounds like a very interesting day to me." he said. "Go ahead if you want to."

"They will be expecting me at church," Julie said.

"Oh, they will survive one Sunday without you," he replied.

"You had better get on your walking shoes," Corley said. "You can't get a car to Grandpa Fletcher's, and you sure can't get one to the Keefer place. Also, it's kind of cold this morning."

She appeared very excited and went to get her coat. Her dad looked at Corley for a minute and said, "I wouldn't mind hearing that myself sometime."

"Well, the Keefer boys never play anywhere except at home, but maybe you could go with me sometime."

"I'd like that," he said.

Corley decided again that old man Meadows was alright, a hell of a lot better than his wife.

They climbed into the old pick-up and, with the guitar and fiddle in the cab, there wasn't much room for Julie. But they managed to get the doors closed. They drove as far as the road went, then got out to walk.

"You carry the fiddle," Corley said, "and I'll carry the guitar."

He had managed to get him a cheap guitar case with some of the money that he earned playing at The Beeches. It wasn't much, but it kept the weather off the guitar. When they got to the top of the hill to where the Fletcher place was visible, Julie was obviously impressed.

"What a lovely place," she commented. It looks so neat and so alone."

"Well, it's pretty and it's alone alright. That's the way Grandpa likes it."

The meadows were all cleaned up and each sported a neat haystack. Corley remembered how the haystacks got there. There wasn't any snow, but it was still a pretty sight, even with the browness of the end of November. When they got down to the house, his grandmother was in a flurry. She said that she did not have a thing to eat and didn't know what she was going to do. But Corley had heard that story many times before and he knew that in no time at all she would produce a beautiful meal. His grandfather was really looking Julie over as they sat down in front of the stove to warm up a little. He had been to church and had on his best clothes.

"You two going to get married?" he asked.

He was always saying that kind of stuff. He thought everybody ought to get married and if anyone showed up at his house with a girl, he would start on them.

"No, nothing like that," Corley replied.

Julie was looking at the floor and trying not to laugh.

"There is nothing as good as a good woman, but nothing as bad as a bad one," he said pensively.

Corley thought he would have a little fun with Julie so he carried the conversation forward.

"Which do you suppose that Julie is?" he asked.

"Well, she certainly is a pretty one, but you never can tell about that. I've known some pretty ones that were pretty bad news."

Julie was blushing, but smiling.

"I haven't decided which she is yet, Grandpa," Corley said.

"She is awfully contrary sometimes."

"That's just the nature of women," he replied.

Corley was really quite impressed with Julie's grasp of the situation. She was totally out of her element but she took his grandfather's teasing very well. She offered to help in the kitchen but was chased out. When they all sat down to eat, Corley decided again that it was worth the walk just to hear his grandfather say the table grace. Once more, he couldn't tell what he was saying, but he said it with such style.

The meal was pretty typical for the Fletcher place. They had canned pork, mashed potatoes, green beans, corn, peas, some kind of relish, and homemade bread. There was blackberry cobbler for dessert. Corley noticed that Julie was a bit overwhelmed by it all. He figured that folks who did not live out in the country and raise their own food did not know much about eating. Julie lived in the country, but Corley doubted if her mother knew the first thing about fixing a good country meal. All she could do was flash a phoney smile, but she was good at that.

Julie was allowed to help with the dishes and Corley and his grandfather talked a little farming. Corley had thought about farming for a living some day. The only thing that bothered him about it was that all of the farmers that he knew had everything that they wanted except money. And, at that particular time in his life, money seemed important. He doubted that he would ever really be a farmer, but he liked to talk about it.

It was getting along mid afternoon when he and Julie got to the Keefer place. Old Frank was all smiles when he saw Corley at the door.

"Why come in, Corley. Who in the world you got with you there?"

"This is Julie Meadows. She is my neighbor over on the river."

Frank looked her over. "Pretty as a speckled pup, ain't she Albert?"

"Danged if she ain't." Albert said.

Even Frank's wife, Zelda, looked on admiringly.

"You guys been playing any music?" Corley asked.

"Oh, we play quite a bit," Frank answered. "Sure will be nice to have a guitar player though. Get that thing out and let's get tuned up. Zelda will probably make some coffee. You drink coffee don't you Julie? I know that Corley does."

"She'll drink some," Corley answered for her. " I want you to show me some fiddle licks after while."

"I'll do that, but let's just play awhile first. I do like to hear those bass runs on the guitar."

Frank started with "Lost Indian" and it was one of Corley's favorites. It was one of those old minor key tunes that got him right down in the small of his back. It was kind of strange, Corley thought, how Frank and Red played so differently. They were both excellent fiddlers, but their styles were worlds apart. Sometimes, it was difficult to tell when Frank completed a line because he threw a little drag lick in there, but that was one of the things that made the music so neat. Frank and Albert ran through about fifteen tunes before taking a break. They put all kind of names on them, "Forked Deer," "Leather Britches," Elzic's Farewell," "Yew Piney Mountain," and on and on.

"Let's play "Blue Eyed Girl," Frank suggested. "I always liked a blue eyed girl." He twinkled at Julie. She was quite enthralled by it all and her eyes were glued to Frank.

"You ain't danced yet, Corley," Frank said.

As they began playing "Blue Eyed Girl" Corley got up and did his best flatfoot shuffle. Julie was visibly embarrassed so he did not dance long. But it felt good dancing to Frank's fiddle. The music was definitely going right to Corley's soul. When the music stopped and Corley started to sit down, Zelda spoke up.

"I'd like to see you two waltz," she said. "I'll bet Julie is a good dancer."

Frank started playing "Over The Waves" and Corley pulled Julie to her feet. He locked his eyes right on hers and began to move her around the small room. She was genuinely moved by the moment. Corley could tell by the way she danced, and he could also tell that she had waltzed before. But he doubted that she had ever danced to "Over The Waves."

"That was very beautiful," Zelda commented.

"Thank you," Julie replied. "Corley just leads well."

Zelda served cake and coffee while they took a break, and Frank and Albert spent some time showing Corley some old time licks on the fiddle. They showed him how to start some of the tunes and assured him that once he started into the tunes he would find his way. Corley wanted to play like them so bad that he could hardly stand it, but doubted if he would ever master it. He thought that maybe it was genetic.

The afternoon was fading and Corley knew that they were going to have to get started or it would be a dark walk back to the truck. They hustled off, stopped and paid their respects to his grandparents, and made it to the pick-up just as darkness was falling. Julie was humming one of the old fiddle tunes and was obviously still high from the experience. It had been a learning experience for her, no doubt about that.

"How in the world do they keep all of those tunes in their head?" she asked.

"I'm damned if I know. I used to think that they were just putting me on. I thought that they just played something and put a name on it. But, they play the exact same notes each time, note for note. And, Christ, do they play a lot of notes. Most fiddlers shuffle the bow a lot and leave out notes, but Frank seems to put more in. He's remarkable."

They drove to the Meadows place mostly in silence, but when they pulled up in front of the house, Julie snuggled close to him.

"I just can't get over all of the things that you do," she said.

Then she moved in and put one of those burning kisses on him and it only took one of those to put Corley in agony.

"I don't suppose that you want to see me any more," she said as she pulled away.

"Well, I'm not going to say that. I don't believe that I can stay away from you. I've tried, but I always seem to come back."

"I'm glad that you do," she smiled. "I always have such fun with you. I must say that you are completely different from anyone that I have ever known. I still think that we can have fun without getting serious."

"I hope so, Julie, I really do, but you are going to have to slow down on those burning kisses of yours."

She just smiled and slid out of the truck and went inside.

As he was driving home, he wondered how the hell a man was supposed to be on the receiving end of one of those burners of hers and not get serious.

XVIII

Corley returned to school after the Thanksgiving break feeling better about everything. He had gotten his buck, he had made peace with Julie, sort of, he had gotten out of the Saturday night gigs at The Beeches, and he was not really sure where he was with Lucy. And, things always slowed down for him in December. There wasn't much to do on the farm except milk and feed and he found himself with a bit of free time on his hands for the first time in months.
He decided that he would keep Julie at arm's length, go through the motions of school, and just enjoy being alive. His mother had already mentioned a Christmas tree so he knew that there was an adventure coming up.

He had been stealing a Christmas tree from old Cecil Russ since he was twelve years old, and he wanted to do it just one more time. The only reason that he did it was because old Cecil was such a horse's ass. He could have cut a nice tree on their own farm, or a dozen other places, but he always stole one from Cecil. It had become a tradition with him. Old Cecil had it coming, Corley figured, because of the way he treated him the first time he was sent to cut a tree when he was twelve years old.

During that first outing, he was out scouting around, trying to find a really pretty one. And, while going through Cecil's place, he spotted one just about like he wanted, the right size and everything. He had always heard that Cecil Russ was a nasty man, but he figured that if he asked him for the tree, he would let him have it. So, he knocked on his door and asked him if he could have the tree, and that if he wanted, he would pay him a fair price for it. But old Cecil had yelled at him something awful, and told him to get off his land or he would set the dogs on him. He was still ranting and raving as Corley went out of sight.

Corley was shattered and when he was about half way back home he decided that he would just go back and get that tree. He figured that there was just no reason for a man to act like that. Any other person in the whole damned county would have been glad to give a boy a tree. It wasn't like there was a shortage of them. So Corley waited a couple of hours and went back to the Russ place. He crawled on his belly up to the tree and slowly and quietly sawed it down. The tree was not visible from the house but Corley was scared that he would hear him and set the dogs on him. Once he had it severed he grabbed it up and ran nearly all the way home. He decided that it was the prettiest tree that they had ever had and he was proud of it. Every year after that, he had stolen a tree from old Cecil's place.

So on the following Saturday he went up and hollered Sam out. He had been so busy that he and Sam had not spent much time together. And, not only had he been busy, but Sam was spending most evenings over at the Phillips' place. He was getting in pretty deep. He and Sam had just sort of gotten on separate tracks. They had talked some at school but really hadn't done anything together.

"Steal a Christmas tree?" Sam said. "Who the hell ever heard tell of stealing a Christmas tree?"

"Don't knock it if you haven't tried it," Corley replied.

"From what you say we are liable to get our ass shot off, and all for a scrubby pine tree. Hell, they're growing everywhere. Why steal his?"

"For two reasons," Corley said. "First, for the challenge of it, and mostly because old Cecil Russ is a horse's ass."

"Well, it's something to do I guess. Let's do it."

When they got to the Russ place, they cut one tree that was well out of sight of the house and put it beside the escape trail. Then they crawled through the broomsage to where they could see the house and where they could survey most of the trees. Suddenly, Corley saw the one that he had to have. It was about thirty yards from old Cecil's house.

"That's the one," he said to Sam as he pointed out the tree. It was sort of standing alone and was perfect in every way.

"You're crazy as hell," Sam replied. "That one is nearly in his yard."

"To hell with him, let's go get it," Corley said.

They crawled through the broomsage side by side, flat on their bellies until they were right under the tree. The trick was going to be in getting the tree sawed off and pulled out of there without being discovered either by Cecil or his dogs. Corley sawed slowly. The pine cut easily so it was a fairly easy task and the tree was soon down.

"Now what?" said Sam. "We going to run, crawl, or just lay here."

"Let's just make a run for it," Corley replied.

Corley said "go" and they made a mad dash for the shelter of the woods. Just as they reached the ridge line and safety, they heard a dog bark twice and when Corley looked back he saw a dog coming on the run and he was not barking. That was a bad sign, Corley figured, because he had always heard that a barking dog hardly ever bites. When they reached the edge of the woods where the first tree had been stashed, they stopped to face the snarling dog. It was not a big dog, but it was big enough. They knew that they could not outrun him, that was for sure. The dog ran right at Sam and jumped for his throat. Sam caught the dog in the side of the head with a haymaker right and knocked him toward Corley. Corley kicked as hard as he could, catching the dog under his belly. The dog rolled over, got up and showed his teeth and growled. By that time Sam had secured a club and moved toward the dog. The mutt had obviously seen a club before because he tucked his tail and ran for the house. Almost immediately, they heard old Cecil call for the dog. They picked up the trees and ran out the ridge. Once they had put some distance between themselves and the edge of the Russ property they rolled in the leaves with laughter.

"Now wasn't that more fun than buying a tree or cutting one elsewhere?" Corley asked.

"Hell yes. Let's get another one," said Sam. "I creamed the hell out of that dog didn't I?"

"He would have eaten you up if I hadn't kicked him," Corley said.

"Bullshit, I had him on the run," exclaimed Sam.

"Yeah, and Eisenhower is a Democrat," Corley replied.

The stealing of the tree was only the beginning of the good times that the Christmas season usually brought to Vandalia County. Corley had always enjoyed

Christmas to the fullest and he especially enjoyed the warmth that the season generated among the people who lived along the river. They were busy people and since most of the homes were located a considerable distance apart, there was really very little house--to-house visiting. The men got together during the summer haying season, and the women yakked in church, but as far as visiting one another in their homes, it just wasn't done to amount to anything. Yet, for about a two week period around Christmas, neighbors and relatives just popped in almost every evening. And, while most of the people in the valley were non-drinkers, they did take an occasional nip during the yuletide season. There was always so much to eat that it was indeed incredible.

But of all the people who came to visit, no one created excitement like the Tawney boys, at least not for Corley. He looked forward to their visit the way he used to look forward to Santa Claus. You never knew when they were coming and that made it even better. Corley rarely went anywhere during the evening for fear of missing them. They exuded more warmth and good cheer than all of the other people combined.

He had a feeling that they were going to come to the Malone place on Sunday evening this year. They knew that two of Corley's brothers were home so he figured they would want to see them. He was so sure that he had gone and picked up Lucy. He had been neglecting her lately and he figured that bringing her to the farm for the evening might be a good way to make it up to her. Typically, the real winter was setting in as the West Virginia Christmas approached. And, it had been snowing most of the day. The ground was white as he picked Lucy up at her house and the old north wind had begun to blow when they got back to the farm.

"They'll not come tonight, it's too bad," Corley's mother remarked.

"Those boys don't mind the snow," his dad had replied, and Corley sort of agreed with his dad.

The oldest of the four Tawney boys was about thirty-five and the youngest was in his mid twenties. They had been coming around for about five years. They would make their rounds up and down the river spending perhaps thirty minutes at each house. They were the best singers that Corley had ever heard, and they did it with such style. One of them usually brought a guitar.

The Malones were about to give up on them for the evening when they heard laughter outside and the sound of men stomping snow off their feet on the front porch. Roy, Frankie, Parker, and Oak Tawney came through the door in an absolute explosion of good will.

"What you got good to eat, Mrs. Malone?" Roy began as they all headed for the kitchen.

They always sampled all of the Christmas goodies at each house. And, while Corley's parents were non-drinkers, they usually bought a little good cheer for the holiday visitors. The Tawneys took advantage of such offers, as did Corley's brothers. Corley did not risk drinking in front of his folks just yet.

The Tawneys were about ready to sing when Oak discovered Lucy sitting quietly in the living room.

"My, my, who is this?" he said looking at his brothers.

"She's awfully pretty," Frankie said slyly, "bet she belongs to Corley."

They converged on her to her disbelief and pulled her under the mistletoe and each of them planted a kiss on her crimson cheeks.

"Corley, you ought to share anyone that pretty more often."

They all laughed and Corley thoroughly enjoyed the moment. He really thought that Lucy enjoyed the attention even though she appeared embarrassed.

But the boys were ready to sing. Parker was taking the guitar from its case. It was an old Martin and a beauty. They did not necessarily sing Christmas music. They just sang whatever was on their minds. You would never hear four part harmony sung any better than they could sing it. Corley really wanted to listen, but they insisted that everyone sing with them. Corley noticed that Parker played all kind of weird chords on the guitar. He decided that he was going to have to learn some of those someday.

They sang several old songs that everyone knew. But, when they sang "Lorena" everyone stopped and listened. It was a beautiful old song anyway, but the way they sang it would have chilled anyone's spine. Corley noticed the moisture in his mother's eyes when they finished.

"You boys get better ever year," she said.

"We get better looking too," Roy added, and everyone cracked up over that.

Too soon, they were getting ready to leave. They had been with the Malones for about forty-five minutes, but it seemed like a flash. They went out the door amid smiles and kisses and backslapping. They got into their car and made it on to the next house. The Malone house seemed so empty after they had gone.

"Boy, if they aren't something," Lucy said. "They were kind of scary at first, but my how they can sing."

"They can do that," Corley's dad agreed. "You had better put chains on the pick-up and throw some blocks in the back if you're going to take Lucy home tonight. I expect the road is bad," he added.

There was nothing Corley hated worse than putting chains on the pick-up but he knew that his dad was right. He made Lucy go with him out to the shed where they kept the old truck. She held the flashlight while he crawled around in the dirt and secured the chains.

The wind had blown the clouds away and the sky was sprinkled with stars as they drove back down the river. There was only an inch or two of snow but it was enough to enhance the night landscape. As Lucy snuggled close to him, he thought how lucky he was to live in such a beautiful place and among such good people.

XIX

Bryson Hill sounded like someplace where a bunch of soldiers had fought a battle in some old war, but the name belonged to a slight built, sandy haired boy who attended Bolton High School. Corley had seen him a million times, had passed the time of day with him, but really did not know anything about him. He was one of those guys who was always smiling. Nothing ever seemed to bother him. He looked at the world as if it were a parade and he was just watching it go by. He never made any trouble for anyone. Actually, he was the sort of person that Corley liked. He just minded his own business and did not meddle in other people's affairs.

He approached Corley the first day of school after Christmas vacation.

"Hey, Corley, you still playing the guitar?"

"Sure am," Corley answered. "Don't suppose that I will ever stop doing that."

"Let's get together and play a little dab some night," he suggested.

"I didn't know that you played any music," Corley responded.

"Well, I got an old electric guitar that I fool around with some. Don't know if I am much good or not. I really haven't played much with anyone other than myself."

"What kind of stuff do you play?" Corley asked.

"I like to fool around with the new stuff. Rock and roll, you know, that jerky stuff that people are dancing to."

Corley never thought of Bryson Hill as a guitar picker, and he had never played with a rock electric guitar, but it did sound interesting.

"Where can we play?" Corley asked.

"Why don't you come over to my place. We have a room in the back of the garage where we can play without bothering anyone. Come on over Friday evening and we'll see what we sound like."

Bryson's folks lived over near the Blair County line in a nice brick home. Corley knew the place. His father owned a small-time coal operation and the Hill's were pretty prosperous by Vandalia County standards.

Corley took the old Gibson and drove over on Friday evening. Bryson met him outside and took him through the garage. There were two other boys already there. One of them was tuning a stand up bass and the other was sitting behind a small set of drums. They were evidently Blair County boys because Corley did not know either of them.

"Corley, that's Jerry on the bass and Doug on the drums. They go to Blair High."

Corley shook hands with them and got the old Gibson out of the cheap case. Bryson picked up a very expensive looking electric guitar. Corley thought that he was probably out of his element.
He had fooled around with some of the new songs, but he had never tried them in a group.

"I doubt if we know any of the same songs," Corley ventured. "I haven't played much except bluegrass and country."

They tossed a few titles around and failed to establish common ground. Finally, Bryson came up with "When My Blue Moon Turns To Gold Again." It was an old bluegrass tune which Elvis Presley had recorded with the new tempo.

"I know that one," Bryson said. "Let's try it."

He took off on the electric guitar and Corley was stunned. Old Bryson Hill was all over the neck of that slick guitar and his rhythm and timing were perfect. Corley fell in and sung the words, and it sounded pretty good. They missed a lick here and there but they got through it. Corley had never played with a drum beat in the background and he decided that it really added something. They tried a little of several of the new songs and had a really good time. Corley did not know all of the words to very many of them but he knew enough until they could struggle through.

As Corley walked to his car, Bryson followed along with excitement in his voice.

"I'm trying to get a little group together," he said, "just to play some local gigs, you know, high school dances and such. You interested in that kind of thing, Corley?"

"Well, I don't know. I just got out of one band. Don't know if I want to get tied down in another one or not."

"We need a lead singer and you could sure do that for us."

"I'll give it some serious thought," Corley said.

He really did think about it on the way home. This was quite a different group than Red's band. Corley always felt kind of out of place among Red's group. They were all older and seemed to take everything for granted. Mostly, they just liked to get high and have a good time. But, Bryson and his boys seemed hungry for the bright lights, and they had the potential to be pretty good. Then, that song that he had been thinking about and trying to write came into his head. It occurred to him that it fit the music that he had just been playing. He had written the words long ago, but never could quite find the right music for them. As soon as he got home he raced to his room, got out his guitar, and it came together with a bang. He sang it over and over and over. He did not read much music so he couldn't write it down. He was afraid that he was going to forget it before Monday. The first thing he did the next morning when he got out of bed was to sing it again. It was still there. He liked it. He called it "River City Girl."

Monday morning he sought out Frank Kerns, the band director, and got him to put the song on tape. Corley felt better after he got the song recorded. It would have been a tragedy, he figured, if he would have forgotten that damned song before anyone else got to hear it. Mr. Kerns was not too impressed, but Corley felt that it really wasn't written for his generation. Later that day he found Bryson and told him that he wanted to try this new song that he had written with the group.

"Good deal," Bryson said with his ever present smile. "I'll run over to Blair County this evening and have Jerry and Doug to make it over Friday night. Can't wait to hear it."

"It's a damned good song," Corley said, "even if I did write it."

That evening after school he stopped by the office where Lucy worked to tell her about the new song and the new group. She was very excited to see him and said that she had felt neglected lately.

"You have hardly been to see me since you stopped playing The Beeches," she complained.

Corley hadn't really thought about it, but it was kind of strange. It just seemed that Lucy and The Beeches went together, and now that he had not been to The Beeches for over a month, Lucy seemed somehow less important. But as he was talking to her he could smell her hair and he remembered how good she felt in his arms. He reached for her hand and squeezed it.

"We'll do something soon," he said. "I really have missed you."

But Corley was so excited about his song that he could not keep his mind on anything else. When he got home that evening he sang it again and again, changing it just a little each time, but not much.

As he was milking that evening, it occurred to him that he had been doing a good job of staying away from Julie Meadows. He had come to the conclusion that the only way he could live with that situation was to stay away from her. She was not haunting his mind as much as she used to before he went to sleep at night and he thought maybe, just maybe, he was getting her out of his system. He had not talked with her since Christmas, but she flashed those eyes at him at school, and the thought of her laying one of those burning kisses on him still sent a chill down his spine.

He thought that Friday night would never come, but it finally did, and he made it over to Bryson's house. They were all there waiting for him and anxious to hear the song. They listened as Corley went through it, listened again, and the third time they began playing along with him. It was a pretty simple song, three basic chords and a quick A minor every now and then. It sounded even better than Corley thought it would. He felt compelled to move it a little faster when they played with him and that was good. It needed a little quicker beat. Before the night was over the group was adding a little voice background which helped it even more.

At the end of the evening Bryson had them all convinced that they had the makings of a good group. He said that if everyone agreed he would start booking some gigs. They all agreed but they realized that they needed to do a lot of work to get a good professional sound. They decided to practice every night. Corley knew that he was going to be hard pressed for time, but he decided that it was something that he really wanted to do. He figured he would be alright during January and February, but he was a little concerned about the spring months when the farming chores picked up. He decided to take it one day at a time and worry about spring when spring came.

The band nearly consumed him during the remainder of January. When he was not practicing he was thinking about a new song, or trying to come up with a way to improve some of the songs that they were already doing. Every night they had a discussion about what they would wear once they landed their first gig. Dress bothered Corley some. Red never gave a damn about dress and Corley liked that part of the gigs at The Beeches. Bryson was concerned about alienating parents and he leaned toward a coat and tie. Since it was his dad's money that was backing the band, they all tended to agree with Bryson's suggestions. Corley thought that it was kind of strange that all the members of the group lived within ten or twelve miles of one another, but they were all very different from him. He thought that they were a bit immature. He doubted that any of them had been in a beer hall, and it was very obvious that they knew little or nothing about girls. They were pretty much in the gee whiz, golly gee stage of life. He worried about that some because he had difficulty making conversation with them at times. But, he kept telling himself that the important thing was that they played well together.

He was particularly impressed with Jerry Moss, the bass player. Good acoustic bass players were pretty hard to find at any age and Jerry played very well. He was a big kid and cut a pretty good figure as he handled the big instrument. And Bryson Hill could have played lead guitar with anyone around. Corley felt adequate but he certainly did not feel musically superior to any of them. They played an hour or two each evening and soon had twenty five or so tunes that they could get through pretty well. Finally, Bryson made the long awaited announcement. He had booked their first gig. It was a Valentine's Dance at one of the high schools in Charleston. He billed them as the "River City Rockers." And, they agreed that they would wear gray dress pants, dark blue jackets, and black bow ties

When the big night arrived they all traveled to Charleston in Bryson's station wagon. It was a big Ford and had plenty of room for instruments and equipment. They rolled into Charleston pretty impressed with themselves. Corley felt pretty stupid in his coat and bow tie but he figured it was part of the price for becoming a star. They strutted around Charleston like aristocrats and drew all kinds of stares from the masses as they ate in a restaurant. They were going to make fifteen dollars a piece so they were living good. Corley decided that he was going to like being a star, he could tell already. He began to think of all of the people with whom he was going to stop associating just as soon as he made his first million. And, he envisioned taking a Cadillac back to Bolton in a year or so that was so long that he had to back it up to get it around the corner.

The gig was like nothing that he had ever experienced. Everyone was dressed to the hilt and he had never seen so many good looking girls in one room in his entire life. There must be fifty girls here that look as good as Julie Meadows, he thought to himself, almost as good anyway. People began dancing as soon as they started to play. They opened with a couple of slow ones so that people would get their confidence level up before they showed their rock and roll step. These kids know how to rock and roll, Corley thought. They seemed to show a little more class than he was used to seeing at The Beeches. They liked the music. That was obvious from the start.

About halfway through the evening, they hit them with "River City Girl." They did not say anything about the song, who had written it, or where it came from. They just wanted to see how it went over. It was a slow dance song and it was really the first opportunity that Corley had to sing. He saw an occasional glance from some of the girls that were dancing and noticed that others were listening intently. He even got a little applause when the song ended. He loved those glances that he had gotten while he was singing. It gave him a feeling like he had never had before. It was a good feeling. Corley's impression was that the song went over pretty well and he felt pretty good about it.

During their break Corley mingled through the crowd a little, just like he had seen Red do so many times. He kind of wished that he had some of Red's liquor so that he would have a little more courage. He figured that if he was going to be an international lover this would be a terribly good place to start. He isolated one of the girls who had given him the eye as he was singing. She had the prettiest hair that he had ever seen. It was very dark and silken like, and hung nearly to her waist.

He opened the conversation with a line about not knowing Charleston and perhaps she could give him some ideas about where to go after the dance. Once he broke the ice he moved forward with her trying to remember all of the advice that old Blackie had given him about women.

"What's your name anyway?" he asked.

"Joy," she smiled.

"You have a phone number?" he said, remembering to take the direct approach.

"Yes, I have a phone number," she answered, but she did not say anything else. She just looked away and ignored him. Corley loved that.

"If I knew what it was I might give you a call sometime when I am in town."

"I don't give my number to everyone," she said.

"I'm not everyone," Corley replied. "I'm just someone who thinks that you're awfully pretty and would like to get to know you better."

"Lot's of people think I'm pretty," she said, looking away again.

"But how many boys from up on the Vandalia River who play the guitar and sing think you're pretty?"

"Only you," she responded.

"There, you see, I'm not just everyone. I'm someone different that you should get to know," Corley said confidently.

Just then Bryson yelled at him and as Corley turned to answer, she walked away. He tried to find her the rest of the evening to see if he could get another glance from her, but it was so dark in the room, and so many couples, that he could not find her. But when the dance ended, she came to the bandstand and told him that she had enjoyed his music. She pressed a piece of paper in his hand as she walked away. He looked at the paper and smiled broadly.

>Joy Kelly
>1212 Hilcrest
>285-4602

So this was what it was like to be a star, Corley thought. He could certainly get used to this kind of stuff. For the first time in his life he felt the drive of his ego. He really did have one after all, he thought. And Bryson was walking around like he was already the king of pop music. He was flashing his best smile and taking all of the compliments that he could get.

It was after midnight when they finally got the station wagon loaded. By the time Corley got home it was nearly three a.m. He was exhausted. He left a note on the kitchen table pleading for his mother to do the morning milking. It was a Saturday morning, but he still did not relish the thought of getting up after about two hours of sleep. It started to come home to him how tough it was going to be to keep up with the band, and to do his chores on the farm.

He slept until noon, got up and ate a big dinner, and decided to go over and see Julie Meadows. He wanted to tell her about the group, how well they had been received at the Charleston dance, but mostly he wanted to see if he still got excited when he saw her. The river had large chunks of ice floating in it so he had to be extra careful with the boat. He took a couple of hits from small icebergs, but nothing serious.

When he got to Julie's house she came flying through the door and threw her arms around him. She was so damned excited that she could hardly talk.

"I found out only yesterday and I have been dying to tell you. I'm so excited I don't know if I can get it out."

"What is it?" Corley asked.

"I'm going to New York," she screamed. "Not Buffalo, New York, not Albany, New York, but New York, New York. I am actually going to New York City."

"What the hell for?" Corley said, trying to contain her.

"I've been accepted to the Juilliard School of Music. I'll be going in September."

Corley did not know anything about the Juilliard School of Music. He had heard of the Juilliard String Quartet somewhere but he was not sure where they came from. But, considering the excitement level of Julie, he figured that it must be a really big deal. She was excited.

"Listen, I'm happy for you," he finally managed to say.

Her charming mother who had been watching the scene butted in to make her contribution.

"We are all thrilled to death. We have planned on this for so long and we can hardly believe that it is happening. Of course, some of my relatives in

Connecticut have some connections there. We do want the best for Julie. I hope she will do alright.

"Oh, she'll do fine," Corley said. "I've never known a more talented musician."

And, she was all of that. She was one of those people who could put it together musically. Corley had always known that some people learn all there is to know about music, but still are not able to play a damned thing because they had no natural talent. Then, there were some, like himself, who had a little talent but who were too damned lazy to try to learn anything about the structure of music. But, old Julie had it all. Corley had realized that the first time he heard her play. She could play some really difficult stuff, and she played it with feeling. He was indeed happy for her.

After listening to all of the excitement about the Juilliard, he did not even want to bring up the Charleston gig. He was sure that no one there would be even remotely interested in the "River City Rockers." Julie finally contained herself and began to remember her manners.

"But, Corley, how selfish of me to go on like this. You come over so seldom, and I just had to tell someone all about it. You will forgive me for getting so carried away."

"Of course, Julie. I just came over to see how you were getting along. I have hardly had a chance to talk to you lately. I guess we have both been busy."

"Yes, we have," she said. "Do sit down."

Actually, Corley wanted to get out of the situation that he was in but he did not quite know how to go about it. He did not feel like he ought to be there, didn't really know why he was there, but he was there and he had to stay at least a few minutes. It was a cold afternoon and he sure could not ask her to go for a walk. But Julie, being the keen girl that she was, read the situation very well. She sensed his discomfort and came to the rescue.

"Let's take Daddy's car and go for a little drive. We haven't talked for ages and I want to know about all the things you are doing."

"Great idea," Corley said.

It was kind of a pretty February afternoon. The sky was clear except for a scattered white cloud here and there, and there were patches of old snow hanging around on the north slopes of the hills. The sun was bright but it really did not provide much warmth. It was very cozy in the car from the effects of the sun shining through the glass. Julie drove up to the top of the hill and pulled over at a spot which afforded a tremendous view of the valley. Corley could see his house way off in the distance.

"What have you been doing with yourself, Corley? I see you at school and you smile and speak, but you haven't really had much to say."

"Well, I guess I really haven't had much to say to anyone lately. I've been busy and I've had a lot on my mind. I've missed you Julie. I did not realize how much until now."

"Corley," she cut him off, "I think I should tell you that I have been seeing someone on a pretty regular basis."

"Someone besides Denny?"

"Yes. His name is Mark Wells. I don't suppose you would know him. He's older. He has already finished college and he works with my dad.

Corley had never seen her look so concerned and he had a very sinking feeling. It occurred to him that somewhere in the back of his mind he had clung to the hope that he and Julie would end up together somewhere on down the road. It seemed to him that it was just meant to be.

"I don't know how serious we are," she continued, "but he has asked me to not see anyone else for awhile and I told him that I wouldn't."

Corley looked away for a moment, then totally lost his cool.

"Now that's just great, Julie. One minute you tell me that you are going to New York and hit the big time and the next minute you tell me that you are in love with some slick college man. What the hell is it with you anyway?"

"Don't you yell at me," she replied. "He's not slick, he is a very nice person, and I still intend to go to New York. I didn't say that I was getting married."

Corley fell silent. As he thought about it, he guessed that he was mad at himself more than anything else. He had tried so hard to stay away from her because he saw her potential and did not want to interfere with her future. He especially did not want her to disappoint her lovely mother. But, it occurred to him that everyone was not so considerate. He did not quite know what to say so he just got out of the car. He climbed up on the front fender where he could see down the valley and tried to forget where he was. It was colder than hell out there and he decided that it was no time to be dramatic. He walked around to her side of the car and she got out.

"Listen, Julie, why don't you just drive me back down to your house and I'll go home and mind my own business."

"Now why do you say things like that?" she said.

"Well, it's pretty damned obvious that there is no place for me in your life anymore. I suppose that I always knew that it would come to this."

"You're jumping to conclusions," she said. "I've told you before that I have a lot ahead of me in my life. I'm not getting married next weekend or anything. Mark is just a very fine and considerate person and I like him. He's a joy to be with and he has asked me to go steady. It's as simple as that."

He looked at her for a full minute, standing there in the cold with no coat on, pretty as anything or anyone that he had ever known, and realized that he now knew the difference between passion and love. Passion was good. Love was bad. He wanted to tell her how much she meant to him, but he was not about to do that. He just walked around the car and got in. She got under the wheel, smiled at him, and drove the big Dodge back to her house. Corley got out, pinched her cheek a little and walked away. It was a long, cold walk back to the boat, and once he was in the river he maneuvered through the ice chunks without giving it much thought.

When he got back to his house, he went to his room and got the ribbon that he had taken from Julie's hair one night as he kissed her. He took it out to the barn, tied it onto the barbed wire fence and lit a match to it. He stood there with a lump in his throat and watched Julie Meadows go up in smoke. He did not want anything around to remind him of her. But, he pinched out the flame and saved a short piece.

XX

As March approached Corley's life was being consumed by the band. They practiced every night and were playing somewhere every weekend. Bryson Hill was devoting his entire life to promoting the group. Corley figured that it must be costing old man Hill a bundle the way Bryson got around. And, Bryson had gone out and bought a recording outfit so that they could hear themselves and polish their mistakes. Corley hated playing songs over and over again, trying to make every lick exactly alike. It sure took all of the fun out of playing music as far as he was concerned. He remembered telling Julie one time that he did not want to become a professional musician because it would turn music into work. It appeared that he had just about arrived at that point. But Bryson was a perfectionist and was dedicated to what they were doing. Corley admired him for that, but he found it all very tedious.

The band had done his composition of "River City Girl" so many times and so many ways that Corley was sick to death of it. He was almost sorry that he had ever put it to music. But Bryson thought that it was their best shot and he kept working on it. What really bugged Corley the most was that he never had any time for himself. By the time he got his work done at home, rehearsed, and played a weekend gig, there was no time left for him to do some of the things that he really liked to do. He had not taken a Sunday morning boat ride for ages, and he and Sam had not been out getting into mischief since he did not know when.

He was considering giving it all up, and was just trying to think of a good way to break it to Bryson. Then, one day at school, Bryson came running up to him in the hallway all excited.

"Corley, I have a man in Charleston who wants to hear us. He has heard one of our tapes and says he thinks he can get us a hearing at Sun Records in Nashville. It might just be the break that we have been looking for."

"So what does he want us to do?"

"Wants us to come to Charleston Friday night and play for him at his place. He has a small recording studio and he tries to promote local talent."

"What's his name?"

"Kenneth Frazier, ever heard of him?"

"No, can't say that I have," Corley said. "Have you talked this over with Doug and Jerry?"

"Yes, they're ready to go. What do you think, Corley?"

"Hell, let's give it a shot. Never know I guess."

They practiced that night until Corley swore that he would never sing again. But Bryson still was not happy with everything so they practiced again the next night. They concluded that they were not going to get any better and that once they got there, it would come together.

Friday night, they loaded up the station wagon and headed for Charleston. Bryson introduced the group to Ken Frazier and they set up in his studio. It was a professional looking place with sound proof material on the walls and overhead. Corley thought that the guy must be for real. They cut "River City Girl" after about two dozen attempts, and a little upbeat thing that Bryson and Corley had put together called "Rock'n with Freda R." Corley thought that both tunes sounded pretty good, but he had heard them so much that he really did not know. He figured that after you play a song so many times, it became disgusting, no matter who wrote it.

Kenneth Frazier was a Texas bullshit type who began telling the group about all of the important people that he knew in Nashville and New York. Corley doubted if he had ever been to New York, but he humored him with smiles and some phoney gestures of awe. He was very positive and told them that he would have some people listen to the tape in Nashville next week, then give Bryson a call.

It was still early when they left the studio so they decided to cruise around Charleston for awhile before they went home. After all, it was Friday night. They drove through all of the drive-in restaurants and looked at the girls. Doug kept referring to all of them as "pretty babies". Corley thought that there must be a song there somewhere so he made a mental note of it. Bryson mostly smiled and drove. They finally pulled into HoDos, the hot spot for teenagers in Charleston. This was where all of the teens came to show off their cars, and their girls, and it was really busy on this Friday night. They got them something to drink and watched the traffic. Then Corley had a thought. He got out of the car and went to the phone booth, dug out the phone number that Joy Kelly had given him, and gave her a call. She answered, but there was so much noise in the background that he could hardly hear her.

"Joy, this is Corley Malone, how are you?"

"Who?" she said.

"Corley Malone, you know, the River City Rockers guy. I talked to you at the Valentine's dance."

"Oh, yes, I remember. Hold on a minute while I go to another room."

Corley waited until she came back on the line, wondering what the hell was going on.

"I'm having a little after the game party, just some of the kids from school. Why don't you come over?"

"Well, I'm with the band, we played in town tonight."

"Bring them all," she answered. "This is just an informal get together."

"OK, I'll see if they will come. Where is Hilcrest?"

"It's on the south side. Cross the river, get on MacCorkle Avenue, watch for the Hilcrest sign. It turns up the hill."

It took Corley a few minutes to talk the boys into going, but they finally agreed. They found the place with little difficulty. Corley knew Charleston pretty well. What a place it was. Corley realized when he saw it that he was definitely going to be out of his element, but he figured what the hell, he was, after all, on the road to stardom. Joy met them at the door and took Corley's hand.

"Everybody, this is Corley Malone," she shouted. "His group played for our Valentine's dance. Corley, introduce your friends."

There were about thirty teenagers at the party. They were drinking soft drinks and some of them were smoking cigarettes. They were certainly a loud bunch, Corley thought. He had forgotten how pretty Joy Kelly was. She was a "pretty baby" to use Doug's term. She had very intriguing bosoms. They were not especially large, but right where they ought to be. Corley had noticed that some girls wore them too high, or too low, but Joy's were right on target. He had a time trying to talk with her over the noise but did establish that she was a senior and that she did not have a steady boyfriend. He decided that it was time to make his move.

"I'll tell you what, Joy, I would like to come back down tomorrow night and take you to a movie."

She looked at him for a moment or two before she answered.

"I've always thought that country boys were shy and retiring," she said. "I'm beginning to think that you are not country."

"Oh, I'm country alright. And I'm usually very backward around people, but you are a very inspiring girl, bring out the best in me I guess."

"You wouldn't take me to a drive-in movie on the first date, would you?"

"Now do I look like the sort of boy who would do something like that to a girl of your caliber?"

"Yes, you do," she answered.

"I'll take you to any kind of movie that you want to go to, and I guarantee you that I will be a perfect gentleman."

She smiled the biggest smile that Corley had ever seen then replied, "I'll go with you if you make it Sunday afternoon."

"I'll bet you already have a date tomorrow night."

"I'll bet that you are right," she smiled.

"Then Sunday afternoon it is. You look like a girl who is worth a day's wait, not more than a day though.

You had better get back to your friends or they will think I'm trying to dominate you."

Corley noticed that the boys in the band were not doing bad at the party. They were mixing in very well. Doug was even dancing with a girl. People began leaving about eleven, so Corley decided that they had better not wear out their welcome. He got a slight squeeze on the hand from Joy as they departed. He tried to brush by her bosoms, but missed.

When they got back into the station wagon, Bryson began telling everybody that he had gotten a date for the following weekend. Corley was stunned, but pleased. Maybe he had underestimated the boy after all, he thought. He evidently had eyes for something other than his guitar. He was glad to see that he was a human being. Doug confided that he had never seen so many "pretty babies" in one bunch and Doug, the quiet one, smiled in agreement. Corley was beginning to feel a little better about the boys after the party. He was beginning to think that they were a bunch of duds. And, he decided that he really had to think about that phrase "pretty baby". There had to be a song there. He did not tell them about Joy Kelly. He decided that he would wait until after the date, then tell them. After all, he might get stood up.

It occurred to him that he had the next night free. He had not had a free Saturday night in weeks. For some reason he decided that he did not want to see Lucy. He knew that he would feel guilty if he took her out knowing that he was going to see Joy Kelly the next day. He decided that he would holler old Sam out the next morning and try to get something going.

His plans were altered slightly the next morning by the appearance of Porter Belk as he was coming back from the barn. Old Porter is up early, Corley thought. He pulled his Jeep up into the yard, got out, and came toward Corley with his typical quick step.

"Hey, Corley, how'd you winter this year?"

"Not bad I guess. How about you?"

"Oh, stayed fat and sassy. Listen, I need to get the camps cleaned up. I always have some fishermen who want to rent it in early spring. Suppose you and Sam could go up and give them a once over today?"

"I expect so. I'll holler Sam out as soon as I eat breakfast. If he can't come, I'll be glad to do what I can."

"Hey good, Corley. I'll look for you after awhile."

Corley ate a good breakfast and went up to get Sam. He was outside chopping up some firewood.

"Sam, you able to go up and help me clean up the camps today?"

"Hell yes," he answered. "I'm broke flatter than hell. You could not have asked at a better time."

"I'm getting a little low myself," Corley replied. "We need to get started if we are going."

They worked all day at the camps, giving them a general cleaning. It was mostly a matter of cleaning up the dust that had settled during the winter. They brought in wood for the fireplaces and stacked it neatly. Porter's wife fixed their lunch and for the first time Porter offered them a beer.

"You boys are getting old enough for a beer now and then. A good cold one tastes good with a sandwich."

The boys exchanged a knowing smile and enjoyed the moment.

They earned eight dollars a piece for the day and on the way home they decided that they needed to get rid of some of it. Sam had a date with Sue Phillips, but decided that he would drive over to her house early and talk her out of it. They wanted to go to Blair County and do a little hell raising.

Sam secured his dad's Ford and it was after eight by the time he got back and picked up Corley. There was a warm breeze blowing and it was one of those evenings that reminded a person that spring was just around the corner. A light denim jacket was all that was needed for comfort. Corley slipped the .38 under his shirt as he went out.

"Let's drive down to The Beeches first," Corley suggested. "I haven't been down there for ages on Saturday night, and besides, old Troy Carr will probably sell us a six pack."

The Beeches was just starting to get underway for the evening and Corley was not surprised to see a group of young rock and rollers setting up on the bandstand. It was kind of sad not seeing old Red up there with his fiddle, but Corley was comforted by the fact that he had been right in reading the changing times.

Old Troy was his usual jovial self and greeted Corley warmly. He said that he had heard about his new band and asked if they might want to play there some Saturday night. Corley told him that he doubted it, explained the composition of the group, and how they were not oriented toward the kind of crowd that The Beeches tended to draw.   "Well, if you ever change your mind, let me know. Give these boys a beer on me," he said to the girl behind the bar.

They drank the beer slowly and watched the crowd for awhile. The rock and roll band was ready and they opened with "Blue Suede Shoes". It was the hottest thing around in the spring of '56. They were not bad, but Corley quickly concluded that the River City Rockers could do it better.

They secured a six pack from Troy Carr and started up the river. When they got up to Camp Creek, Corley noticed that there was a revival meeting going on at the Camp Creek Methodist Church. It was a small church located right alongside the road. The meeting was already in progress, but several people were standing around outside.

"Pull over Sam. We've only had one beer. Maybe we could go in and sing a few songs, look the women over."

"You crazy bastard," Sam said. "We can't go in there smelling like a brewery. They would throw us out."

"Hell, they are not going to throw out a good singer. Come on."

Sam parked alongside the road and they started toward the church. But their walk was halted abruptly because Corley spotted a man leaning against an old '46 Ford. One quick look at him told Corley who it was. It was Paul Dudley, the oldest of the bunch of riff-raff that had rocked the hell out of him and Sam last summer when they were camping. He had not recognized Corley so he pushed Sam on toward the church. When they got out of hearing, Corley turned to Sam and whispered.

"You know that son-of-a-bitch leaning on that Ford?"

"No, who is he?"

"It's that goddamned Paul Dudley, you know, the one who stole all of our stuff last summer."

"The hell you say," said Sam. "Is he alone?"

"I'd say he is. Probably up here looking for a stray piece. What do you think?"

"I think that we ought to throw his ass in the river," Sam replied.

"Think we can do it?"

"Hell, he won't know what hit him."

They surveyed the situation for a moment. He was leaning on his car, facing the road. They were going to have to get behind him, push him across the road, and over the river bank. Once they got him started down the river bank it would be easy. They planned their strategy. Corley positioned himself directly across the road from him and stopped. He was standing there casually smoking a cigarette.

"Hey, Dudley," Corley said. "You know me?"

He turned quickly and looked Corley over. The only light was coming from the outside light on the front of the church so he could not see very well. Corley was not sure that Paul Dudley knew him anyway.

"Who are you?" he asked.

"Why don't you come and see," Corley answered. "I hear all of you Dudleys smell like turkey shit and I'd like to find out."

He started toward Corley, stooping down and straining his eyes, trying to see who he was. Just when he got within reach of Corley, Sam plowed into him from behind and pushed him over the bank. Corley went right behind him and when they both got hold of old Dudley, they tossed him into the cold Vandalia River, right on his head. The boys whirled around, raced to the Ford, and Sam laid down a loud strip of rubber as they roared out of sight.

"You think he knew who we were?" Sam asked.

"I don't know and I don't really care. All I know is that he got his ass wet and that I feel pretty damned good about it. Served the son-of-a-bitch right. Slow down a little, Sam, I want to try a couple of road signs."

"What the hell you doing with that thing?" he asked, looking at the .38.

"I want to shoot the hell out of some signs tonight. Haven't done that for ages."

Road signs were very good target practice and they were safe targets. Signs indicating curves were often located out in the middle of nowhere, no houses and no people within miles of them. And, the slug did not really do much damage, just knocked off a little paint. And, if a person was moving along at 45 miles per hour or so, they were not an easy target with a pistol. It was a fairly common sport around Vandalia County. Corley emptied his gun at one and hit it only twice.

"You're a damned maniac, Corley, damned if you're not."

"Hell, it's our tax money that pays for the signs."

"You ain't never paid no taxes in your damned life," Sam said.

"Guess not, but my dad does. I'm getting his money's worth."

They drove on over to Blair, county seat of Blair County, and just generally goofed around. They stopped at every joint they came to out along the road, went in, and just watched for awhile. Corley always got a kick out of just watching other people have a good time. If he saw some guy dancing with a girl, or his wife, and they were holding each other tight and smiling a lot, it gave him a warm feeling inside. And, he enjoyed watching a couple who could really dance well together. To him, that was a good time, just watching other people having a good time.

As the hour grew late they drove back down the river, found a wide place where they could pull off the road, and just sat there and drank the six pack that they had gotten from Troy Carr. They had a good talk.

"What the hell you going to do when we graduate, Corley?"

"Damned if I know. I've been giving it some thought. I suppose that a man could go over to Cleveland or to Detroit and get a job, but I don't particularly want to work in a factory. Ain't no future in it. Sometimes, I wish I had the money to buy me a farm."

"Oh shit, Corley, you don't want to farm for a living. You wouldn't never have a damned thing."

"Guess not, but I don't really want much. Would like to have a good car though, can't drive the old man's much longer."

"Yes, and besides that, one of these days you'll want a wife, and a wife means a house, and then you are talking about a hell of a lot of money."

"Yeah, I guess you're right, but I sure don't like to think about a regular job. How bout you, Sam? What are you going to do?"

"Hell, I don't have any idea. I suppose that my dad could get me a job around the mines doing something. I done told him, I'm not digging no goddamned coal."

"Can't blame you for that," Corley said.

"If I were you, Corley, I'd try my luck with that old guitar. You do a pretty good job and you got more damned nerve than you need."

"I'm afraid that I got more nerve than I got talent."

"Hell, there's a bunch of people making a living singing that can't sing a damned lick. Look at old Ernest Tubb, he never could carry a tune."

"Well, there's some truth to what you say, but I don't know if I really want to or not. All that traveling around would bother me, and all the drinking. Hell, I'd be a damned drunk in two or three years. Look what happened to old Hank Williams."

"What about all of the women that you would get? Could you stand that?"

"I could stand that," Corley said. "In fact that may be what I'll do with my life. I'll just be a cock hound."

"It takes money to do that too," Sam said.

"Damned if it don't," Corley concluded.

"You ever thought about going into the service?" Sam asked.

"Yes, I've thought about it. Two of my older brothers were in during the Korean War and they tell some pretty interesting tales."

"Slayed all of the women in the world, I suppose."

"I'd say, if they got all that they say they did."

"Might not be too bad if there wasn't a war going on," Sam said philosophically. "But I don't want to get my ass shot off in some crazy-assed war."

"I hear that," Corley said. "What about Sue Phillips? You thinking about marrying her?"

"Christ, I don't want to get married. I probably won't be able to support myself. What about you? You going to get married?"

"Hell no. I'm too damned good looking to get married."

They laughed over that because they were beginning to get a little high on the beer.

"What about your friend over across the river? Have you given up on her?"

"She's dating some slick-assed college man from Charleston. Says she doesn't want to see anyone else right now."

"I told you that she was out of your league," Sam said.

"And, like I told you earlier, you are probably right. But it's kind of a weird thing. I have always liked her, but hell, I don't want to be tied down and I don't think she does either. She says she is going to New York next September to a music school."

"She'll probably go up there and marry one of those goddamned yankees. Be good enough for her."

Corley agreed, but at the same time, it gave him a chill down his spine to think of her with a slick yankee husband.

They finished their beer and Corley took the six bottles across the road and placed them in a line against the hill. Sam turned the car so that the headlights pointed toward the bottles. Corley got the .38 and sat down on the front fender. The .38 spoke six times and four of the bottles shattered into tiny pieces.

"Not bad," said Sam.

XXI

There was not a cloud in the sky and there was a warm wind drifting up from the south when Corley got up the next morning. As he went out to milk, he could feel the ground giving beneath his feet and thought to himself they would soon be living in a sea of mud. There is no place quite so repulsive as a West Virginia barnyard in spring, he thought. All of the mud and manure that has been frozen all winter produces about a six inch base of pure yuck. He wasn't looking forward to that, but he was looking with fondness toward some nice spring days. He always enjoyed the winter, but it was starting to wear thin. The snow was all gone but February had remained cold as had early March.

As he was preparing for his Charleston date that afternoon he started thinking that he did not want to spend an afternoon like this one sitting in a movie theater. This was the nicest day that had come along in months and it would be a shame to waste it. Going to the movies with a girl was a corny thing to do anyway. He wanted to ask Joy to do something else, but he couldn't think of a thing. He had noticed in the movies that men were always asking ladies to dinner. "How about dinner tonight?" they would say. Corley always liked the sound of that, but hell, he had eaten supper at five o'clock all of his life, and rarely ate anything after that. He never did understand people who ate in the middle of the night.

He put on his jeans and his chambray shirt and drove the Buick down the river. He stopped at the first pay phone booth that he spotted, dug out Joy's number, and gave her a call. He was glad that she answered the phone because he had not even met her parents.

"Joy, this is Corley Malone."

"Are you calling to tell me that you're not coming?"

"No, I'm almost there as a matter of fact. I was just wondering if we could alter our plans a little bit?"

"What do you have in mind?"

"Well, I thought maybe you could put on some old clothes, some jeans or something, and we could drive up the Vandalia River. I can show you the sights up that way. It's just too nice a day to sit in a movie."

"It sounds very interesting," she said, "let me ask my mother."

She was gone for quite awhile and Corley was about to get a sinking feeling. But she came back on the line and said that she would be ready in a jiffy.

Her mother answered the door when Corley knocked and he was somewhat taken aback. She was one of those mothers who looked like her daughter's older sister. She was probably no more than forty and did not look that. Corley had an impulse to ask her if she wanted to go and just leave Joy behind. But, she immediately turned into a mother and started giving him the third degree, asking him if he were a careful driver, and made him swear that he would not drink anything. He was expecting her to swear him to celibacy next, but she stopped just short of that. He was very glad to get out of the house and into the seclusion of the Buick.

"Have you ever been up the Vandalia?"

"Only a few miles. I don't suppose that I have had an occasion to go any farther."

"Tell you what I'll do. I'll take you up to our place and we'll go for a boat ride. You can swim can't you, in case we would sink?"

"Yes, I can swim," she smiled.

Corley kept looking at her out of the corner of his eye. She looked pretty good, he thought. Her hair was her best feature. It was very beautiful. And, her figure, while slightly thin, left nothing to be desired. He was very pleased to be with her, but the excitement he felt around Julie Meadows, and the comfort he felt around Lucy O'Brannon were both absent. For the moment, it was almost like riding along with a casual friend. She sat a respectable distance away, not against the door, but very near it. She made no comments about the natural beauty that was so obvious along the river and that bothered him some. He was afraid that she would be bored to death in the old john boat.

She did show a little excitement when they pulled down into the Malone place.

"I've never been on a farm," she exclaimed.

"Well, this isn't really a farm, it's just sort of a country place. We don't farm for a living, we just sort of enrich our lives with it, I suppose."

"It looks like a farm to me," she said.

Corley thought that she was a little shocked when she went into the house because it was obvious that she had not seen anything quite like it. The linoleum floor probably looked a little stark to one who had been oriented to carpet and shinning hardwood, and the Malone furnishings were very simple and practical with little or no emphasis on style and motif. Corley's milking coat and his boots were by the kitchen door where they had always been. He never thought about it before, but they looked sort of crude there. His dad was at work and his mother was doing some kind of needle work as they came in the back door.

"Mother, this is Joy Kelly from down at Charleston. I'm going to take her for a little boat ride."

"Pleased to meet you, Joy. It's a nice afternoon for a boat ride, but you two be careful. It would be mighty cold if you fell into the river."

"I might just push her in to see how tough she is," Corley joked. "We're going ahead down while the sun is still high."

The river bank was still soft and muddy from the winter floods and they touched for the first time as a result of the hazardous walking. She first took hold of his hand and then clung to his arm with both hands. Corley got her into the boat and pushed off into the deep water. He got his hand and arm wet and decided that his mother was right about one thing, the water was cold. Joy sat in the stern and as Corley got into the rowing seat, he took a long look at her. He was reminded of the time that he had rowed Julie Meadows up the same river in the same boat. Joy was nearly as pretty, but he certainly was not as excited as he was that fateful evening that he made his singing debut.

"It must be nice to have such a pretty river in your backyard so that you can go for a boat ride anytime you want to," she said.

"Well, it is nicer than you can imagine. The river provides so many things for a person to do. We have a fine place to swim here in the summer, and there is always good fishing. I really don't know what I would do without the river. It has been a big part of my life."

It was a beautiful afternoon on the river. The sun was strong and it felt more like a day in May. Corley rowed up the river for a quarter of a mile or so, staying in close to the shore so he did not have to buck the current. Then he crossed over to a place where he knew they could walk up to the railroad track. As he helped her out of the boat, he could not help noticing those intriguing breasts of hers.

They walked up the hill and onto the railroad track. She took hold of his arm and for the first time he felt the pressure of her breasts. Almost impulsively he pulled her around and kissed her very lightly. She felt very good against him, but she pulled back after only a brief encounter.

"Do you kiss everyone on the first date?" she asked.

"I kiss everyone every time I get a chance," he answered, "and I've been wanting to kiss you all day."

"Are you disappointed?"

"Hardly, in fact, I'm thinking of doing it again."

This time she cooperated a little longer, but pulled back before he got carried away.

"I'll bet you bring all of the girls over here."

"No, actually, you are the first girl that I have ever had over here. In fact, I have had very little experience with girls. Would you believe that?"

"No, I wouldn't believe that."

"Then there is no use in my telling you if you aren't going to believe me. One thing that bothers me about you if you don't mind my asking."

"Go ahead, ask away."

"How come a beauty like you is not tied down to some good looking quarterback from one of the high schools in Charleston?"

"I've been tied down a couple of times, not to quarterbacks, but I'm getting ready to go to college next fall and I don't want to be tied down to anyone right now. Maybe you haven't recognized it, but I have a very independent and strong will."

"Oh, I recognized that the first time I ever talked to you, and I admire that in people."

"It seems like every boy that I have ever dated a few times wanted to own me, and I am not ready to be owned by anyone. How about you? You ever been tied down?"

"Not exactly, I suppose. There is a girl that I see on a pretty regular basis, and another one that I like so much that I avoid, but that's about it."

"Well, you are an honest sort," she said. "That's refreshing."

"We had better get the boat back across. It will be chilly on the river before long."

When they got back into the boat she insisted on rowing, and since they had to go back downstream, he put her in the rowing seat. She splashed around some at first but really was doing fairly well by the time they got back to the landing.

"My friends will never believed that I rowed a boat," she said.

"You can also tell them that you got kissed on the railroad track," Corley added.

"I don't know if I will tell that or not," she smiled.

The evening chill was beginning to set in as they walked back toward the house. It was not yet spring and when the sun went down, Corley was sharply reminded of that fact. They stopped at the house for a moment and Corley had a cup of coffee. Joy was not a coffee drinker so she and Corley's mom had tea. Corley noticed her eyes roving all over the house as she sipped her tea. She would probably have a story to tell when she got home. And, next fall, when she was out with some college boy, she would probably tell him about how this boy took her for a Sunday drive up in the country and she found out how simple people lived. He thought about that as he sat there watching her drink her tea. Yet, she remembered all her manners and pulled the visit off very well. Corley's mom seemed very comfortable with her.

It was dark when they started back down the river towards Charleston, and for some reason, Corley talked better in a dark car than anywhere else in the world. In fact, on this particular evening, he talked far too much. He told Joy Kelly things about himself that he shouldn't have, and was guilty of talking about all of the things that he was interested in without first finding out if she was also interested.

He started telling her how it really bugged him for people to stand around and say that there wasn't anything to do.

"Seems like that is all I ever hear at school. Everyone stands around and says that there is nothing to do around this place. That is the most uttered phrase at Bolton High. But, for me, it has always been the opposite. I could never find enough time to do all the things that I wanted to do. And, if I ever run out of anything to do, it just takes me a few minutes to discover something that needs to be done. The way I figure it, people who cannot find anything to do don't really want anything to do."

He could not see her face in the dark so he did not know how she was reacting to all of his ramblings, but he just kept on talking. He talked all the way to

Charleston about all of the things in life that bothered him and Joy did not say a word. After they got down to where the lights of the city made him more visible, he began to quiet down a little. When they pulled up in front of her house she looked at him for a moment or two before she spoke.

"Well," she said, "this is the first time that I have had two sermons in one day. I got one in church this morning and one from you this afternoon."

"You must think that I am some kind of a nut," he said.

"No, I don't think that at all. What I really think is that I'll think about you when I am thirty-five and wished that I had married you. I'll bet that you will amount to something one day."

A lot of people had said a lot of things to Corley, but Joy was the first one who had ever said that he would amount to anything. He found some comfort in that, but also gathered that for the moment, he had not made a very big impression.

"I suppose that what you are saying is that you don't really want to see me anymore until I'm middle aged."

"No, I'm not saying that at all. If you are ever in town and I am not busy, I would enjoy going out with you."

"I think busy is the key word," Corley said. "This is the first weekend that I have had free for ages and the remainder of the spring looks worse. As you know, this is the season for proms, dances, and parties and the band is booked pretty solid for weekends until graduation."

"I don't doubt that," she said, "but you keep me in mind, especially when we are both about thirty-five."

They both laughed and he walked her to the door. Those little breasts felt awfully good against him as he gave her a very polite and dignified goodnight kiss.

On the way home he started feeling guilty about Lucy O'Brannon so he drove up and talked with her for awhile. He told her the truth about Saturday night, told her that he and Sam had gone out hell raising. But, he lied to her about the afternoon. He told her that he and Bryson Hill had been out looking for bookings for the band. Then, on the way home, he felt guilty and really low down. It was not his nature to be dishonest with people, especially someone he liked as much as Lucy O'Brannon.

XXII

Bryson Hill caught Corley just as soon as he got off the school bus on Monday morning. His eyes were wide with excitement.

"Hey, Corley, I got a call from Ken Frazier last night. A man in Nashville liked our tape and wants us to come down."

"The hell you say; wants us to come down when?"

"This week, soon as we can. Can you go this week?"

"I suppose I can. I'd have to miss school, but that would not be a big deal."

"You're going to be rich, Corley, no use to worry about school. I'll set it up with Doug and Jerry tonight. We'll leave Wednesday and come back Friday. Remember, we have a gig at Blair High Friday night."

"How are we going to go?"

"Ken is going to ride with us in our station wagon. I've already talked to my dad about it and it's all set."

"Guess we had better practice every night this week," Corley said.

"I'd say," Bryson answered, "and we have some rough spots we're going to have to clear up."

Corley hated to hear that. He knew that they were going to have to play parts of the songs over and over. He shuddered at the thought.

"Better come over about six this evening so we can get an early start."

"OK, I'll be there."

Corley discussed the exciting news with his mother that evening and, to his surprise, she was very understanding and cooperative.

"Your father and I are very aware of the fact that you may be leaving home soon," she said. "Many of the things around here exist just so that you will have chores to do, and I expect that once you are gone, many things will change. Your father does not have time to look after all the things that you have attended to, so he will adjust the place accordingly."

Corley was very comforted by her words because he was beginning to wonder who was going to do all the things that he had been doing. It never really occurred to him that his dad just wanted to make sure that he had enough to do, but as he thought about it, he was kind of glad that he did. He had enjoyed the work, and he had enjoyed the fruits of his labor.

Somehow, the excitement that should have been with him as they rolled toward Nashville just wasn't there. Oh, he was excited to be sure. He had never been out of West Virginia, let alone to Nashville, and he was full of anticipation about what it was going to look like. He was especially thrilled at the possibility of seeing some of the people that he had heard on the radio for years. But the thought of becoming a star just had not quite hit him yet. Somehow, he just couldn't quite grasp the concept. But Bryson's dad was financing the trip and he certainly did not want to appear unappreciative.

They got into Nashville late Wednesday night and checked into a motel. It was his first experience in a motel and it felt a little strange to him. Ken Frazier made sure that everyone within ear shot knew why they were there. He assured the desk clerk that the next time these boys were in Nashville they would be staying in more opulent surroundings.

They were down at the studio by nine the next morning and Corley did not like the atmosphere around the place. There were several other groups scheduled that morning so there was an entire waiting room full of dumb looking people. Corley bought him a package of cigarettes and lit one so that he would not look as uncomfortable as he felt. Since he hardly ever smoked, the cigarette made him look even more ridiculous. Every now and then a man would come into the room and shuffle folks around. He was a loud, abrasive man and he gave Corley the creeps just to look at him.

Finally, he heard "River City Rockers move this way." For the first time, it really dawned on him what a corny name for a group that really was. The abrasive man herded them into a studio and showed them where to set up. He looked at Corley as he was getting the Gibson out of the cheap case.

"Do you not play an amplified guitar, kid?" he asked.

"No sir, I'm mostly the singer and I play rhythm."

He looked at Corley like he was a moron or something and went on about his business. Hell, thought Corley, Elvis Presley did not play an amplified guitar, and the old scratched up Gibson sounded as good as any guitar he had ever heard.

The abrasive man began pushing Corley around and stuck a microphone right into his face. He told him to face one way, then the other way, then the other way. Corley looked at Bryson and the sweat was rolling down his forehead. He had never seen Bryson upset before, but he definitely looked uncomfortable. Then, he noticed Ken Frazier standing over against the wall smoking a big cigar and playing the role. Corley decided that he hated that phoney bastard. When they got organized and in tune, a man behind a glass enclosed booth started talking to them through a microphone.

"OK, I want you to give me your best number. I might want to stop you so keep an ear open and watch me for a signal. When I drop my hand, start your song."

He dropped his hand and Bryson hit the introduction to "River City Girl". He was visibly shaken and missed a run right away. When Corley came in to sing his voice was shaking and he had not sung three words until the man in the booth stopped them.

"Relax group," he said. "You guys are shaking like hell and look like a bunch of hicks off the farm. Come on now. This is a professional setting. Let's act like professionals."

They started again and the second introduction was worse than the first one. They stopped themselves and Bryson yelled at the man that we wanted a fresh start. The man barked his approval angrily.

"Look group, I don't have all damned day. You guys are supposed to be ready."

Corley had now regained his cool and was pretty settled down. The third time was better. The beat sounded right and Corley could feel the pulse of the song. His voice came in strong. He saw the man behind the glass relax and light himself a smoke. When Corley got to the first bridge he tried to forget where he was and pretended that he was singing to Julie Meadows, sitting in the back of the boat.

Just a River City honey without enough money
To get out of this town, and make all the rounds
Just a child of the mountains, fresh as a fountain
With a face that's so pretty, in Old River City.

They got through the song and Corley thought that he sounded pretty good, or as good as he was capable of sounding. Everyone in the group breathed a sigh of relief.

"OK, let's hear your second number," the man yelled.

Bryson hit the introduction to "Rock'n With Freda R". It was mostly instrumental with a typical rock beat, and they all sang one line in unison at the end of each chorus. It was kind of like the old Glen Miller tune "Pennsylvania 6-5000," except the music was different. Bryson and Corley had put it together one night when they were just fooling around. Corley thought that it was pretty catchy. The man in the glass booth showed no reaction one way or the other to the second song. He just sat there and watched and listened. When the song ended, he yanked off his headset and walked out in front of the booth.

"That's it group. Move your stuff out of the way and come back at three-thirty for a critique of your session." He handed Ken Frazier a slip of paper.

Corley was really glad to get out of there. He noticed that Bryson didn't look too happy. Doug, who rarely said anything, unleashed his wrath after they got outside.

"Did you hear that bastard yell at us? I did not come down here to be yelled at. Who is that son-of-a-bitch anyway?"

"Now you boys just settle down," Ken said. "That is all a part of the business. All of those guys get excited and yell around. They don't mean anything by it. It just goes with the profession."

"Hell of a way to make a living," Corley commented.

"Just cool it guys," Bryson said. "Let's see what happens at the critique. I thought we did a damn good job."

They had about four hours to kill so they spent some time touring the city. At least Ken Frazier was good for something, Corley thought. He knew his way around town. He took them to the Rhymer Auditorium, home of the Grand Old Opry, and Corley got pretty excited about seeing the place. He had listened to the voices that came out of there many a Saturday night, and he knew the names of everyone who had ever performed there. He had many fond memories of listening to country music.

Later, they got something to eat and walked around downtown Nashville. They gawked like a bunch of farmers, just as the man in the booth accused them of being. Corley mostly looked at girls and had thoughts of beginning his career as an international lover right there in Nashville. He found himself wanting to be a little older, a little wiser, and a lot more prosperous.

Too soon they had to head back to the studio to hear the results of the session. Ken Frazier gave the slip of paper to a top heavy girl and she led them to a conference room. The man who had been in the glass cage came rushing in and he laid it right on the line.

"OK group, we have listened to your tape and discussed your session and here is what we think. You have a decent sound, but you lack experience and professionalism. We cannot offer you a record contract at this time. We will press a record for you at your expense and try to promote it for you. It will cost you right at one thousand dollars. If you guys get a little more experience and a little more exposure, we might be interested in working out a contract with you."

Corley was dumbfounded. He did not know a damn thing about the record industry and this was the first time that he ever heard of anyone having to pay a thousand dollars to get a record made. He always thought that the record company paid the people who made the records. He never knew that you had to pay to be a star. But Ken Frazier was wise to the ways of the fast moving record promoter. He jumped up and pumped the man's hand and told him that we appreciated his time and that we would be in touch. But, when they got back in the station wagon, he looked pretty depressed.

"Well, fellas, we didn't make it. I was hoping that they would offer you a contract. You see, if they offer you a contract, they will cover everything and pay you royalties on the record. Otherwise, the cost of production is up to you."

"Hell, we are not used to that kind of pressure," Corley said.

"That's for sure," Bryson added.

"What you need to do is to go back and get some more experience," Ken said. "You guys are plenty good and you show a lot of promise. You keep working and we'll try again. Don't give up. Most people don't make it on the first try."

Bryson Hill was visibly upset. He was really expecting big things from the trip and was really disappointed. Corley was certainly disappointed, but not terribly surprised. He thought that they were pretty good, but at the same time, he realized that there were a lot of groups around who were "pretty good." He was not convinced that they were anything special. He also knew that you had to have some influence somewhere and he doubted that Ken Frazier had any clout. Red had always told Corley that it was really tough to break into the record business, and that if you did not have some inside help, it was nearly impossible. He had also told Corley that if you were a girl you could screw your way to the top of the industry. Red had been around some and Corley had more respect for him than he did Ken Frazier. But, Corley still believed that "River City Girl" was a good song and had a thought that maybe he ought to try to get some established singer to cut it. Then, reality sank in again because he really did not know too many established singers.

    He tried to put it all out of his mind as they rode back to Vandalia County. The dance at Blair was something to look forward to, he was also looking forward to seeing Lucy O'Brannon again. Maybe the River City Rockers could not make music together, but he and Lucy definitely could. And, he also fantasized about Joy Kelly. He wondered if there was any way in the world that he would ever manage to get into her britches. He thought that it was probably impossible, but a man could never tell what the future held.

XXIII

Corley noticed two or three cars in the yard as Bryson's station wagon pulled down into the Malone place. He recognized one of them as one of his older brother's. And, as he walked into the kitchen, he realized that the Nashville trip was going to have an even sadder ending. Before he could say anything, his mother spoke.

"Your grandfather died this morning."

"Which grandfather?"

"Fletcher."

The news took a lot out of him. He had an impulse to cry, but it was only momentary. He tried to concentrate on the positive. His grandpa Fletcher had lived a full life, had watched his children grow up healthy, and had seen most of his grandchildren reach adulthood. And, as he had related to Corley when they were working in the hay, he had been his own man. A man could not ask for much more out of life, Corley figured. Still, he was saddened. He was a man for whom Corley had a great deal of respect and he thought fondly of the hours they had worked together during the past summer. Corley had marveled at his strength and endurance at that time.

Death brought out the very best qualities of the people of Vandalia County. By nightfall dozens of people had come by the Malone place. The women brought food of all sorts, so much that an army could not have consumed it in a week. All the men wanted to know when they could help dig the grave. A dozen offered to keep the chores up at the Fletcher place until things got back to normal. His grandmother would be left alone now and would, in all probability, move in with Corley's mom and dad. That was the general custom in the area.

Corley decided that he would go ahead and play the Blair High gig that night. He could not see any way out of it really, so he got ready and went over to Bryson's place. Bryson offered to call and cancel out. That's the way he was. He was the most considerate person in the world. But Corley assured him that he was fine and that he could get through the gig alright. They drove over to Blair County, picked up Doug and Jerry, and went on to the dance.

Actually, Corley was kind of glad that he went. It took his mind off things, and they had a really good time. The Blair High kids even requested a couple of country songs and Corley thoroughly enjoyed singing a little country. It felt really good to be playing without being watched and criticized; and the band had a very enjoyable evening.

When Corley got back home about one in the morning everyone was still up. They had brought his grandmother to the house and she was sitting in the kitchen among all of her friends and family. Corley hugged her tightly when he came in and apologized for being gone all evening. She appeared to be holding up remarkably well. She and his grandfather had been married sixty-two years and Corley could not imagine losing someone who had been your constant companion for that long. And, they had been constant companions because Grandpa Fletcher had never worked at a job away from the farm. She told Corley once that they had never spent a night apart since they were married.

Next morning, several of the area men went to the Fletcher family cemetery which was located high on the hill above the Fletcher farm. Corley's great-grandfather Fletcher was buried there, and his great-great grandfather Fletcher was buried less than a half mile away. The Fletchers had held a grip on this part of the county for a long time. Corley remembered helping his grandpa shore up the fence around the cemetery during his stay with him the past summer. There were seven strands of barbed wire around it and there was never any doubt in his grandfather's mind that he would be laid to rest there.

It was a warm, dry day and a total of thirty men showed up by about ten o'clock in the morning. They all brought some kind of a digging tool. Sam's father brought some dynamite in case they might run into some rock. Grave digging was far from a sad occasion in Vandalia County. The men enjoyed the fellowship of working together. The banter that went on among the men was something akin to that of the hayfield. Only one or two men could work at the same time in the grave. Everyone else just watched and talked.

There were many comments about Corley's grandfather. Most of them concerned how strong he was in his youth. Someone said that he was a good man with a mowing scythe and everyone agreed. Corley remembered how close he had mowed with the scythe last summer. Corley's Grandpa Malone, in his middle eighties, was there and he remarked that Mr. Fletcher was the best man with a broad ax that he ever saw when he was young.

"He could get out crossties with the best of them," he said "He was strong as an ox."

"He had a pretty good education for his day," Corley's dad said. "He was pretty well read."

The comment about education got everyone started on the upcoming school bond election which was to occur in early May. The money from the bond was going to do several things, but the big issue was the elimination of the one room elementary schools. There was to be one central elementary school built in Bolton, and all of the one room schools were to be torn down. The men gathered at the grave were all against it.

"I don't see any damned use of it at all," Corley's Uncle Ken said as he shoveled out the loose dirt that Corley had just dug up with a mattock.

"Nor do I," his dad added. "The Broad Run School was good enough for me and all of my kids. It's still a good building and I don't see any use of spending good money on a building that we don't need. If them sons-a-bitches in Bolton want a new school, let them build one with a city bond or something. There is not a damned thing wrong with one room schools."

Old Thort Evans, in his sixties, exploded in a rage. "It's coming to the point where everyone knows what's best for us. The damned government seems like they know what is best and they act like we don't have enough sense to live on the earth. If you take a school out of the community, you destroy one of the main places where people congregate. A local school holds folks together. I'm no damned politician, but I know that."

He looked down at Corley who was busy digging with the mattock and asked, "What do you think, Corley, you fer it or agin it?"

Corley looked up at all of the faces above him and decided that there was not but one answer.

"Hell, I'm, agin it," he said.

Everyone smiled approvingly, and Corley figured that he had said the right thing.

Around noon, someone showed up in a Jeep with all kinds of food and several jugs of coffee. Everyone took a general break for about thirty minutes, then went back to the chore at hand. The grave was all done by about three in the afternoon, and folks began leaving. Corley and his dad covered both the grave and the fresh pile of dirt with a big piece of canvas in the event of rain. Corley marveled at the good job that they had done.

It was the custom at that time and at that place in the universe to take the body to the home of the deceased so that friends could call the evening before the funeral. Many times people would stay up all night. It was not a sad occasion at all. There was laughter and fellowship. But, because Corley's grandfather lived in a spot that was inaccessible by car, it was decided to leave the body at the funeral home. It was the longest evening that Corley could ever remember going through in his entire life. He did not like seeing his grandfather there and wished that he could remember him throwing hay up into the barn, and not lying there stark and cold. Lucy came by and spent an hour or so with him and he deeply appreciated that. Lucy was as good as they made them. Corley realized that more every day.

He never knew how many friends that his grandfather had until the next day. Even though he lived in isolation, and no one ever thought of him as being a social person, a lot of people evidently knew him, or knew about him, and came to pay their respects. The little church which he had attended so faithfully was filled to capacity. It was a warm, beautiful Sunday afternoon for March and several people stood outside.

Julie Meadows showed up and Corley got his first look at her big time boyfriend. He was tall, handsome, and prosperous looking. Corley had not expected anything less. She came over and gave Corley a slight caress and made the introduction.

"Corley, this is Mark Wells. Mark, Corley Malone."

Corley shook hands with him but he had an inner thought that he ought to hit the son-of-a-bitch right in the teeth.

"Julie has spoken of you," he said politely.

"I believe that she has mentioned your name to me," Corley answered.

"I'm really sorry about your grandfather," Julie said, remembering her manners. "I recall the wonderful meal we had with them the day we went to visit the Keefer boys."

"He lived a good, full life," Corley said, as he turned away.

Corley took his place with the family inside the church and looked around at the crowd. He knew all of them. The men all looked terribly uncomfortable in their ties, but their women looked so proud of them. Mark Wells looked very comfortable in his. Corley even spotted Sam back in the back and was pleased to see him. He knew that Sam would have preferred to sit this one out, but he was there.

The minister was an older fellow, unknown to Corley, and he arose to make his remarks.

"Now I see some folks crying around the room and I want you to know that there is no use in that. Either we believe this stuff or we don't, and if we do believe it, we should not be crying. Mr. Fletcher believed in God more than anyone I have ever known. There was never a doubt in his mind that he was going on to a better life. He lived the scripture as close as you could live it. I never knew him to drink, nor swear, and he was a devoted family man. He certainly never bothered anyone and we could all live by his example. The Lord has told us that he has gone to prepare a place for us. Henry Fletcher is going to claim his and we should all be happy for him."

That was all that he said.

Someone read from John XIV, the first three verses. Corley loved the King James Version and that was indeed one of the more moving passages from the entire Bible as far as he was concerned. They then called the Tawney Boys up to sing. Corley had done fine up to that point, but when they begin to sing "Angel Band," he choked. It was one of Corley's favorite hymns and they sang it as well as it could be sung. There was not a dry eye in the house when they finished and Corley felt like someone had stuck a straight razor down his throat. He was glad when it was over and felt very relieved to get outside and into the sunshine.

They drove the coffin to where the road ended and then loaded Henry Fletcher on to a horse drawn sled for his final ride to the top of the hill. Corley could not stand to watch his grandmother's grief at the graveside so he walked back down the hill alone. Then, he decided to walk all the way home. He felt an overwhelming need to be alone so he spent the evening down by the river.

XXIV

Warm, dry weather persisted after the sweeping away of death and Corley's father decided that it was getting dry enough to plow the land. It was early, but he held to the old theory that if the soil was turned early, the last freezes of spring would kill the insect larva. Corley was not sure that he believed in the theory, but if it made his father feel better, he was all for it.

The Malones had always used a one-horse turn plow and alternated two horses so as to rest one of them all the time. Using the turn plow was not really hard work if a person knew what he was doing and let the horse do the work. The only hard part was turning the plow blade at the end of each row. Then, occasionally, the plow would hit a rock or a root and slam into your hip, but other than that, Corley enjoyed it. He took his time. It was really the first hard work that he had done since last fall so he did not want to overdo it. He liked to smell the fresh plowed ground, and he liked to stop at the end of each row and just enjoy the scenery. The Vandalia River Valley was beautiful anytime of the year as far as he was concerned. It was almost too warm for March. The hills were still totally brown and there was no sign of green grass. Yet, by late morning the sun felt nearly hot on his back.

He plowed the potato patch and three small plots where they raised the vegetable gardens. His dad had spread manure from the barn on the vegetable plots and the odor made the plowing there slightly less than pleasant. But, Corley knew that it was the best fertilizer in the world. His dad always reminded him that you couldn't just keep taking from the soil. You had to give something back in return.

Corley had thoughts all day about farming for a living. It was pleasant work, it was independent work, and he liked being out- of-doors. But, there was no money in being a small time farmer. His dad had given up the idea years ago and had gone out and gotten himself a job, and had actually found a pretty nice balance. He had continued to enjoy many of the things that living on a farm provided, but the job had also permitted him to have the things that modern life demanded; things like automobiles, clothes, washing machines, televisions, guitars, fiddles, and other necessities.

Late that afternoon while Corley was plowing the large field where they always planted their field corn, he saw a big blue Cadillac pull down in front of their house. He thought that it looked like the car that Bryson Hill's father drove, and when the man got out, he saw that it was indeed Roy Hill. He walked over to the barn and talked to Corley's dad for a few minutes, then made his way toward Corley. Roy Hill was a slick talking business type and he had a little nervous, dishonest laugh that infiltrated all of his conversation. Corley figured that the laugh was a cover for the guilt he felt for all of the people that he had cheated in life.

"Hello, Corley, Ha Ha," he began. "Farming today are you?"

"Just a little," Corley said, wondering what the hell he wanted with him.

"I wanted to tell you that Bryson had a little wreck last night. Nothing serious, ha ha, but he did break his arm in two places, and got a bump on his head. They are holding him for observation in the hospital down at Charleston. He wants to see you if you can get down."

"I'm really sorry to hear that Mr. Hill. I'll make a point of going down to see him this evening."

"That boy thinks a lot of you, Corley, Ha Ha, I do hope you can get down."

"I will, I will, don't worry."

He reached out and shook Corley's hand and departed with his little laugh. He hurried back across the field to his Cadillac.

Now this is a revolting development, thought Corley. It sounded as if Bryson was going to be unable to play any guitar for quite some time. They had four dances to play in April and May and Corley was not sure where that left them. There was no way the group could operate without Bryson.

He kept at his plowing until supper time and was able to get it all done. After he ate and did his evening chores, he fired up the old pick-up and headed for Charleston. He could not remember ever being in a hospital and decided as soon as he entered the door that it was not some place he wanted to be. But, he could hardly suppress a laugh when he first saw Bryson lying there. His arm was in a big cast all the way up to his shoulder and he had a big patch on his head. But, the ever present half grin was still on his face.

"Hey, Corley, glad you could make it."

"I'll be damned if you ain't a mess," Corley said. "You in any pain or anything?"

"No not now, but I was in some when I got here last night."

"What the hell's the matter with you? Can you not drive a car?" Corley joked.

"I don't know. I was just going down the road and all of a sudden I was all over the place."

"Wasn't drinking anything were you?"

"Nothing but water," Bryson grinned. "But, I guess we got a problem on our hands with the band. You want to try to pick up another lead guitar player?"

"Hell no," Corley quickly interjected, "I wouldn't know where to begin looking for a good lead guitar player. Besides, no one but you could cover my singing."

"I'd have to agree with that," Bryson laughed. "Guess we had better cancel out real quick so that folks can make other arrangements. My dad has all the numbers to call so I will have him break the bad news to everyone."

Corley had two thoughts as he sat there looking at Bryson. One was that he was going to have a lot of free time on his hands between now and graduation. The other was that he was going to have less money. The band had not made him rich, but it had kept him in spending money. He really felt sorry for old Bryson, lying there looking kind of pitiful. Yet, he got the feeling that Bryson's spirit had been broken by the Nashville trip, and maybe he was just a little relieved to be out from under the pressure of the band. He didn't appear to be as sad over the demise of the group as he might have been earlier.

"Don't you worry none, Bryson, we'll get things going again after your arm mends," Corley said. "We'll make that arrogant bastard in Nashville sorry that he ran our ass out of town."

"I might forget how to play," Bryson said.

"Naw, hell, you won't forget. You'll be better than ever after you get that arm going. Besides, it will give me a chance to practice, and then maybe I can keep up with you."

"You keep up alright," he smiled.

"Well, at any rate, I'd better be getting up the river. Maybe I can find me a good band to get in. You never know."

They shared a good laugh over that and Corley left him in a good mood.

It was still early when he got back to Bolton so he drove up and talked to Lucy. They cruised over to the drive-in restaurant and Corley drank some coffee. He thought that Lucy had been acting kind of strange ever since she got into the car so he was not too surprised when she started on him.

"Corley, you are going to be out of school in a couple of months. What are you going to do with yourself?"

"Get a job, I guess. Everyone has to go to work sometime."

"Get a job where? They're pretty hard to find around here I'm told."

"Well, I'd like to stay around, but if I can't find anything, I suppose I'll have to go where the work is."

He was not about to tell Lucy, but lately he had been thinking that he was going to have to get out of Vandalia County, at least for a year or two. He was beginning to look around him and see a lot of guys who had never been away from the place. They had graduated, acquired that "fat married look" that Hemingway wrote about, and had become a slave to some job. He was beginning to think that he did not want any part of that scene. He had also noticed that after about six months of marriage the wives moved over against the other side of the car, and the guys looked miserable. And, what really got him was watching the poor bastards coming out of the A&P store on Saturday evening carrying a couple of sacks of groceries. He had really started to think about that kind of stuff a lot.

Then, on the other hand, he worried about Lucy. He wasn't sure that he had been fair with her. He had made her no lasting promises, had not led her to believe anything. She was damned good company, and, after all, she had seduced him in the first place. Yet, he did not want to hurt her feelings and he wasn't going to if he could help it.

"You have any place in particular in mind?" she asked.

"No, not really. Cleveland maybe, or Detroit."

"Are you ever going to come back and see me?" she asked.

"Hell yes, I'll come back to see you. I'm not even sure that I am going anywhere yet."

"Somehow I just can't picture you hanging around," she said. "Sometimes when we're together I get the feeling that you are really somewhere else already."

That line sent a chill down his spine. She was hitting too close to home. Before he could answer she continued.

"I can't help wondering what is going to happen to us."

"Listen Lucy," he said. "Let's give it some time. I really enjoy being with you. I don't think that I have ever enjoyed anything as much as the times we used to have at The Beeches. You will never know what a thrill it was for me the first time we danced there."

And, he was sincere in what he was saying. They did have a good time together. His experience with women was very limited, but Lucy seemed awfully good to him. And, maybe somewhere on down the road he would get serious about her, but not now. He could not envision himself coming out of the A&P store on Saturday night with a sack of groceries, not at eighteen years old.

"I'm sorry for bringing all of this up," Lucy finally said. "It's just that I worry when I think that you might leave and never come back."

"I'm not going anywhere yet," Corley said. "Let's just enjoy the time we have together now."

They decided that it was time for them to get their lives back in order. They made plans for both Friday and Saturday nights. Friday night, they would go to Charleston and act civilized. Then, Saturday night, they decided that they would go over to Blair County and hit the night spots, do some dancing, and act like the good country people that they were. He drove her home and damned near got carried away in the seat of the old pick-up. They laughed as they untangled her skirt from the floor shift.

XXV

The final week in March turned wet and cold, a bitter reminder that winter was not quite over in the hill country. It was the sort of weather that made it impossible to do any kind of outside work on the farm. Yet, everyone sort of had the farming fever. It was the kind of a time when men stood around the barn or a shed somewhere and talked about what had to be done. The weather was totally unpredictable. Corley's dad called it March weather. On a given day it would rain, snow, and be sunny all within a five hour period. For Corley it was just a plain frustrating time.

For the first time in his life he was faced with a series of uncertainties. He did not know what to do about a job. He did not know what to do about Lucy. He could not decide whether or not to try to do anything with his music. If he could have gotten out and worked, plowed, planted, or something, he would have felt better about things. But, as it was, he just had too much time to think.

Evenings were getting longer and that made the days even more difficult. He sawed around on the fiddle some and he and Sam tried some muskie fishing, but it really was not good fishing weather. He had been so busy all fall and winter and now everything had just stopped on him. He was beginning to feel like that bunch of fools at school who stood around and complained that there was nothing to do. He was bored to death with school and was just going through the motions. They were reading *Macbeth* in senior English and he was enjoying that, but English class only lasted fifty minutes.

Early April was not much of an improvement, but he did notice that the daffodils were blooming and that was an encouraging sign. But, he had remembered has grandfather Fletcher saying that it would always snow on the daffodils at least once after they bloomed so he did not want to get too excited about spring just yet.

April eighth was indeed a milestone for him. He was finally eighteen years old. It really meant a lot to be eighteen in West Virginia in 1956. He drove to Charleston the day after his birthday and registered for the draft. Very few people were being drafted at that time, but there was a certain distinction in having a draft card in your wallet. You could flash that baby and buy a beer any damned place that you felt like it, or go into any pool room that you wanted to. Sam was not going to be eighteen until June and he was very envious. Corley started referring to him as "kid" immediately.

By mid April things began to look much better. The ground was drying out some and there was beginning to be a few traces of green here and there. Even the yuck around the barn was showing some improvement. There was still plenty of mud around on the secondary roads, but dry times were coming. The second Saturday in April turned out to be one of those sterling spring days and the Vandalia Valley became a beehive of potato planters. It was past the traditional potato planting time but folks had been held back by the wet weather. Corley put in a long hard day's labor and it felt really good to be out working. Working outside had always been an outlet for his frustrations and at this particular point in his life he had a surplus of frustrations to get out of his system.

He kept thinking all day that there were really two people within him. One of them wanted time to stand still so that he could continue to stay on the farm, eat his mother's cooking, run around on Saturday nights, and hunt and fish when the season was right. But there was another force within that wanted to get away, to see the world, and to seek new adventure. But the adventurous side of him kept asking difficult questions. Where would he go? What was he going to do when he got there? How was he going to support himself? What would he do when hunting season came and he was not there to enjoy it? Were there any more girls in the world as good as Lucy? Could he really bear seeing Julie Meadows marry someone else?

That evening his already frustrated world was complicated a step further as he was washing up for supper. He heard a car coming up the drive toward their house and as he looked out the window, he thought that it looked like Julie's Dodge. She pulled up into the yard and blew the horn. Corley walked outside, still drying his hands on a towel, trying to act like he was not surprised to see her.

"What are you doing, Corley?" she greeted him.

"I was just getting washed up for supper. You want to come in and join us?"

"No, I want to talk to you. It's kind of important."

"Right now?"

"Yes, right now."

He looked at her and thought about his supper, but, he had to admit, he would have talked to her any time or any place. All she would have had to do was to ask. She knew that.

"Let me get a shirt," he said.

He left the house with his mother yelling at him about supper getting cold and got into her car.

"Where can we go to talk?" she asked.

"Go down and drive up Sugar Creek where we parked that night."

She drove to the spot without saying a word, shut the engine off, and looked at Corley like she had never looked at him before. The blue eyes did not look right to him.

"Well, what the hell is it, Julie. I gave up a good supper for this."

She immediately started crying. She put her arms around him and cried and cried and cried until there was nothing left inside her. She trembled and sobbed until he really felt sorry for her. He did not say anything. He just let her cry it out. Finally, she spoke.

"I've got to tell someone about this or I am going to explode."

"Well, for christ's sake Julie, get it out."

"Corley, I think I'm pregnant."

Somehow he knew she was going to say that, but he still got nauseated when she spoke the words. He had idealized her for so long, placed her on a pedestal so high, that it was hard to believe that she was saying what she was saying. All he could think about first were his own selfish thoughts. He had controlled his own desires for her, stayed out of her way, tried to please her snobby mother, and for what? So some high and mighty college man could knock her up. He wanted to just knock the hell out of her. Finally, he started saying words without really knowing what he was saying.

"For christ's sake, Julie, haven't you ever heard of rubbers. What in the hell have you gone and done some dumbassed thing like this for?"

She started crying again and he was sorry that he had said anything.

"Have you not told anyone else? Mark or your mother?"

"No, I will never be able to tell my mother. She has so many plans for me. She is just absolutely going to die. There is no way that I can ever tell her."

"Well, you sure to hell had better tell Mark Wells because he is going to have to get his act together. Are you really sure that you are pregnant?"

"Pretty sure. I missed last month's period and I've been getting sick every morning, sometimes at noon. But you know what makes me so mad? We only did something twice, just two times, and I didn't even enjoy it either time, I was so scared."

"They tell me that it only takes once and that it does not matter whether or not you enjoy it. That's what I've been told," Corley said.

"What am I going to do, Corley?" she asked.

All sorts of things ran through his mind. He considered for a moment asking her to marry him, but laughed that thought right out of his mind. He was in no position to get married, and the thought of raising that phoney college man's child did not set well with him at all.

"Do you love Mark enough to marry him?" Corley asked.

"I don't know. I do and I don't. I like him a lot, but I don't want to get married. I've looked forward to going to college for three years. I just don't know what to do."

"Well, it seems to me that the first thing that you had better do is to tell Mark Wells all about it. He looks like a responsible sort to me and I am sure that he will do the honorable thing."

"I suppose that I don't really have a choice, do I?" she said.

"Julie, if there is anything that I can do, any arrangements that I can make, you know that I will do what I can."

"I know," she smiled. "Thank you so much for listening to me and letting me cry all over you. I had to talk to someone and you are just the best someone that I know."

As Corley sat there and looked at her he almost blamed himself. If he had been more aggressive, had taken better care of her, this would never have happened. If he had not fled in fear every time he thought he might get in too deep, things might have worked out better for both of them. If he hadn't been such a doodle bug! On the other hand, Mark Wells was certainly in a better position to take care of her than he was. If he had gotten her pregnant, he thought, her dear mother would have had a heart attack. The truth was, he did not know what he did think.

"Mark is coming up tonight and I'll just have to spill it all," she said.

"You do that," Corley answered. "And if he does not treat you right, I'll just shoot the sorry son-of-a-bitch."

"I don't suppose that you will ever stop talking dirty," she laughed.

At least she was laughing, he thought, as she fired up the Dodge and drove Corley back to his house. It was good to see her laugh. She leaned over and kissed him lightly as he got out.

"Thanks again," she said.

He had a date with Lucy that evening but his heart was not in it. He took the pick-up and they drove up to The Beeches. They listened to the band awhile, danced a couple of times, but Corley just was not in the mood to party. After about an hour, he decided that he had to get out of there.

"What's wrong with you this evening?" Lucy asked as they were getting into the truck.

"I don't know. I guess my life is closing in on me again. Seems like all I do anymore is contemplate my place in the universe. Life doesn't seem to be as much fun as it was a few months back."

"You're just growing up, Corley. Don't worry so much."

She was right, Corley thought. He was growing up, but he never thought of it as being so painful. Only a year ago life seemed like a big puff of wind within which a man could blow around and have a good time. Now, all of a sudden, it had become a major pain in the ass.

They drove to Lucy's house under a glittering starlit night and the air was warm and pleasant. The thoughts of a long Sunday alone the next day haunted him, so he decided that he would rather go through the day with some good company.

"Why don't I come down and get you in the morning and we'll spend the day together. We can eat dinner with my mother, then go for a long walk on the hill. There should be some wild flowers blooming and it will be good for both of us to walk. You could stand to lose a couple of pounds anyway," he teased.

She laughed and said that she would be ready by eleven.

Corley went home, went to his room, and found that tiny piece of ribbon from Julie's hair that he had saved the night he burned it. He took it outside, lit a match to it, and watched the last symbol of Julie Meadows go up in smoke. He went to his room and spent the night somewhere between being awake and being asleep. He had a thousand visions of Julie Meadows coming down the aisle in a white wedding gown with big round tears falling down her cheeks.

He stirred just when the first sunlight hit his window. He could hear the birds singing loudly and he could hear dew dropping from the maple trees in the yard, a sure sign that there was no frost. It was one of those spring mornings that inspire poets, song writers, and young lovers.

He got up and went to the barn and did the morning chores, momentarily feeling sorry for folks who lived in the big cities where the changing seasons went unnoticed. There was an indescribable smell in the air. It did not smell like anything in particular other than spring. He came back to the house with a huge appetite and enjoyed eggs, sausage, biscuits, and coffee, lots of coffee.

After breakfast, he got the old guitar, went out on the back porch, propped his feet up on the bannister, and sang a concert for the world to enjoy. No one could hear him except his mother. He sang all the old songs that he had ever heard and they sounded awfully good to him. He thought about that son-of-a-bitch down in Nashville. He would probably have scoffed at the concert on the porch. But, that was the best thing about singing on the porch. If it sounded good to him, it did not matter what the rest of the world thought.

Soon it was time to go get Lucy. He went out to the shed, fired up the old pick-up, and headed down the river valley. As he passed the Big Run Methodist Church he wondered if Julie were in there playing piano for the souls, pretending that she was as pure as the water that was running out of the hills.

Lucy looked lovely. She had on blue jeans, rolled up to the knees the way all the girls were wearing them, white socks, and oxfords. She never wore much makeup and always looked like she had just scrubbed her face. She met him on the porch as she almost always did. He could not ever recall having to wait for her. She took hold of his arm and dragged him playfully toward the truck. He looked at her, pretty as a young kitten, and thought how fortunate he was that she liked him. She was the best thing that had happened to his young life. She had been his anchor.

After they had dinner they sat on the back porch for awhile. He sang to her a little as they let the meal settle, then started off on their walk. They made the long pull up the first hill and began to follow the ridgelines. The sun was warm and pleasant and there was not yet enough foliage to provide any shade. Once they got into the woods they were rid of the mud and the walking was pleasant.

"Where are you taking me?" she asked.

"I am going to take you for the longest walk that you have ever thought about, and I'm going to wear your little fanny out."

"Oh, I don't know. I'm pretty tough. I've walked a few hills myself you know."

He sat a pace for the old Smith place which was about a three mile walk with a steep climb or two thrown in. The Smith place was an old abandoned farm which was located right on top of one of the highest knobs around. It afforded one of the best views in the entire area, but most people never took advantage of it because it was accessible only by foot, and it was a long walk from anywhere.

They noticed a few flowers along the way. The dogwood was budding but had not yet popped out. It was a little too early for a wildflower walk, but it was an inspiring day even without flowers. When they first walked into the clearing of the old Smith place, Lucy was properly impressed.

"God, how beautiful," she said.

And beautiful it was. You could see the hills for as far as the eye could see, one hill behind the other until they became a part of the blue that was the sky. Corley had stood in that same spot dozens of times while hunting, or just fooling around, but it seemed more beautiful each time he came there.

"It was worth the walk," Lucy said. "I have really never seen West Virginia as I see it now."

"Nor so much of it at once," Corley added.

The old barn was still being used by someone for the purpose of storing hay. They cut the old meadows around the barn, stored the hay in the barn, and hauled it off later with a horse and sled. They walked into the shed of the barn and looked at some of the old tools and pieces of horse harness that had been there for ages. No one had actually farmed the place for thirty or forty years.

Corley pulled her into the hayloft and they lay down in the soft hay. He kissed her once and she pulled back suddenly.

"I want to make love," she said, almost like an excited child.
"I have read about people doing it in the hay, seen it in the movies, and I have always wondered what it would be like." She was unbuttoning her blouse.

"This hay is going to be scratchy," Corley said. "Let me see if I can find something."

He went below to search for a reasonable facsimile of a blanket. All he could find was three old feed sacks. When he got back into the loft she was nude and was sitting with her arms across her breasts. She laughed at his modesty as he got undressed. Corley wondered if it was the inspiration of the natural setting or just what it was, but Lucy had never been so anxious. Her breasts were high and rigid and appeared extra sensitive to the touch. Even her mouth was more sensuous and sweeter than he had ever known it to be. He kissed her and kissed her and simply could not kiss her enough. The double backed beast, so aptly named by Shakespeare, was soon unleashed and they became oblivious to the discomfort of the hay.

They got dressed and worried about the lateness of the hour. They had a couple of hours of daylight left, but they were going to have to hustle back. The sun was going down behind the hills by the time they got back to the house, but it was still warm and pleasant. They had a snack with his mother before he took Lucy home. He took her home in the Buick because he figured a girl like Lucy deserved a comfortable ride home. She sat so close to him that he could hardly drive. It was sessions like the one that he had just experienced that caused men to give up their freedom and go to the grocery store on Saturday night. He could feature himself being content with Lucy forever. Yet, he had a deep fear that his aspirations of being an international lover could get lost in the A&P store if he was not careful.

He kissed her on the front porch and all of his desires were immediately rekindled. She tasted every bit as good as she had on the mountain top and he wanted her again. She pulled herself away, fighting her own desires.

"You'd better go home and cool off," she said.

"I'd rather go somewhere and cool off with you," he replied.

She turned him around and pushed him toward the car.

"You go home. Stop by the office and see me tomorrow."

Corley went back to the Buick, fired it up, and started back up the river, a firm believer that passion and love were one in the same.

XXVI

Suddenly it was May and there was no time to be bored. The weather improved daily and the hills and meadows were coming alive. Corley was back into his more normal schedule when there was not enough time to get everything done. There was a whirl of social activity at school and there was much to be done on the farm.

He had to help get all of the gardens planted and to get the place generally ready for summer. In addition, he was trying to get a lot of things done that he could have normally attended to later in the summer. He kept thinking that he was not going to be around long and he did not want to leave the place in a mess. The barn roof needed painting, fences needed mended, and there was general repair to be done everywhere he looked. He even stayed home from school a couple of days and worked. There wasn't much academic activity going on for seniors anyway.

In fact, school was fast coming to a close. There was a banquet of some kind, a dance, or a party nearly every night. Corley passed most of them up since Lucy was out of school and not eligible to attend. They did make an appearance at the prom and hung around for a couple of hours. He also took in the annual awards banquet thinking that he might get the "least likely to succeed award."

Julie was there, looking splendid in a white dress and the ever present ribbon in her hair. She was called forward and presented with the certificate for being the best musician. She certainly deserved that. Henry Holt made a speech about what a fine girl she was and told everyone how she had been accepted to study at the Juilliard School.

"That's quite an accomplishment for a girl from Vandalia County," he concluded.

Julie carried it off superbly just as Corley knew she would. He was somewhat worried about her so he isolated her outside afterwards. It was a misty evening so he got her to sit in the truck with him.

"We're going to run away Sunday after commencement," she said. "It's all set."

"Have you told your mother?" Corley asked.

"Heavens no," she replied. "I'm not going to tell her until it's over. Then, I think I'll call her. I'm just praying that she won't notice anything."

"Well, you are certainly looking well," Corley said.

"I'm feeling great, haven't been sick for a couple of weeks."

"You'll be a beautiful mother," Corley said.

She dropped her head on that one and didn't answer.

"Do you have all of the arrangements made?"

"Yes," she replied, still looking down. "We're going to Virginia to be married and Mark has an apartment for us in Charleston."

"Let me know if I can help."

"Thanks, Corley, I will."

He got out of the truck, walked around and opened her door, and she walked briskly away.

Seniors got out of classes one week before school actually ended and Corley took his last ride on the school bus. He had been driving to school nearly every day but decided to take one more ceremonial ride on the old bus that he had hated so much. As he got off the bus that evening and started toward the house he saw a black 1949 Ford sitting in front of the house. He did not recognize the car and wondered who was there. As he approached the house he was met by his dad on the porch.

"Who does the Ford belong to?" he asked.

His dad smiled a warm smile and said, "It's yours."

"You're not serious," Corley replied.

"Yes, it's yours. We have saved some money from the calves we have sold since you were born. It's not much, but it's transportation."

Corley was overwhelmed. It was a seven year old car but it looked to be in excellent condition, and he noticed that it was a V-8. His dad handed him the keys and he fired the engine and took his test drive. It drove like a dream. And, it gave him a sense of independence that he had never known before. It was the first good thing that had happened to him in awhile.

Commencement night finally came and as Corley was getting ready he decided that he really did not have any emotional feelings about it. The biggest thing that bothered him about it was that he did not know what he was going to do with himself now that it was really over.

He and Sam rode to school that evening in the Ford. They were both uncomfortable in their ties, Sam more so than Corley because Corley had half gotten used to wearing one while playing in Bryson's band.

"I don't know why we have to go through this bullshit?" Sam complained.

"It's for the parents, I guess," Corley replied. "They get a big kick out of this stuff. They talk to other parents and feel some kind of pride I guess."

"It wouldn't be so bad if we didn't have to listen to some ignorant bastard make a speech," Sam concluded.

"Well, maybe if we all look bored, he'll cut it short," Corley said.

It was a beautiful late May evening and people were standing around under the maple trees when they arrived. The girls all looked fresh and pretty in their dresses. The boys all looked miserable in their ties. They all stood around and pulled at their shirt collars, and they looked stiff when they walked, like they were afraid that they were going to break.

Old Bryson Hill was there, his arm still in a cast and the ever present smile on his face. Corley made his way toward him.

"You playing any guitar yet, Bryson?"

"No, not yet, but it won't be long. First thing I have to do is to get this stupid cast off my arm."

"We'll have to get together and play some when you get it off, see if you still have your touch," Corley said.

"Yes, we'll have to do that," he replied. "I sure have missed the band and I hope we can get it going again."

"We'll work on it soon," Corley said.

Corley surveyed the crowd under the maples and spotted the great Denny Lewis with a blonde on his arm. Corley did not recognize her but figured her for a Charleston girl. Denny did not appear to have suffered any emotional damage from his relationship with Julie. He was strutting around, giving everyone the glad hand and introducing his blonde. Corley avoided his path.

He saw Julie across the way, standing with her parents and her intended, Mark Wells. He looked cool and comfortable in his tie. Julie was wearing her white dress and still showed no signs of motherhood. Corley thought that she looked better than he had ever seen her look. Her mother was beaming with pride, probably telling everyone how her baby was going to knock New York on its ear.

Lucy arrived in her car bringing Sam's friend, Sue Phillips with her.

"My, you look handsome tonight, Corley," Lucy said.

"I feel like a damned moron," Corley replied.

When the seniors lined up to go into the program the two M's, Malone and Meadows, were together. She was right behind him in line. The high school band played the "March from Aida" as they walked in and it caused a bit of chest swelling on the part of Corley. Pompous music always did that to him.

The program itself was not too bad. It could have been worse. They had to listen to Henry Holt ramble around awhile about what fine boys and girls they were, but he was fairly brief. Then, Dr. Somebody from the University of Somewhere, ranted around about how these had been the best years of their lives. Corley was slightly amused with that line. Just because that ignorant bastard had made himself miserable ever since he graduated from high school didn't mean that the rest of the world was going to, Corley thought to himself. Then, the speaker turned and said that he challenged all of them to do better than they had thus far and Corley figured that was a pretty easy assignment for him. He had not really done much of anything yet.

The choir sang a couple of songs and Corley enjoyed watching Frank Kerns at work. His choir put on their usual sterling performance. Corley made a mental note that he was going to write Mr. Kerns a letter letting him know how much he appreciated him while he was in school. He had a thought that if it had not been for Frank Kerns, he really might have quit school.

After the program was over they marched out of the gym and back into the room where they initially congregated. Everyone was presented with their official diploma and there was hand shaking and embracing everywhere. Julie Meadows, who did not say a word to Corley while they were going in, during the program, or coming out, made her way toward him. He was taking off his cap and gown when she turned him around. She put those blue eyes on him in a stare that would be with him forever. He saw one tear go down her face as she embraced him. She put her head into his shoulder and held it there for a long moment. When she pulled back, the tear was gone.

"I'll never forget you, Corley Malone," she said.

Then she whirled around, got that haughty look on her face, and walked out of the room like she was going to the Miss America pageant. Corley walked over and looked out the window and tried to forget those goddamned eyes that had haunted his life for over a year. She was gone and it occurred to him that he would probably never see her again. He felt a hand on his shoulder.

"I saw that, Corley. Wish things could have been different with you two."

"Hell, it's like you said in the beginning, Sam, she was out of my league."

"I don't know, Corley, maybe you were out of hers."

"Why don't I get the Buick and we'll take the girls somewhere," Corley suggested, regaining his composure.

"Good idea," Sam replied. "You get the Buick and I'll round up the girls."

Corley spotted his parents standing in the back of the gym talking with a group of people.

"How about trading me vehicles, Dad?"

"For how long?" he kidded.

"Oh, just for the evening. I'll give it back tomorrow.

"You boys be careful," he cautioned. "You know every year you read in the paper where some kids get killed commencement night, so watch your sledding. I need someone to do the milking."

"You be extra careful," his mother added.

Everyone was already sitting in the Buick when Corley got there. Sam and Sue were in the back seat and Sam looked like a Philadelphia lawyer getting ready to run for Congress.

"Let's go to one of those fancy-assed restaurants in Charleston and get something to eat," he suggested.

"You think you know how to act in a place like that?" Corley asked.

"Hell, it's time I learned. You heard what the man said in there, he wants us to do better."

They drove to Charleston, showed off their girls by driving through all of the drive-in restaurants, and admired all of the cars. It must have been commencement night at several area schools because there were ties all over the place. They cruised around the city awhile and settled on a restaurant.

"Table for four?" a nice looking lady asked.

"No, a table for six," Corley replied. "We're expecting more people."

Everyone looked at Corley as she led them to a big table. After they were seated, Sam looked at Corley.

"Who the hell is coming?"

"No one, I just wanted a big table."

"You're a crazy bastard, you really are," he said.

It was nearly eleven o'clock when they finished their meal and Corley and Sam decided that they should take the girls home so they could get some beer before midnight. By the time they made it to The Beeches it was nearly twelve. They got a smile and a handshake from Troy Carr and he gave them a six pack of Falls City. It was his graduation present, he said. They drove up the river, parked alongside the road, took off their ties, sat down on the fenders of the Buick, and talked it all over.

"What do you think, Corley? Are the good times all gone for us?"

"Well, they probably are here. I think that we are going to have to stop being boys and start looking for a way to make a living. Hell, I guess I could stay around home for as long as I wanted as long as I did the chores, but I can't do that. Got to do something."

"I hate like hell to go to work for a living," Sam added.

"That makes two of us," Corley replied.

They drank the beer in silence and thought about it for awhile. They discussed the possibility of trying to get on with one of the pipeline construction jobs, looking around at some of the chemical plants in Charleston, or perhaps trying one of the natural gas outfits that were scattered all around the area. But none of those possibilities really appealed to either of them.

"You know, Sam, I'll bet that there are a bunch of good times left out there in the world somewhere for a couple of young fellows like us. Maybe we have used up all of the good times in Vandalia County, but there is a big world out there. Maybe what we should do is to get the hell out of here for a couple of years. We're not helpless. We know how to use tools and I'll bet we could pick up work just about anywhere we went. Let's you and I climb into that Ford of mine and head out. Maybe we can head south, work a month or so in one town, then move on to another. Hell, we can make it. You might even get a job blowing up buildings."

"I am good at that," he replied.

"What about the girls?"

"I don't think that we need to worry about the girls. Hell, they're both pretty as they can be. They might miss us for a week or two, but some horny bastard will be after them as soon as we are out of sight. They'll be alright."

"I guess you are right about that, Corley; the likes of us shouldn't be too hard to replace."

"That's for sure," Corley said. "Then, let's look at the other side of it. These poor bastards who get married and stay around here and work don't really have much to look forward to. When they are down at the A&P store on Saturday night buying groceries, you and I will be out on the town somewhere, screwing everything with a skirt on, international lovers at last."

"You make it sound good, Corley."

"Hell, it will be good. We'll worry about amounting to something when we're thirty-five."

Sam threw his can over the river bank. "Hell, might as well. It's something to do."

When Corley got home and put the car away he decided that he would walk down to the river. There was a light moon and he could see pretty well. He walked down to the edge of the river, picked up a flat rock, and skipped it across. The rock made contact with the water four or five times and jumped out on the bank just about where Julie Meadows used to come down to go swimming.

The End

Made in the USA
Middletown, DE
10 January 2023